TREACHEROUS
STRAND

Also by Andrea Carter

The Well of Ice

Death at Whitewater Church

TREACHEROUS STRAND

AN INISHOWEN MYSTERY

ANDREA CARTER

OCEANVIEW PUBLISHING
SARASOTA, FLORIDA

ISBN 978-1-60809-398-4

Oceanview Publishing • Sarasota, Florida

www.oceanviewpub.com

10 9 8 7 6 5 4 3 2

PRINTED IN THE UNITED STATES OF AMERICA

For Geoffrey Victor William

Chapter 1

PANIC IS A hangover cure. This I discovered one morning in September as I tore along the coast road from Glendara to Ballyliffin, managing to avoid about one in every three potholes. My old Mini was not happy – her springs conveyed their displeasure in no uncertain terms. The windscreen wipers screeched as they did battle with the heavy rain. The car was humid, the windows fogged up from the inside. The sky was an angry mix of yellow and charcoal and the sea was that particularly bleak shade of gunmetal gray it so often is on Donegal mornings. Visibility was lousy.

I wiped the windscreen with a filthy pink rag I'd picked up God knows where, but it didn't make a damn bit of difference. The splitting head I had woken up with two hours previously had been replaced by a pins-and-needles-type sensation that was traveling down my neck and into my shoulders. Peering over the steering wheel, I caught sight of the mannequin advertising the Famine Village just in time to slow down, take a sharp right and cross the narrow causeway, over the mudflats and on to the Isle of Doagh. This morning the shrieking gulls and little oystercatchers held no interest for me; the dread in the pit of my stomach was all-consuming. Guilt made me nauseous, a bit like a hangover but a lot less cosy. Panic and guilt – now there was a song I knew by heart. I felt like running around in a circle, waving my hands in the air and screaming at the top of my voice.

Instead, I continued along the narrow road that snaked through the center of the island, scraggy hazel hedges blocking the view on either side. Unable to see fully around the next corner, I swerved suddenly to allow a tractor to pass by with a trailer full of cattle. Then I remembered. It was Wednesday – Mart Day in Glendara. The office would be like a zoo. But there was nothing I could do about that now; I had to find out what had happened.

I emerged at a wide grassy clearing where the sea appeared again in front of me. The tide was out and the long beach was just about visible as a biscuit-colored stripe beneath water and sky – providing, that was, you could see past the three squad cars and I counted seven gardai blocking the view. *Every guard in Inishowen must be here,* I thought. Tucking the Mini in behind the last squad car where it wouldn't be seen from the road, I tugged hard on the handbrake. The salty wind that lunged at me as I clambered out of the car made me pull at the collar of my coat and hunch with my arms crossed as I made my way towards the blue figures. At least the rain was easing off.

A tall guard was bellowing into a mobile phone, trying his best to be heard over the wind: Sergeant Tom Molloy – a native of Cork, honest, principled, and utterly committed to a job he arrived at late, after an abandoned career in science. I've known Molloy for seven years, although sometimes it feels as if we've only just met. Which makes things difficult for me since I've been thinking a lot about him lately. What began as a working relationship became a friendship of sorts, but then nine months ago something changed between us, culminating

in a moment when we had almost . . . *Almost* because Molloy
had pulled back. He still hadn't told me why. It was clear there
was something holding him back, but we'd brushed aside what
had happened and carried on as before. The problem was, I
cared about him, more than I wanted to admit. And I knew he
cared about me; he had shown it when I had needed him most.

He caught sight of me out of the corner of his eye, finished
his call, and came over.

"Ben, what are you doing here?"

My parents' fondness for an obscure fifth-century Italian saint
has landed me with the middle name Benedicta, which did not
make my convent school days any easier. Ironically, it's now
the name I use — or a shortened version of it. And thankfully,
despite his dislike of nicknames — which I suspect comes from
the difficulties in trying to police an area where nicknames are
rife — Molloy has managed to make an exception for mine.

"Is it true you've found a body?" I tried to sound less breathless than I felt.

Molloy raised one eyebrow. He has dark eyebrows, framing
deep gray eyes. "Where did you hear that?"

"Oh come on, Tom, it's all over the town. Do you know
who it is? Is it Marguerite — Marguerite Etienne?"

He relented. "We think so. One of the Malin guards was
able to identify her."

"Is he sure?"

"Yes. Seems she wasn't in the water that long. Did you know
her?"

"She was a client." That was enough for now, I decided.
"When was she found? Who found her?" My voice sounded
shrill. I'd like to have blamed it on the wind, but it wouldn't
have been true.

"Iggy McDaid. He's over there talking to McFadden." Molloy nodded in the direction of a man with a face the color of a ripe plum, talking to a young guard. "He was out checking lobster pots about seven o'clock this morning when he came across her washed up on the shore. All knotted up in the seaweed. Came close to standing on her, according to him. He was pretty upset."

I looked over at the two men. Uncharitably, it occurred to me that McDaid's starring role in the whole drama was compensating quite a bit for the shock. He was leaning against one of the squad cars talking animatedly while McFadden took notes. Every so often he'd grab the notebook, take a look at it, point something out, and hand it back.

I cleared my throat. "May I see her?"

"Christ, Ben, why on earth would you want to?" Molloy said.

"It's just something I need to do."

He shook his head. "I can't let you. The state pathologist is on his way up from Dublin. He should be here in about half an hour."

"Please, Tom. I just need to be sure it's her."

Molloy paused for a second and made a quick decision. "Right. Okay. I suppose it couldn't hurt to have a second ID. Come on."

He led the way through the rough marram grass, over the dunes and along the narrow pathway leading down to the beach; his long strides forcing me to trot after him, my high heels sinking into the wet sand.

He spoke briefly to the young guard at the bottom of the path then continued over the stones, on to the beach and towards a cluster of craggy black rocks about twenty meters to the left. As we approached, a large white tent covering part of the rock came into view with another guard standing outside it. He was stamping his feet and clapping his hands together to warm them against the wind but stopped abruptly as soon as he saw the sergeant approaching.

"Are you sure you want to do this?" Molloy asked me.

I nodded.

He walked over, lifted the flap of the tent, and went inside. I took a deep breath and followed him. A smell I didn't recognize assaulted my nostrils. Salt mixed with something else I couldn't identify. Something unpleasant. My stomach lurched. Next to the rock, looking at first glance like a pile of shiny red ribbons, was a stack of dulse seaweed.

Molloy stayed back as I took a step forward, slowly. Tangled up in the midst of the seaweed, lying in a fetal position and cradled by the rock, was a woman's body. From a meter away it looked as if she was naked, but as I approached her, I could see that she was wearing sheer, lacy underwear. Short dark hair was plastered against her forehead. I forced myself to look at her face.

"Well?" Molloy was beside me. He touched my arm. "Are you okay?"

I swallowed, then turned to look at him. "It's her. It's Marguerite."

"There wasn't really any doubt. Did you notice this?" He squatted down beside the body.

Clearly visible on the left upper thigh was a crude black mark like a tattoo. It consisted of two intersecting arcs, one end of each extending beyond the meeting point. From one angle, it looked like a fish. From another, a noose.

Walking back across the beach with Molloy, I made a decision.

"She came to see me yesterday," I said.

Molloy kept walking, but I knew he was listening.

"Professionally, I mean. At the office."

He stopped and looked at me.

"She wanted to make a will," I said.

"I see."

"I know what you're thinking."

"What am I thinking?"

"Tying up her affairs. Suicide."

"Well, it is the most likely cause of death," he said. "We found her clothes and shoes on Lagg, and her keys were in the pocket of her jacket. You know that stony section just before you turn the corner to come on to the main beach?"

I nodded.

"With the way the currents are, if she'd gone into the water over there, this is where she'd wash up. And very quickly."

Molloy was right. The Isle of Doagh is an island attached to the mainland by a narrow causeway. Directly across from it, on the other side of Trawbreaga Bay, is a long golden stretch of beach called Five Fingers Strand, so named because of the five pointed rocks sticking out of the water on its western side. The locals call it Lagg, after the townland. But the currents in Trawbreaga Bay are dangerous and unpredictable. Bréag in Irish means falsehood, lie: Trawbreaga or Trá Bréige is Treacherous Strand.

I remembered walking on the beach at Lagg when I first came to Inishowen and seeing some teenaged boys playing with an old football. One of them kicked it out to sea and he stood watching it float away like a little boy until one of the others shouted that he knew where it would wash up. *The Isle of Doagh*, he said, *it'll be on the Isle*. And off they sped in their souped-up car to drive the twenty-odd kilometers by road in search of their ball, circling the inlet. Whether they found it or not, I have no idea, but the memory – in light of what we were talking about now – made me feel ill again.

"She can't have committed suicide," I insisted.

"Why?"

"Because she didn't sign her will. I haven't even drafted it. She had to come back in. Why would she have gone to the trouble of coming to see me, give me instructions for a will, and then kill herself before she signed it? That doesn't make sense. If that's what she was doing, tidying up her affairs."

"Maybe she didn't realize she had to come back in. Thought it was all done and dusted."

Molloy lifted the cordon, and I walked through. The rain had started again. I shivered, whether because of the chilly wind or the memory of what I had just seen, I couldn't be sure.

"She knew," I said, as we made our way back up towards the road.

Molloy smiled at me for the first time since I'd arrived. A wry one. "Are you sure about that? You're not the clearest sometimes, you solicitors."

"Thanks."

"Look, we won't know anything until the pathologist gets here. We may not even know then. It's not easy to tell with drowning."

"The pathologist. It's not . . . ?"

Molloy shook his head. "No. It's the Assistant State Pathologist this time, I think."

"Will you call me after?"

"Look, Ben, I'll try. But you know what it's like."

Chapter 2

THE OFFICE WAS the last place on earth I wanted to be. My feet felt as if they were encased in cement as I walked towards the town square from the County Council building where I parked the Mini.

I looked at my watch; it was half past ten, which meant that the Oak was not yet open, which meant no decent coffee till eleven. So I walked on towards the office, past McLaughlin's Bar with its clutch of all-day drinkers smoking in the doorway – the only pub in Glendara with a Fisherman's licence allowing it to open at 7 a.m.; past Doherty's Surveyors; McLaughlin & Son Auctioneers and Estate Agents; Doherty's labyrinthine second-hand book shop and McLaughlin's newsagents. Much of the town is owned by Dohertys and McLaughlins – not all the same people, however, and in most cases not even related, just people who share the same surnames. This is something a blow-in like me struggles to handle, but the locals seem unfazed by it, any confusion deftly avoided by a reliance on nicknames. Patrick McLaughlin the newsagent, despite standing as straight as a rod, is Pat the Stoop because of the way his grandfather used to walk, bent over an old ash stick. His son and two daughters are lumbered with Stoop too. While Phyllis Doherty, the bookseller, will always be Phyllis

Kettle since her family had a stall in the square selling pots and pans two generations before.

Dohertys and McLaughlins are people who belong in Inishowen, have always belonged. *I* do not belong here. Although I have lived here for seven years, I will always be an outsider. In many ways this peninsula has saved me, for my position as an accepted outsider has allowed me to keep my past to myself, to be only who I choose to be and not what my past has made me. But it's never as simple as that, is it? For the one person you can never escape is yourself.

Marguerite had been an outsider too: a French woman living in Inishowen. Stupidly, it occurred to me for the first time that maybe that was why she had chosen to come to see me. Kindred spirits or something.

I pushed open the door of the cramped terraced house that serves as my office – O'Keeffe & Co. Solicitors – the most northerly solicitor's practice in Ireland.

Leah looked up expectantly as I walked into the reception area. Leah McKinley is the "& Co." in O'Keeffe & Co. Solicitors. She is my sole employee, the one who manages to fulfil all roles from A–Z, and she's not one to hold back with her opinions.

"Jesus, you look like crap," she commented.

"Thanks."

"Well?"

"Yeah. It's her."

Leah's face fell. "Oh, God, I'm sorry. That's awful. Do they know what happened?"

"Not yet. Pathologist is on his way, apparently."

"God, Ben." She looked at me sympathetically with her chin resting on her hands.

"I know. Suppose I'd better get some work done though. Nothing else I can do at the moment."

"Right." She handed me a stack of files. "Your morning's appointments. First one is due back in ten minutes. I sent them off for half an hour. Said you had to step out."

"Thanks, Leah."

I climbed the stairs to my office, dumped the files on my desk, sat down, and finally allowed my mind to replay the events of the day before.

It had been District Court day in Glendara. Still called "law day" by some of the older townspeople, as if it is the one day when the town is forced to acknowledge the existence of a national government and an obligation to obey a wider set of rules than those made locally. But that's probably just my city view of things.

At half past five I had emerged from the old courthouse, eyes watering, and yawning like a horse. I was so tired my teeth hurt, and it was still only the beginning of the week – a hell of a long way to go to get to Friday. Things hadn't been great lately, and so I'd been looking forward to having dinner with Maeve and her family that evening. I made a decision to drop my files into the office and then head home to a long bath and an even longer glass of wine.

Nice plan. Although I could tell it wasn't to be, when I caught Leah's expression the moment I walked in the door.

"Ben, I'm sorry," she whispered. "I know you're probably wrecked, but there's someone here to see you. She seems pretty anxious. She's been here for two hours." Leah cast her eyes in the direction of the waiting room. "I told her you wouldn't be able to see her today, but she insisted on waiting."

I hoped the look of dismay on my face wasn't too obvious when my eyes met those of the woman sitting stiffly in the waiting room. It took me a second to recognize her out of her usual context.

"Marguerite."

She stood up expectantly. Marguerite was my yoga instructor. That sounds more glamorous than it was. She taught an evening class in the local hall – in an empty room with peeling walls and a draught.

She walked towards me, displaying the toned, willowy body of the lifelong practitioner. As usual she wore no make-up. Although forty or so, I guessed, she had no need of it. Her skin was coffee-colored, her features delicate, eyes dark and long-lashed. I remembered now that she had asked at the end of the last class if she could come into the office, but I thought she would have understood to make a bloody appointment.

She smiled a tight smile. Although tiny lines were beginning to form around her eyes, she was still very striking. But today her eyes looked as if they belonged to someone who didn't sleep very much; they even seemed to have a slightly yellowish tinge. Strange, I thought, for someone who managed to instill such a sense of peace in others, myself included. Yoga was the one healthy thing I did, unless you counted my crazy year-round dips in the sea when things became too dark and I needed a jolt.

Gratitude for her contribution to my sanity didn't make me any more pleased to see her now, but I faked a smile and led her upstairs. In my office I sat at my desk and offered her a seat.

"Is this about your will?" I asked. "You mentioned something . . . ?"

"Yes, I hope it is okay. You did say I could come and see you." Marguerite spoke softly, but her accent was unmistakable. French. With the tiniest sprinkling of Donegal.

"Yes, it's fine," I said brusquely, removing an attendance pad from a drawer. "I can take some instructions from you now. Have you thought about what you want to do?"

She took a deep breath before replying. "I want to leave everything to my daughter."

"Okay." I took a note. "Do you have any other children? Any other family?"

When the expected response did not come, I looked up. Marguerite's hands were clasped tightly together in her lap, the whites of her knuckles showing through her brown skin, her eyes anxious. She was biting on her lower lip.

I put down my pen. "I don't mean to be overly intrusive. But the Irish Succession Act makes certain provisions about the inheritance rights of spouses and children which can override a testator's wishes, so I'm going to need a certain amount of information to be able to advise you properly."

A further pause and more lip-biting followed, until finally, I was rewarded with a nod followed by an answer. All in a rush.

"My parents died in a car crash when I was a student, and I lived with my grandmother. I have no other children. Just my daughter Adeline."

I noted what she had said.

She cleared her throat. "What would be the situation if I did?"

I looked up. "Sorry?"

"Have more children. What would happen if I had more children?"

"Well, you can make another will at any stage. You can make as many wills as you like. For some people it becomes almost a hobby. Every time they fall out with a relative, they get disinherited."

I smiled, trying to lighten the mood. Unsuccessfully as it turned out; the French woman's expression didn't change.

"And if I don't make another will?"

"Well, a child has a right to make an application to your estate under Section 117 of the Succession Act." I explained the provisions of the section as simply as I could.

Marguerite nodded, but I had no idea if she had really registered anything I had just said. It was at this point I realized I didn't have the patience this evening to drag instructions out of a client. I needed a drink.

I turned over a page. "How old is your daughter?"

"Twenty-three." No hesitation this time.

"Okay, she's not a minor so no complicated trusts needed. And what about Adeline's father? Are you married?"

Marguerite's eyes darted towards the door. She picked up her bag from the floor and clutched it on her knee, looking as if she was about to bolt. Exasperated, I pretended not to notice and carried on.

"Under Irish Succession Law, a spouse has inheritance rights whether you make a will or not – that is, if you are still legally married when you die and the rights have not been waived."

Marguerite put the bag down again. "No. I'm not married," she replied slowly. "At least, I don't think so. I don't think we were ever legally married. His name was . . ." her voice lowered almost to a whisper ". . . Alain Veillard. He died about a year ago."

There was something about the way that she said her ex's name that made me feel as if I was expected to recognize it. I didn't, and I certainly hadn't the inclination to pursue it.

"I met him when I was seventeen," she continued. "When I was in school in Toulouse. I had Adeline when I was nineteen. I was very young." She leaned forward suddenly. "This is all completely confidential, isn't it?"

"Of course," I assured her. "Nothing you say to me will go outside of these four walls."

She nodded, unclasped her hands, and began playing with something on her wrist. It was a bracelet, a black metal bangle with some kind of engraving on it.

"When the light came on and I left Alain, Adeline stayed with her father. I had no choice about that. I haven't seen her in a long time."

She tapped the surface of the bracelet with each of her fingertips in turn, one by one. When she was finished, she repeated the action again and again. It was very distracting and a little irritating. I tried to ignore it.

"Do you have an address for Adeline?"

Marguerite lifted her bag again from the floor and drew out a small piece of paper. I took it and placed it beside the instructions I had taken. I then drew up a list of her assets in Inishowen, which amounted to little more than a small bank account and a car.

"Do you have any assets in France?" I asked.

She looked down. "Not anymore."

"That's fine. You won't need to make a French will."

I moved on quickly to explain the role of an executor and the necessity of appointing one. "It's generally advisable to appoint someone the same age or younger. A relative maybe? Someone you trust."

She brightened a little. "I should like to have my friend Simon Howard. The sculptor. He lives in the cottage next to mine."

After she had described where she lived and I had taken a note of the address, I glanced at the clock behind Marguerite. It was twenty past six. I had given her forty minutes. Enough was enough, I decided. As it was, I would have to go straight to Maeve's without heading home first. I replaced the lid of my pen and put it back in the holder on the desk.

"Okay, Marguerite. That's it. Your instructions seem pretty straightforward and it's a simple enough will. Give me a couple of days, and I'll be in touch for you to come in and sign it."

The expression of alarm on her face took me by surprise. "Oh. I thought I would be able to sign it today," she said. "I could wait. I have plenty of time."

"I'm sorry. It needs to be typed up, and we must have two witnesses to your signature so we'll need Leah here when you sign it. And she'll have left at this stage," I added pointedly.

Marguerite didn't respond.

"I'll give you a call when it's ready," I said again and stood up. The implication was clear. This meeting was over.

Slowly, Marguerite got to her feet. "So I should just wait to hear from you?"

"Yes."

I walked her down the stairs and showed her to the door, but she stood without moving in the doorway, examining the carpet.

"Was there anything else?" I asked, my hand on the doorknob.

Marguerite looked as if she was trying to make her mind up about something, staring down at her wrist and doing that strange thing with her bracelet again. I waited.

Eventually she shook her head. "No . . . no . . . thank you."

I opened the door, relieved, but instead of walking through it, she turned to face me again.

"Are you sure it would not be possible for you to do the will now, and I could just wait here while you do it?" she said. "Maybe you could just witness it yourself? I can wait as long as you need."

"I'm sorry, Marguerite. It has to be two witnesses. And I don't have time to do it this evening, I'm afraid," I said.

"Could you have it ready tomorrow? I could come back tomorrow?" she said nervously. "There's something else I think I might like to talk to you about."

I sighed. "Yes, yes, okay. I'll draft your will in the morning and give you a call."

I don't think I have ever encountered a client who doesn't harbor some sneaking suspicion that giving instructions for a will would result in them being mowed down by a bus within hours of leaving the office. In fact, I'm pretty sure I would feel the same way if I ever got around to making my own will — which I haven't, of course; the cobbler's child is always barefoot.

But looking back, I knew now that Marguerite had been really on edge. Way more than the usual client-giving-instructions-for-a-will type of "on edge." Let's face it, I knew it at the time too. I just hadn't cared. With a sickening feeling, I realized what I had known the second I had heard the news this morning. Marguerite had been frightened when I had seen her at the office. And I had practically shoved her out the door.

Chapter 3

I CLICKED MY pen while I stared at the wall. I should have recognized Marguerite's fear but I had been too damn self-absorbed. I had been feeling on edge myself of late. It was nothing I could put my finger on, but I hadn't been sleeping well and there were times when I had woken in the middle of the night feeling spooked, with the sense that I was being watched. There had been calls too – phone calls from an unidentified number with no one at the other end when I picked up. The calls weren't regular – only two or three in as many months, certainly not enough to do anything about – so I hadn't said anything to Molloy. Uttered aloud, the whole thing amounted to nothing more than a bout of insomnia and a few wrong numbers. But it had left me feeling tense and ill-at-ease.

None of that excused the way I had treated Marguerite. I *knew* something was wrong – and yet I had let her down. The thought was hard to bear, and I could not escape the cold knot of guilt that settled within. The knowledge that it was not the first time I had let someone down in that way made it all so much worse.

I couldn't concentrate on work. As soon as the last of my morning's appointments were finished I made my escape, leaving Leah to lock up before she went home for lunch.

The Oak was cosy, a turf fire crackling in the grate, the dark wood a balm for my frayed nerves. I was prepared to take my comfort where I could today. And it was quiet, since I was about half an hour earlier than usual for lunch. There were only five people in the pub and that included the staff.

The Oak had lost its previous barman, a dope-head and regular client of mine, to Sydney, Australia, during the summer. Lucky Sydney. He had been replaced by his older sister Carole, who had soon made me realize that her brother's lethargy had been less about chemicals and more about genetics than I had given him credit for. When I approached the tiny food counter, she glanced over at me with a loud martyred sigh before shoving her phone into the pocket of her jeans and making her way over.

"Cheese salad sandwich and a Coke, please, Carole. And a coffee. Oh, and a packet of salt and vinegar crisps."

"Comin' up." She threw me out the crisps and a glass of black fizz, then leaned over the bar and lowered her voice. "Any news on that body they found out on the Isle? I heard it was that French woman."

"Seems so."

"She was a bit of a strange one, wasn't she?"

"Was she? Why do you say that?"

Carole clammed up. "Just what I heard."

Information is a one-way street, if you're a barmaid.

For once the armchairs by the fire were free. Just as well, as my hangover seemed to be making a return visit; my stomach was raw and sore and my head felt as if I was wearing some kind of helmet that was too tight for me. But the inevitable salt craving had arrived so I took off my coat and draped it over the back of the closest chair and opened the crisps while I waited for my sandwich.

I was just trying to figure out what the *Wax Auction in aid of Glendara Football Club* advertised by the poster above the fireplace would involve, when the door of the pub flew open, causing a rush of cold air. A tall woman in a pair of blue overalls strode in, spotted me, and came over. Pulling off a massive pair of gloves, she sat down on the arm of the chair opposite.

"Jesus, did I hear right?"

Maeve Sheridan is the local vet. In a rural area where the majority of her patients are cattle, sheep, or horses, she has succeeded in making her way in a male-dominated profession with the minimum amount of fuss, her gender barely even acknowledged by the farmers she deals with. We are friends.

"About Marguerite?" I asked. "What did you hear?"

She lowered her voice. "That she killed herself. The farmers around Malin Head were all talking about it this morning. They're saying your boy McDaid found her – not that that eejit could keep his mouth shut about anything."

I looked down. "It's true, I'm afraid. She's dead – drowned, they think – although it's not clear exactly how it happened. Iggy McDaid found her body on the Isle of Doagh this morning."

Maeve shook her head. "God, that's awful."

"Her clothes were found on Lagg, apparently."

"Where did she live?"

I remembered what Marguerite had told me at the office. "One of those cottages on that left-hand turn after the entrance to the beach, about a kilometer up the hill. One of the three."

Maeve froze. "Which one?"

"The middle one, I think. The smallest. It's kind of out on its own."

"That's Seamus Tighe's old place."

"God. That hadn't occurred to me."

Maeve gazed into the distance. "Isn't that weird? I was just thinking about him yesterday. It's three years ago next week since I went out to test his cattle and ended up having to help fish his body out of a slurry tank. Not something I'm ever likely to forget."

"That was a horrible accident."

"I didn't know Marguerite lived there. I thought that house was empty. I passed by it last night on my way back from doing that Caesarean."

"I don't know how long she was there. I think she was living in town at some stage before that."

"That's really awful news."

"I know. Grim."

"How's the head, by the way?" Maeve asked. "You left early this morning. I didn't even hear you get up."

I groaned. "Don't ask. It's the last time I have dinner with you two on a school night."

"You put away a right lot of that red wine last night. Thank Christ I was on call or I might look as rough as you do."

"You're not the first person to point that out to me today."

Maeve threw the keys of her jeep on the table. "Want anything?"

I shook my head and she headed up to the counter. She was back within a few minutes with a big chicken salad, a huge coffee, and my cheese sandwich.

"It must be all over the town. Carole just asked me if I'd heard." She picked up a fork and started on her salad. "Of course she worked in the book shop too, didn't she? I was in last week with the boys."

"God, that's right, she did. I think she just did weekends." I thought suddenly of our bookseller. "Poor Phyllis."

"She seemed such a gentle sort of person. That lovely, soft accent. The number of times I dozed off in her yoga class . . ." Maeve smiled sadly.

"You didn't notice anything when you drove by her house last night, did you?"

"Mmm?" Maeve spoke through a mouthful of chicken.

"Were there any lights on, for instance?"

"No, I told you. I thought it was empty."

"No cars parked outside it?"

"Outside her house? No. Why?"

"No reason. Just wondering. Can you remember what time it was?"

Maeve raised her eyebrows. "You're beginning to sound like Molloy."

"Humor me." I took a sip of my Coke.

She thought about it for a second. "What time did I get back to the house . . . half past eight? Well, it would have been about ten minutes before that. Why? When did she die? Was it last night?"

I shook my head. "I don't know. All I do know is that they found her this morning. And she was alive yesterday evening, so it must have been last night sometime, I suppose."

"What if I was passing by at the exact time when . . ." Maeve put down her fork, a stricken expression on her face. "I mean, what if I could have done something, stopped her or something?"

"Of course you couldn't. You can't think like that." I reached across the table and put my hand lightly on her arm.

"Why on earth would she kill herself?" Maeve sighed. "She seemed so . . . serene. But then I didn't really know her outside of the class. Did you?"

I shoved my plate away, sandwich only half-eaten. My appetite had been shortlived. "Not really," I said quietly.

"She was single, wasn't she?" Maeve asked, finishing her coffee.

"I don't know, to be honest."

"I never saw her with anyone. Amazing really when you think about it, she was so attractive." Maeve returned to her food. After a few moments she said, "How long was she in Inishowen – two years? We did that yoga class with her the winter before last, remember, and she hadn't been here very long at that stage. That sounds about right, doesn't it?"

I nodded.

"Do you think she was lonely?"

I didn't respond.

Maeve looked up from her food suddenly and examined my face with concern. "Are you okay? Does it remind you of . . . ?"

I cleared my throat. "No. No, I'm fine, honestly."

"Are you sure?" She placed her knife and fork on her plate.

"Yes," I said firmly.

"Okay." Maeve looked at her watch and immediately gathered up her gloves and keys. "Listen, I have to go. I'm supposed to be operating on a cat in ten minutes and I have to get back to the Mart after that. Let me know if you hear anything." She hesitated. "Will there be a wake, do you think?"

Inishowen is one of the few parts of Ireland where the tradition of the wake is still alive and well. The body is laid out for two days and two nights. All clocks in the room where the body is kept are stopped at the time of death, mirrors are covered or turned towards the wall and a window is opened to allow the soul to escape to heaven.

"I doubt it," I replied. "Who would wake her? I don't think she had any family around here, do you?"

"No, I suppose she wouldn't have had."

"They have to do a post-mortem first, anyway."

"Okay. Let me know if you hear anything. I'd like to go to the funeral, if I can."

By ten to two I was back at my desk, head in my hands.

It wasn't something I had wanted to discuss in the Oak, but Maeve was right. Marguerite's death did remind me of something. Of someone. Nine years ago, my sister Faye was killed by my ex-boyfriend, a man named Luke Kirby. And despite our friendship, it had taken until the summer just past for me to tell Maeve the real reason I had come to Inishowen and why I didn't use my real name. I had told Molloy six months before that, and with his encouragement had finally told Maeve too.

What had happened to Marguerite did remind me of Faye, although not for the reasons Maeve thought. What Maeve did not know, but Molloy did, was that I had let my sister down too. Faye had called me repeatedly on the night she died, and for reasons I now regretted more than anyone could imagine, I hadn't answered her calls. Luke Kirby was now in prison, having been cleared of Faye's murder but convicted of manslaughter, but I carried the guilt of that night with me every single day. Now I had let someone else down and she was dead too.

I decided I couldn't wait any longer to hear from Molloy. I had just picked up the phone to dial the garda station when Leah buzzed.

"Those two developers who were supposed to come in yesterday are here," she said. "I told them you wouldn't be able to see them, but they insisted on waiting. Your two o'clock hasn't shown."

"That's okay, Leah. Give me a minute then send them up."

I don't think I have ever seen two more physically different people than the two men who walked through the door of my office. The first was a balding, rubbery-faced man with a thick black moustache. He could not have been taller than five feet nine, but he was grossly overweight. The second was blond and at least six feet four, requiring him to bend down to get in the door of the office.

The tall one spoke with a strange combination of Donegal lilt and American drawl. "Hi, Miss O'Keeffe. I'm Jim Gallagher and this is my partner, Sean Dolan."

I shook their hands and offered them seats. I was concerned for the one Dolan chose.

"That real-estate guy in the square, Liam McLaughlin, gave us your name," Gallagher said. "We may have some business to put your way, if you are interested."

"Sure. Go ahead, Mr. Gallagher."

Gallagher leaned back in his seat and crossed his arms as if he were about to tell a long story by a roaring fire. "Well, Miss O'Keeffe, we've both been away from the old sod for a long time."

"The States, by any chance?" I asked.

The sarcasm went over his head. He nodded.

I felt badly and tried to make up for it by being obsequious. "Well, you haven't completely lost the Donegal accent."

He gave me a toothy smile. "My grandfather was from the Illies. You know where that is?"

I nodded.

"Go as far as the North Pole and turn left."

He laughed loudly at his own joke. It was an old one. The North Pole is a pub at a crossroads on the way to Buncrana. I smiled politely.

"I've been in the States most of my life, apart from the odd trip home to visit cousins and so on. Dolan here is from Cavan. He's the same, pretty much."

Dolan stared at me unsmilingly, his moustache twitching slightly while Gallagher continued.

"We've made our fortunes, so to speak. And now we think it's time we came home and gave something back."

"That sounds very commendable."

"We're interested in acquiring some property here."

"And, of course, it's a good time to invest," I said, unable to help the dig. I wasn't sure how buying land at rock bottom prices from cash-strapped sellers could be seen as giving something back.

"Not bad. Not bad. We're interested in acquiring a piece of property in Malin Head. We've been negotiating for some time and we've finally struck a deal. We want you to act for us in buying it."

"Okay. I don't see any difficulty with that as long as I don't act for the seller. Have you a name?"

"Sure do. Andrew McLaughlin. No relation of Liam's. Nickname of Dancer," he added.

I wondered what the story behind that little gem was as I noted the name on an instruction sheet. "That's fine. He's not a client."

Out of the corner of my eye, I saw my mobile phone light up and wondered if it was Molloy ringing and leaving a message.

I glanced over. *Number blocked.* Distracted, I realized I hadn't caught the last thing Gallagher had said.

"I'm sorry, you said Liam recommended me?"

"Yes, ma'am. He has all the details. There's one condition: the deal is subject to planning permission. We're applying for planning permission to build a hotel on the site."

That brought me back into the room with a jolt. This was a big deal. Time to pay attention.

"A hotel in Malin Head? That would be the most northerly hotel in Ireland. You'll have a job getting planning permission though. It's been tried before."

"Let's just say we're quietly confident." I was surprised to hear Dolan speak for the first time since he sat down. A mix of Cavan and New York. Not pretty.

It turned out to be his parting shot. With surprising agility he was up out of his seat and on his way out the door before I could even respond. Not even a goodbye. Apparently social niceties weren't his thing.

Gallagher stayed long enough to give me their contact details and was gone too.

I wandered over to the window, rolling my head from left to right to ease the tension in my shoulders, and pulled back the blinds to gaze out on to the street. Though still early, the sky was already beginning to darken; it was about to rain again.

I thought about ringing Molloy again. I checked my phone and there was no message.

The rest of the afternoon was spent seeing clients and dictating conveyancing contracts and probate papers: not exactly riveting stuff, but the kind of work that keeps a practice like mine ticking. And I was grateful for the distraction. At least it had taken my mind off Marguerite.

At six o'clock I left the office. I live in Malin town, about eight kilometers from Glendara. I have always assumed the word *town* was added to distinguish it from Malin Head, Ireland's most northerly point, since Malin is most decidedly a village. One of those Tidy Towns award-winning villages, in fact – a picture-postcard place full of pretty little houses, with an old stone bridge and a triangular green dotted with park benches, cherry trees, sycamores, and limes.

I suspected I was no picture postcard myself at the moment. My hangover seemed to be making yet another reappearance as I pulled over to the curb in front of my cottage. Before going into the house, I headed across the green to the shop to buy some cat food and a frozen curry, and when I returned, I was greeted by a disgruntled-looking black cat sitting on my doorstep with his tail curled around him. I leaned over to stroke the little white patch on the top of his head.

"Hey, Guinness. Hope your day was better than mine."

He responded by turning his back on me and facing the other direction, pointedly ignoring me as I turned the key in the lock. There had been no sign of him when I'd stopped in briefly this morning on my way back from Maeve's, and I'd been so hassled I'd forgotten to leave out some food for him. He was clearly put out by my overnight absence.

But he appeared behind me in the kitchen just as I was opening a tin of cat food, hunger obviously getting the better of his pride. After I fed him, I put the curry into the microwave and grabbed a bottle of beer from the fridge. Opening it, I took a long gulp and walked into my tiny sitting room, flinging the jacket of my suit on to one of the armchairs.

I lit a fire log in the grate and threw some turf on top of it, saying a silent thanks for the age of convenience and sinking on to the couch. I jumped suddenly as Guinness took a flying leap from the doorway and landed in my lap, circling and digging his claws into my thighs until finally deciding to settle curled up like a prawn with his head resting on my knee. I was clearly forgiven: cat grudges don't last very long. I scratched his head absently as I flicked on the television and caught the end of the RTE news.

"And tonight Donegal Gardai have confirmed they are treating the death of French woman Marguerite Etienne in Inishowen as suspicious. Anyone with information is asked to contact Glendara garda station, County Donegal, or Letterkenny garda station. Telephone numbers will follow on screen."

Chapter 4

AT 9.02 ON Thursday morning I walked into the public office of Glendara garda station. I had received the summons at half past eight while still mainlining tea, Molloy's usual abrupt telephone manner giving nothing away. Andy McFadden was sitting at the desk behind the counter, ginger brow furrowed in concentration as he tapped away at an ancient-looking computer with two fingers. I wondered if he was typing up McDaid's statement from the day before.

He looked up as I closed the door behind me.

"Morning, Andy. Tom about?"

"Aye, he is. They're waiting for you in the back office."

"They?"

He lowered his voice. "There's a detective up from Letterkenny. Didn't he tell you?"

"No. He didn't."

McFadden threw his eyes up to heaven and showed me into the tiny interview room at the back of the station. I hesitated for a second in the doorway before going in because, frankly, at first glance, I couldn't for the life of me work out how I was going to fit. No small man himself, Molloy was accompanied by a heavy-set, fair-haired fellow who seemed to take up at least half the room. The man was sitting authoritatively behind a large desk which itself seemed to take up the other half, and Molloy was rammed into the corner opposite. He stood as I entered and motioned to an empty chair beside him, so clearly I was expected to join them. I maneuvered my way in as he carried out the introductions.

"This is Detective Sergeant Frank Hanrahan from Letterkenny, Ben. Frank, Benedicta O'Keeffe."

I couldn't remember the last time I had heard Molloy use my full name.

"Thank you for coming down, Miss O'Keeffe. I'm sure you are very busy." Hanrahan struggled to his feet and shook my hand.

"Call me Ben, Detective Sergeant. And it's no problem. Anything I can do to help."

"Good to hear, Miss O'Keeffe." Hanrahan was keeping it formal.

Molloy got straight to the point. "We're conducting a preliminary investigation into Marguerite Etienne's death, arising out of the findings of the post-mortem. The autopsy report has confirmed that she died as a result of cardiac arrest or 'shock' as a result of sudden immersion in cold water, but the pathologist also found traces of bruising on the back of her head which could have been a result of being hit with something before she entered the water."

My stomach flipped. "I see."

"But," Molloy continued, "the bruising could also have been caused by her head hitting against rocks on the sea bed after she died. The water where it's likely she went in is very shallow in parts, and we think she was washed up very quickly on the other side. According to the pathologist it's not easy to distinguish ante-mortem from post-mortem injuries in the case of a drowning."

"Was she . . . ? I mean, I know she was found in her underwear . . ."

Hanrahan cast a disapproving look in Molloy's direction. It was obvious I wasn't supposed to know about the underwear. Molloy caught the look but didn't react. Instead, he responded to my question.

"There was no evidence of any kind of sexual assault."

"That's something, I suppose. But Jesus, do you really think she was murdered?"

"Let's be clear," Molloy stated. "Suicide has not been ruled out. It's still the most likely cause of death. That hasn't changed. In fact, elements of the post-mortem do point to it. But at the moment we can't discount the possibility that there may have been somebody else involved, slim though it is. We're questioning anyone who knew her or saw her yesterday evening."

I shook my head. "Who on earth would do something like that?"

"That's what we're trying to find out, Miss O'Keeffe." Hanrahan had clearly tired of the way this conversation was going and felt that it was high time some information started to flow in his direction. "Sergeant Molloy tells me that Miss Etienne came to you and asked you to draft a will for her but never got an opportunity to sign it, is that right?"

"Yes, that's correct."

"When was that?"

"She came to my office on Tuesday afternoon. She left about twenty past six."

"And what were her instructions?"

"I'm sorry, but I can't tell you that."

The detective's face darkened. "You do realize you've just been informed that this could be a murder investigation, Miss O'Keeffe?"

"I realize that, Detective Sergeant, but the rules of solicitor-client privilege are clear on this. I'm afraid the only way I could give you that information is if I am subpoenaed, and then it would be a matter for a court to decide the confidentiality issue."

I was sure of my ground on this point, having looked up the Law Society guidelines as soon as I got Molloy's call. I was less sure about my initial judgement call with him on the beach the day before. But I convinced myself that telling Molloy that Marguerite had come to see me about a will might in some way have contributed to the guards' closer examination of her death.

But in the cramped quarters of Glendara garda station, it soon became clear that my position was not a popular one. Hanrahan's face began to turn red. It was an odd contrast to the yellow hair.

"I was under the impression that you were willing to assist, Miss O'Keeffe." There was a note of warning in his voice.

"I am. I'm very anxious to help. I want you to find out what happened to her very much. I would be more than happy for you to subpoena me and then I can give you all of the information you want. But if you don't, my hands are tied. Believe me, I wish they weren't."

A purple vein had now become visible on Hanrahan's neck. I was sure that wasn't a good sign. He closed the file with a thump.

"Typical lawyer," he said testily. "Always some old shuffle going on."

I struggled to hold my own temper in check. "That's not fair, Detective Sergeant. The rules exist for a reason."

"Well, if that's your position, Miss O'Keeffe, I'm sure you will understand if we check out the legalities from our end."

"Of course."

I looked at Molloy. He didn't look too enamored with me either. I got the feeling that he might have indicated to the detective that I would be more forthcoming than I was.

"It's really very important that we have all the information available, Ben," he said.

"I know that, but there really is nothing that I can do about this."

It was clear I held no further interest for the two guards. I imagined I could hear the words *interview terminated 9.13 a.m.* as I was turfed unceremoniously out of the office.

But as I walked away from the garda station, a feeling of misgiving crept over me. I had put Molloy in an awkward position. That made me uneasy enough. But what if, and my heart sank at the thought, what if the lack of information meant that they dropped the investigation? That was the last thing I wanted.

I turned on my heels and walked back down the street just in time to see Molloy getting into a squad car outside the station. He rolled down the window as I approached. His expression was hardly encouraging.

"I'm sorry, Tom, but that guy just rubbed me up the wrong way," I said.

"I noticed."

"That's not why I didn't co-operate. I really can't give you the information you're looking for unless you go down the right channels."

"So you said."

"It wouldn't take long, you know. A subpoena."

Molloy nodded towards the door of the garda station. "You know they're not going to do that."

"Why ever not?"

"Resources, Ben. These things are prioritised – you know that. At the moment we have no reason to think it wasn't a suicide."

"But I think she may have been frightened when she was at my office."

He frowned. "I don't remember you saying that yesterday."

"I hadn't quite figured it out yesterday. It needs to be investigated. Someone must know something," I insisted.

"It is being investigated," he said and, making no attempt to conceal his irritation, rolled up the window.

I climbed the steep hill from the garda station to the office with an anxious gnawing in the pit of my stomach. I must have been one of the last people to see Marguerite alive. Why had she wanted to make her will so urgently, I wondered. According to her instructions, she had very little to leave. But in my experience, it's not always about property. People often decide to have their wills drafted when they become aware of their own mortality: mostly when they have children, but sometimes for other reasons. Was that what had happened to Marguerite? Could she foresee her own death?

And then there was the question that had kept me awake half the night: what if there was something I could have done? Maybe Marguerite hadn't wanted to talk to me about a will at all; maybe it was just an excuse. Maybe she had simply needed someone to talk to; someone she could trust. What if she had been trying to tell me something, and I just hadn't listened? Or worse, what if she had needed a refuge, and I had refused to give it to her? All because I wanted to go home for a glass of wine.

My eyes felt gritty as I squinted against the cold morning sun. I hadn't slept well the night before, after the garda appeal on the evening news, and I was even more rattled now. Molloy drove past me without a wave.

The smell of aftershave hit me the second I walked into the office. Two men I didn't recognize were sitting in the waiting room.

"Who are they?" I whispered to Leah. "I didn't think I had any appointments this morning."

"No. You don't. That's Simon Howard."

I looked at her. The name didn't register.

She lowered her voice. "He says he's Marguerite Etienne's executor."

Realization dawned. The sculptor.

"He was waiting when I opened the office. Wanted to know if you would see him without an appointment. He's the older man. I don't know who the younger one is."

I walked into the waiting room. The older man, as Leah had described him, stood up, pushing a lock of hair out of his eyes. Though we hadn't met, I had seen him around the town. He had the sort of face you didn't forget: firm jaw, dark skin, blue eyes, longish brown hair with graying temples. He was also the aftershave culprit.

I offered my hand. "Mr. Howard."

He took it. "Simon, please."

The younger man glanced up briefly, but stayed seated. He was pale and much slighter in build.

"I'm so sorry about Marguerite," I said.

"Yes, bloody awful thing to happen. It's good to meet you. I'm sorry I'm here so early. I'm just on my way back from Derry."

His accent was educated, Scottish, but he would not have sounded out of place in a Welsh choir. His voice was deep and rich.

"No, that's absolutely fine."

"We've just come from the airport. I was picking up my son – David."

The son looked up as if he was surprised to be included. He was older than I had first thought. Maybe it was the way his father had introduced him, but I felt as if I'd been about to address a teenager; looking at his face, I guessed he was actually in his early twenties. Both men had the same blue eyes, but there the resemblance ended. As so often happens in the DNA lottery, when it came to inheriting his father's good looks, the son had not held the golden ticket.

But the real contrast between them was in the way they dressed. Simon was wearing bright purple cords with a gray linen shirt, while his son wore a navy blazer, white shirt, and tie. It didn't take a genius to work out which one was the artist. Both seemed oddly contrived.

Nor, it seemed, had the son inherited his father's geniality. I offered my hand, but he looked away, concentrating hard on the painting on the wall opposite. I withdrew, slightly embarrassed.

"Do you have a few minutes?" Simon asked.

"Of course. Come on up."

I led the way upstairs while David remained in the waiting room, still staring intently at the wall. I was happy to leave him there.

Opening the door to my office, I remembered that the attendance sheets from my meeting with Marguerite were still on my desk. I had left them there earlier while I was checking the solicitors' rules of conduct. I moved quickly to cover them with another file before offering Simon a seat.

He crossed his long legs and stretched his right arm across the back of the second chair. The room seemed suddenly very small but, unlike the garda station, this was not attributable to my visitor's dimensions. I suspected Simon Howard was a man with a big personality. And he knew it.

"I hope you don't think I'm being crass in calling in so soon, but since I was passing by your door, it occurred to me that maybe I should. I'm not at all sure how these things work. Marguerite told me she was making a will with you and that she had appointed me as her executor."

"Well . . . yes," I replied carefully. "She did give me instructions, but I'm afraid she never actually signed a will."

"Oh. I see." He seemed surprised. "I was rather under the impression that it was all done and dusted. So what does that mean?"

"Well, it means there isn't really anything for you to do. If she hasn't made another will somewhere else, her estate here will go to her next-of-kin."

"Right then." Simon uncrossed his legs and got up to leave. "I suppose that's that." He bowed. "Goodbye then, and thank you for your time." He reached for the door.

Before he had an opportunity to open it, I took a chance. "Unless . . ."

He turned.

"You don't happen to know anything about her family, do you?"

He leaned easily against the doorframe. "No, nothing."

"But you did know her pretty well?"

He shook his head. "No, not really. She just lived close by. To tell you the truth, I was rather surprised when she said she wanted to appoint me her executor."

"Really? That's strange. She said you were her friend."

Simon smiled. "I don't think she had very many."

"Well, she obviously trusted you," I told him.

He looked mildly taken aback, as if considering the notion for the first time. "Yes, I suppose she must have. That policeman Molloy interviewed me about her death, but I haven't the faintest idea why. I thought she committed suicide?"

"They haven't actually confirmed that."

"Oh, right." He absorbed that, then: "Anyway, there was bloody little I could tell them."

"When did you last see her?"

He paused for a second before answering. "Tuesday evening – the night she died. Come to think of it, I must have been one of the last people to see her alive. She called in to tell me about the will. Said she had just been to visit you."

"What time was that?"

"No idea. I was working – bit distracted, I'm afraid, wanted to get back to it. Pulled an all-nighter as it turned out." He looked apologetic. "I wasn't really concentrating on what she was saying, to be honest, which is probably why I got the wrong end of the stick about the will."

"I'm sorry about that," I said. "You've had a bit of a wasted trip."

"Not at all. I got to meet you." His eyes narrowed flirtatiously, and I felt myself flush. He explained. "It was David who suggested it might be an idea to call in, as a matter of fact. I knew I'd have to at some stage."

"Does he live with you?"

"God, no. At least not really. I mind his dog. Great Dane, huge donkey of a thing. David travels for work, so he can't take her with him. The sooner he gets himself sorted, the better; he's here most weekends at the moment." He crossed his arms. "So, will you still be administering Marguerite's estate then, with or without my services?"

"I honestly don't know. I suppose that depends on whether or not I'm asked."

"I see." He looked down as if trying to absorb my answer, then told me, "Actually I don't see, but I suppose I don't need to, do I? I'll have nothing further to do."

"No."

"Fine by me. Duty done."

He had half-turned towards the door when something caught his eye on the wall. It was a wooden carving of a head I'd bought a long time ago in Dublin.

"I see you like your art."

"Yes. I did a little in school. But then I had to choose between exams for law and completing a portfolio for art school. Never been sure I made the right choice," I said with a smile. "It was a long time ago now though."

"Oh, not that long, surely. Were you any good?"

"Not bad."

"You could always take it up again. It's never too late."

I shrugged.

"Anyway, I'll leave my number with your secretary just in case you need me. For anything."

He smiled at me again. Rather wolfishly this time, I thought. Although unnervingly, I didn't entirely dislike it.

Chapter 5

I LISTENED TO the stairs creak under Simon Howard's departing tread, feeling oddly disconcerted. I had just met a man whom Marguerite considered a friend, and not just any friend, but someone she trusted enough to appoint as her executor. Yet he claimed to barely know her. He seemed surprisingly unaffected by her death, sympathetic but unconcerned, as though it had nothing to do with him.

Something else had occurred to me during my conversation with Simon Howard. I had been so haunted by that awful image of the dead woman curled up by the rock that I hadn't considered whether or not I had some kind of professional duty here. I tried to work it out. I no longer had a client; my client had been Marguerite. And because there was no will, I couldn't proceed to administer Marguerite's estate without instructions from her next-of-kin. In Marguerite's case, that would be her daughter, but did her daughter even know she was dead? Did the guards even know of the daughter's existence? Simon Howard was supposed to be her friend, and he appeared to know nothing about her family. What if I was in possession of information that no one else had?

I took my attendance notes from beneath the file where I had hidden them. Stapled to the first sheet was the slip of paper

Marguerite had handed to me with her daughter's name and address on it. I had given it only the merest of glances at the time, but I read it now.

I was surprised. Sogn og Fjordane, Norway. I had expected an address in France. I turned the slip over in my hand, but there was no phone number or email. Should I write to her, I wondered. But to say what? A solicitor's usual reason for contacting the next-of-kin is to inform them of the existence of a will. It's rarely up to the solicitor to inform them of the actual death.

Reluctantly, I decided I would wait for a day or two and see what happened. Stay out of it. The guards had the whole thing in hand; Molloy had made that pretty clear.

Leah buzzed. "The Matron from Letterkenny Hospital wants to speak to you."

I pressed the incoming call button.

"Miss O'Keeffe? We have one of your clients here in the hospital. He has asked me to call you to come down and see him. He's not well at all, I'm afraid. We don't really expect him to last the week, but he's anxious to make a will."

The Matron explained that the old man's memory wasn't so good, but that some days were better than others. I agreed to visit the hospital the next morning.

When I finished the call, I rooted out copies of the man's deeds. He was a gentle sort, a bachelor farmer with no children, but many nieces and nephews and much land – a recipe for long sets of convoluted court proceedings if I didn't get everything right at this stage, especially if there were any doubts about his capacity. Deathbed wills are one of the hardest parts of the job; taking instructions and handwriting a will by a hospital bed that you know your client is unlikely to leave under his own steam is incredibly sad. But the safest way to ensure that this man's will could not be challenged was to have a psychiatrist see him and complete an affidavit of mental capacity. The only one in the area was Brendan Quinn. I decided to call him in the morning after I had been to Letterkenny Hospital.

Making arrangements to go there re-awoke that nagging voice in my head, the one that kept asking me why I hadn't just drafted Marguerite's will on the spot. It would have been no trouble for me; I did it all the time. And Leah would have come back in, if I'd called her. The truth was that I had simply seen no urgency about Marguerite's will; hers was not a deathbed will. But now that I suspected that the will wasn't the real issue for her, I needed to find out what she had been trying to tell me. I had to find out more about her.

I couldn't just sit back and do nothing. It was sitting back and doing nothing that had me feeling like this in the first place. What was she afraid of? Had someone been threatening her?

McLaughlin & Son Auctioneers and Estate Agents has one of the most prominent locations in Glendara. Painted a bright cherry red and sitting a good two meters taller than the other buildings on the upper side of the square, it gives the impression of a benevolent uncle leaning over its smaller charges — a fitting premise for the town radar. There isn't a soul in the town or surrounding hinterland that Liam McLaughlin doesn't know.

The ground floor's wide shop windows display properties for sale and lease on the peninsula. Never able to resist, I paused to have a look before I went in. Farms, old cottages, newly built holiday homes, even an island was advertised today. I peered at the photograph and the map; it was a small island with its own beach in the middle of Lough Swilly, just off the western coast of the peninsula. I allowed my mind to drift for a second while I imagined owning my own island. Would the isolation be good or bad for one's sanity? I wasn't sure.

I was just about to push open the door, when I collided with someone coming out. Someone large and sweet-smelling. With a deep Scottish accent.

Simon Howard smiled down at me. "Oh bloody hell, I'm sorry. Twice in one morning. Who's following whom, I wonder?"

I smiled back.

"Getting all my business done at once," he said, by way of explanation.

"Makes sense."

He held the door open for me in an exaggerated ZZ Top pose. "Nice to see you again."

"Hi," Liam greeted me as I walked in, then added in a fake American accent, "Wanna buy an island?"

The estate agent was holding a steaming mug of coffee in his hand and warming his backside against the radiator while his receptionist busied herself replacing brochures in the plastic pockets that were dotted around the walls.

"I just saw it," I said. "Can't say I'm not tempted."

"And you met our Scottish sculptor, I see?"

"I did."

"Like him?"

"You selling him too?"

"He's available. And exciting quite a bit of local interest." Liam gave an exaggerated wink.

"And what makes you think I'd be in the market?"

He grinned. "Well, aren't you? Seems to me you've been single a long time."

I changed the subject. "Do I smell coffee?"

"No coffee in your place, I suppose?" He tut-tutted. "All right, come on in."

I followed him into the back office where he poured me a cup from the coffee pot in the corner, refilled his own, and sat at his desk.

"So what's up? Did Dolan and Gallagher contact you?" He waved to indicate the other seat.

I nodded.

"Any movement?" he asked.

"No contracts as yet. I've written for them. I'll let you know when they come in. Big deal," I added.

"Big players. Give me a shout if you want me to hurry things on a bit. Might be needed in this case, if you know what I mean."

"Will do. Thanks for the nod, by the way."

"No bother." He clasped his hands in front of him. "Any other craic?"

I took a swig of my coffee. "Did you know that lady who was found on the Isle?"

"The French lady?"

"Yes."

"Not really. Just knew her to see her. Did you?"

"A bit."

Liam shook his head. "Terribly sad. Too many suicides around here these last few years. The recession hasn't helped. Wasn't it she who was renting Gallagher's house up towards Knockglass?"

"Gallagher?" There was no shortage of Gallaghers in Inishowen either.

"Jim Gallagher. One of your big players. The Malin Head deal."

"Seriously? He owned her house?"

Liam nodded. "He owns a fair bit of property round here."

"Did you do the lease?"

"No. I don't think he used an auctioneer." Liam's gaze switched to the wall. "Funny, you'd think they'd have had a bit of trouble renting that place what with its history . . ."

"You mean Seamus Tighe's accident?" I said.

"Aye. But then I suppose that French lady wouldn't have known about the accident, being not from around here."

"No."

"And they did do the place up and block off all the farm buildings before they rented it. Pretty house, it is too. Although you can't see the water from there; it's just a bit too far up." Liam disappeared into auctioneer-speak. "Nice as a holiday house maybe. Lonely sort of a place if you're on your own though, especially in winter."

"I suppose."

"Your Scottish sculptor fella is up there, too. His would be a much bigger place now. All those outbuildings out the back." He paused before shouting through the open door: "You knew that French lady, didn't you, Mary?"

His receptionist appeared in the doorway, asking, "Who?"

"That poor French lady they found on the Isle of Doagh the other morning. Marguerite something, wasn't it?" Liam glanced at me for confirmation.

"Etienne." I looked at Mary. "She taught yoga and worked part-time in the book shop."

"I did know her, as a matter of fact." Mary perched on the seat beside me, her arms full of brochures. "A wee bit just. I did one of her yoga classes the winter before last." She shot her boss an accusatory look. "You need something like that in this job."

Liam shrugged as if he had no idea what she meant.

Mary switched her gaze back to me. "She'd just moved here and didn't seem to know many people so I invited her over. But she didn't want to – she was a bit odd actually, unfriendly, very different to the way she was in class. Sort of uptight. I didn't ask her again, I'm afraid. I feel a bit guilty now after what's happened. Maybe she was just shy."

"Do they know what happened exactly? Why she did it?" Liam asked.

"Well, they're not a hundred percent sure it's suicide yet. The guards are still looking into it."

He looked surprised. "I heard that on the news but I assumed it was just a formality." He put his mug down on the desk. "Although it could simply have been an accident, you know. The tides out there are lethal. If she went swimming, she could get caught out very easily, if she didn't know what she was doing."

"Maybe."

He shook his head again. "Strange place to choose to live for a woman on her own. It must have been lonely. Had she any family?"

"None here, I don't believe," I said.

"You'd think she'd have joined something, wouldn't you? I mean, I know she taught those yoga classes . . ." Liam leaned forward. "Take your Scottish sculptor fella, for instance."

"He's not my Scottish sculptor."

"He's only been here six months and already he's involved in all sorts of things: helping with the masks for the carnival, even playing a bit of golf. Now that's the way to settle into a new place. Join a golf club. Great way to get to know people."

"My cue to leave." Mary stood up and headed back out to the front office, shutting the door firmly behind her.

Liam grinned. His golf obsession was well known. "And he's volunteering for the Wax Auction in the Oak."

"What the hell is a wax auction, anyway? I saw a poster for it," I asked.

Liam rubbed his hands together with enthusiasm. "I was going to talk to you about it. Basically some of the local men have volunteered to be waxed. The beauticians from Brid's place are lined up for the job. Raring to go. We're looking for all of the businesses in the town to contribute."

"Waxed? What do you mean, *waxed*?"

"I can see where your mind's going. Back out of the gutter with you. Chest and legs just. But we need people to bid. Businesses especially. I'm doing the auction. Thought we might even persuade Molloy to do it – loosen him up a bit." His eyes lit up suddenly. "Hey, why don't you bid for your sculptor? There's many a local female would pay to see him with his top off."

"I'll take that as *my* cue to leave, shall I?" I finished my coffee and stood up.

"Ah now, you're no craic. Hold on, I'll come out with you. I need a cigarette."

"When did you start smoking again?" I hadn't seen Liam smoke in years.

He shook his head. "Don't ask."

Liam walked me to the door and stood on the step, then gave me his mug to hold while he lit a cigarette. He shook out the match, then exhaled a cloud of smoke, saying, "So why are you so interested in this French lady?"

"It seemed very sad, that's all."

"She may well have had her problems, Ben. No one really knows what goes on in other people's lives."

I looked at him. "Have you heard something?"

He avoided my eye, glanced down at the ground where he had flicked his ash. "No, not really."

"What do you mean, 'not really'?"

"Well, maybe the odd story," he conceded.

"What kind of story?"

"Oh look, that wouldn't be fair, Ben. The poor woman is dead. Far better to let her rest in peace."

He stubbed out his barely-smoked cigarette with his foot, placed his hand briefly on my shoulder, and went back into the office.

Chapter 6

A PHONE CALL from Leah summoning me back to the office and a string of appointments prevented me from asking any more questions on Thursday afternoon. But first thing on Friday morning, I was standing outside a pretty, two-storey Victorian house with a wooden bench outside and a swinging sign advertising Doherty's second-hand book shop – Kettle's, the book shop where Marguerite worked on Saturday mornings. Sitting beside the new County Council offices, the shop has a stubborn look about it, as if it is digging in its heels and refusing to be ousted by progress. A bit like Phyllis Kettle herself.

I pushed open the door and was rewarded with the jangle of an old-fashioned shop bell. Kettle's book shop is an Aladdin's den of books, a place to lose yourself. Sometimes in the middle of the day when I need to run away from the office, I hide behind its dusty old bookshelves and hunt for treasure among the stacks. The problem is, Leah always knows exactly where to find me.

Phyllis Kettle is a notorious gossip, but a kind one. Which makes her incredibly good company. She also has the powers of observation of a cat. I felt sure she couldn't have worked with Marguerite for any length of time without getting to know her pretty well.

Today she was sitting at the counter, head buried in a book, a tomato-colored shawl wrapped around her ample shoulders. When I entered the shop, she slowly removed her half-moon glasses and raised her eyes from her book, the expression on her face in deep contrast with her cheerful outfit. She gave me a watery smile.

"Haven't seen you in a few weeks," she said.

"No time to read anything more exciting than title deeds lately, I'm afraid."

"Well, I suppose they must have their moments too," she replied.

"Believe me, they don't. How are you doing, Phyllis?"

She sighed. "Okay, I suppose. I presume you heard what happened?"

I nodded. "I'm so sorry."

She waved her glasses at the volume she'd just put down. "My books aren't giving their usual comfort today. Poor Fred doesn't know what to think of me, do you?" She addressed a black and white collie on a mat at her feet.

The dog looked up at her, a mournful expression on his face, and I leaned down to rub his head.

"We're closed tomorrow for the funeral," she said.

I stood up in shock. "So soon?" Weren't these things supposed to take longer? And why hadn't Molloy told me this when I had spoken to him the day before? Or had the decision not been made at that stage?

"I was a bit surprised too," Phyllis agreed. "I thought there would be more red tape, especially with the guards looking into it. But it's true. Hal's just been in to tell me."

Hal McKinney is the town mechanic, undertaker, and Commissioner for Oaths.

"Doesn't it seem a bit rushed to you?" I said.

"It does a bit, frankly. But they've done the post-mortem and they tracked down her daughter and tomorrow was the only day she could come. She seems to have been able to make the arrangements very quickly." Phyllis shrugged. "I suppose there was no reason to delay things."

So much for my concern about letting Molloy know the daughter's address, I thought. "So, she's being buried in Glendara then?"

"So it appears. The funeral is after eleven o'clock Mass in the morning."

So Marguerite was a Catholic? Before I could ask Phyllis about that, a noise behind one of the shelves made me jump, and I realized for the first time that there was someone else in the shop.

Phyllis lowered her voice. "Come upstairs with me, if you've a minute. I've some unpacking to do. We can talk better there."

"Are you sure it's okay to leave the shop?" I asked.

She nodded towards the shelves. "They can shout if they need me, and I'll hear the bell if someone else comes in."

I followed her up the narrow winding staircase that led to her flat, or flat-cum-storeroom. Whatever stock overflowed from downstairs ended up in Phyllis's tiny flat. I perched on a windowseat upholstered in bright African colors while Phyllis knelt down in front of a large box, put her glasses back on, and started sorting through books. I watched as she checked the spine of each book and the flyleaf before placing them one by one in a selection of piles. After a while I gazed out on to the square. Phyllis is not someone you needed to interrogate. I was confident she would tell me what she wanted to, in her own time.

"You know I wasn't even aware she had a daughter?" she said eventually. "She never told me."

"Maybe since she lived abroad, it just didn't come up," I said.

Phyllis leaned back on her heels and looked at me over her glasses. "But that's the strange thing. It *did* come up. She did talk about family. The importance of family was one of the few things she would talk about – of knowing who you were, and where you came from. But she was never specific about herself." She paused. "Did you know her at all?"

"A little."

Phyllis sighed heavily. "I think I knew her only a little too. Oh, I tried to get to know her better, I really did. When she started working here, she was so withdrawn. Did you ever meet someone who doesn't quite know where to put them-selves? Uncomfortable in their own skin."

"Yes."

"I thought this job might help her, you know? She used to come in here frequently and she seemed to be spending a lot on books. Said they were company. So when I was looking for someone part-time, I persuaded her to go for it." Phyllis shook her head. "I thought it might take her out of herself. Thought if it worked out, she could maybe even run the place when I head off to Borneo in November."

"I can't imagine anyone not loving working here, Phyllis."

She smiled gratefully. "It's nice of you to say so, but to be honest, at the beginning, it was as if she wanted to crawl under the counter and make herself invisible. It was like trying to make friends with some kind of a wild animal – a deer or something."

I was sure that having a non-communicative workmate would have been hard going for someone like Phyllis. "How long was she working for you?"

"Over a year. A year and a few months, I think. Saturdays just."

She returned to stacking the books with some force. Clouds of dust billowed in all directions, and I coughed, but she didn't seem to notice so I let her work. After a minute or two, she sat back on her heels again as if something had occurred to her.

"You know, she did improve there for a bit. Seemed a little more relaxed. I commented on it, and all she would say was that everything changed eventually if you just waited long enough."

"What do you think she meant?"

"I wasn't sure, but if it resulted in her being happier . . ."

"When was that?"

"A couple of months after she started. She still would never talk about anything even remotely personal, mind. One time she went on holidays, took a Saturday off, and she wouldn't even tell me where she went. Looked at me as if I was the Gestapo when I asked her." Her eyes showed hurt.

"Maybe she was just very private," I ventured again. "Some people are like that, Phyllis."

She shot me a look. "Who are you telling? Sure, wasn't I brought up around here? *Whatever you say, say nothin'.*"

"Was she here last Saturday?" I asked.

Phyllis removed her glasses again. "In body only. She was all over the place. Saying strange things, jumpy, confused, mixing prices up. She couldn't use a computer, not that that was a problem working here, but she needed to be able to use a calculator. She'd been fine before and then suddenly she was hopeless. She was like that the last few weeks, come to think of it."

"Do you think she was worried about something?" I asked.

Phyllis examined my face. "I don't know. It seemed more physical, if you know what I mean – almost as if she had a hangover. If I asked her if she was okay, she said she had a headache. But once I offered her an aspirin, and she wouldn't take it. She said she didn't touch any kind of medication, that she'd be all right."

Phyllis lifted a couple of paperbacks she had been about to stack, then slapped them on the floor in frustration. "Oh, what the hell happened to her? And why the hell didn't I see it?"

"I don't know, Phyllis."

"God, I feel absolutely sick about the whole business. I really do. Responsible."

"But you were so kind to her. Why would you feel responsible?"

"I was the one who encouraged her to work here."

"Why on earth would you feel guilty about that?"

We were interrupted by a gray head appearing at the top of the stairs. "Shop, Phyllis! Can I pay for these?"

Phyllis struggled to her feet and headed downstairs. We didn't have a chance to finish our conversation.

The rest of the morning passed in a haze of appointments. For lunch I bought a takeaway sandwich and a coffee from the Oak and took it back to the office, my conversations with Phyllis and Liam playing in my head.

I opened the drawer of my desk and took out my attendance notes from my meeting with Marguerite – I still hadn't been able to bring myself to file them away – and read through them. They weren't exactly detailed.

On the first page I had written

All to daughter Adeline. 23 yrs old. A's father (Alain Veillard) died last year. Was not testator's spouse.

I sat back, realizing that the name Alain Veillard was familiar, after all, although I couldn't for the life of me think where I'd heard it or in what context. I switched on my computer, typed the words *Alain Veillard* into a search engine site, and turned my attention to unwrapping my lunch while I waited for the results. Seconds later I looked back at the screen – 15,000 results. I nearly choked on my sandwich.

Results 1–10 appeared onscreen. I could see that the first two were Wikipedia entries so I clicked on the first and read through it. It was an account of the early life and career of Alain Veillard: a world champion motorcyclist from Monte Carlo. Was this Marguerite's ex? I read on through the motorcyclist's later life and death. He had died in a crash in Brazil. But the page indicated that he had had no children. I checked the date of his death – five years ago. He didn't fit. According to Marguerite, her Veillard had died only a year ago.

I exited the page and moved on to the second Wikipedia entry. This time I checked the date of death before reading any further. This Alain Veillard had died exactly a year ago; this one fit. But what I read about him made me sink back into my chair.

> *Alain Veillard – born 25 December 1948 died 18 September
> 2013. Founder and leader of the notorious French religious
> cult the Children of Damascus, known also as the Damascans.
> Known by members of the cult as the Teacher. Tried (and
> acquitted) in 1994 for the murder of 16 members of the cult,
> Veillard subsequently moved the cult to Norway to escape what
> he termed as "religious persecution" in his native France.*

Here was Norway again; Marguerite's daughter lived in Norway. I clicked on the words *Children of Damascus* and they led me to a listing for a website called childrenofdamascus.com described as *The official website of the Children of Damascus Christian Unity Group; a group dedicated to sharing God's word and love with others and offering comfort to those who need help.*

I opened the site. The home page was like a Benetton ad. It showed photographs of Children of Damascus members from all around the world: France, India, South Africa, and the United States. Image after image appeared on the screen – of happy smiling faces, adults and children of all races and cultures. I read their mission statement.

> *The Children of Damascus has been in existence since 1980*
> *and now has 18,000 full-time members, working in over 20*
> *countries. Our members live in large family communities or*
> *"centres" where work, education and socialising take place.*
> *Our mission is to devote our lives to spreading the word of*
> *God amongst the community and to live as He decreed.*

So, I thought, Alain Veillard's cult still existed despite his death. More than existed – it was massive. There was a picture of the Damascans' beloved founder and a brief biographical note on the website. He was a striking-looking man, with a serene smile, a shock of poppy-red hair and eyes that were almost black. The biography described him as a prophet. It said that he had died during the autumn of the previous year and although mourned by his followers, they fully believed he was still leading them from the grave. The website painted an idyllic picture of a utopian family-oriented existence.

I looked up from the screen and gazed at the wall in front of me, my thoughts racing. So this was Marguerite's past. A religious cult. This was where she had met Adeline's father. Something Marguerite had said that day at the office came back to me: *"When the light came on and I left."* Now it was starting to make sense. I realized I had come across that expression before, used in the context of breaking away from a cult.

Did this strange past have anything to do with her death? From what she had said, she had left the cult a long time ago, long before Veillard's death. I wondered if her daughter was still with them. There was no mention of her – in fact, Veillard was the only name which appeared on the website from what I could see. So I clicked the "contact us" button and found a phone number and address for what appeared to be the cult's headquarters in Norway. I compared it with the slip of paper Marguerite had given me with her daughter's address. It was the same as the one on the website. Adeline was still living with the cult.

I switched my gaze back to the computer, transfixed. I was just about to move on to the next search result when the phone buzzed. It was Leah announcing that my first afternoon appointment had arrived.

Chapter 7

I STOOD UP in surprise when I realized that the very beautiful-looking boy who strode into my office was wearing the dull gray uniform of Glendara Community School. Before I had a chance to speak, he offered his hand.

"Miss O'Keeffe. I'm Hugh O'Connor."

I found myself accepting an exceedingly firm handshake. He grinned when he saw my expression.

"It's all right, no need to panic. I'm over eighteen. Allowed to visit a solicitor on my own. Among other things."

For some reason I felt completely wrong-footed. "Okay." I returned to my seat and motioned for the boy to sit too in a feeble attempt to regain control of my own office. "So, what can I do for you then, Hugh?"

The boy pulled a neatly folded sheaf of papers from his jacket, leaned forward, and handed them to me across the desk.

"Maybe you would have a look at these for me."

He sat back in his seat expectantly. I picked up the sheets of paper and separated them, examining them one by one. The first was a bail bond which meant that the boy had been released by the guards on station bail after charge. The bond was followed by a number of charge sheets, seven to be precise, all for the same time and place. I leafed through them slowly, scanning the offences. They were the usual little-boy-racer collection of road traffic offences: no insurance, failure to produce; no driving licence, failure to produce.

The boy waited for me to reach the last sheet, a more serious offence – a Section 53, dangerous driving – then sat forward, clasped his hands between his knees and looked me in the eye.

"I can't afford to get a conviction."

"You've no other convictions, then?"

"Always been a good boy." He grinned again, showing perfectly white teeth.

Ridiculously, I had to stop myself from grinning back. I hadn't realized I was so shallow.

I didn't get it. The boy's smile was completely disarming; usually this kind of cocky attitude would get completely under my skin. I decided to remove myself by getting up from my desk and walking over to the bookshelf by the window where I took down my offences handbook. I brought it back to the desk, flipping through it until I found the section on road traffic offences, then I took an attendance pad from the drawer and made a note.

When I had finished all of this, I looked up. "Okay. First of all, do you have any of the documents they're looking for?"

"I do. I *was* insured; the car was taxed and I have a licence. Just didn't get around to going to the guards with them."

"Right. Well, we should be able to deal with those charges, then. And we'll see if we can get the non-production charges dropped. We should be able to, if you've never been in trouble before, but you'll need to bring me in the paperwork. Now what about the dangerous driving?"

"Mmm. That might be a bit more difficult. I was probably being a wee bit daft."

I suspected his sheepish expression wasn't sincere.

"Section 53 Dangerous Driving carries a mandatory disqualification. If you get convicted, the judge will have no choice but to disqualify you."

He shook his head. "That can't happen," he said.

"Okay, I won't go into any details with you now. First we need to find out what the guards are saying happened. You are entitled to be given copies of the witness statements, the custody record, a map if they have one, and anything else they might have. When we have them, I'll take full instructions from you."

He nodded.

I checked the bail bond. "You're remanded to appear before the district court in town next week. So we'll ask the judge to make a disclosure order and put it back to another date so we can have a look at what they have. That okay with you?"

"You know what you're doing."

I sat back. "So why can't you afford to get a conviction? Not that I'm suggesting you will necessarily, I haven't seen the evidence. But I'll need something to put to the court, if I have to make a plea for you."

"I'm going to run for election."

"Ah. You're interested in politics." I couldn't keep the amusement out of my voice. But if he detected it, the boy didn't seem to be offended in the slightest.

He smiled again. "You wait. Watch this space. I'm going to be a cabinet minister."

"I will. Good luck with it."

I closed the book. If a smile could get you elected, this boy's future was sorted.

★   ★   ★

I was still smiling myself when I went downstairs five minutes later to see if the post had come in.

"Well, what did you think of our Hugh?" Leah handed me a bundle of envelopes and messages.

"He's a bit of a rock star, isn't he?"

She grinned. "You're not far off. He played Romeo in the school production of *Romeo and Juliet* last year. My wee sister reckons the whole school's mad about him."

"I'm not surprised. He's a pretty boy." I started to sort through what Leah had given me.

"Although he nearly lost the part. Got suspended for some fight in the school yard."

I looked up. "Really? What happened?"

"No idea. It was with some new kid in the school apparently – family just moved up from Dublin. Anyway, the new kid made some crack about Hugh's grandfather and Hugh lost it entirely, according to my sister. Nearly broke the other kid's jaw."

"Why would someone make a crack about his grandfather?"

Leah looked surprised. "You know who he is, don't you?"

I shook my head.

"God, I should have told you before I sent him up to you, but I thought you'd know. That kid is Hugh Big Hugh."

"You've lost me."

"His grandfather was Big Hugh O'Connor. Ex-Minister for Defence?"

Now I got it. I hadn't heard the *Big* part before, but you didn't need to be from Donegal to have heard of Hugh O'Connor; it was said that if you sliced the ex-Minister down the middle, you would find the word *politician* there, like a stick of rock. Hugh O'Connor was one of the old school in terms of entitlement and straightforward arrogance, but utterly adored by his constituents, of course.

"Ah, I see. Young Hugh has political ambitions too, it seems. Wants to run for election. Sorry," I corrected myself, "says he's *going to be* a minister."

She grinned. "That's not surprising. It's in the genes."

"So what happened after the episode in the school yard?"

"Oh, he was suspended, but his mother made a plea for him and he was back within a week. The school couldn't afford for him to be out for too long. He's captain of the football team and on the county minor team too. Even without the acting, that makes him king of the school."

"I'll bet." I knew how important Gaelic football was in Glendara.

"He sorted himself out after that incident apparently. Nice kid, according to my sister. Friendly to everyone, despite the good looks."

"So he's started early with the baby kissing."

I left the office at six after a crazy, conveyor-belt afternoon. Donegal's factories close at half one on a Friday so their workers can take the opportunity to chase up their solicitor, dentist, doctor – insert appropriate profession. I was tired and irritable and I couldn't wait to get home.

After dinner I took my glass of wine and headed into my study, switched on my laptop, and brought up the results of the search I'd done in the office that morning. I took another look at the official Children of Damascus site, but after a few minutes it became clear that there was very little real information to be gleaned from it; it read like propaganda. I was far more interested in the events that had led up to the cult's move to Norway; the mention in the Wikipedia entry of Veillard having gone on trial for the murder of sixteen people, and having been acquitted.

So I did a further search on French cults and I came across an article from an American newspaper from February 1993. The headline was *sixteen cult members die in mass suicide*. I read on:

The bodies of sixteen members of the French cult the Children of Damascus were found this morning in a swimming pool at a house owned by cult member François Dumain, in Toulouse. It is believed that Monsieur Dumain himself, an accountant, may be among the dead. The organization's leader and founder Alain Veillard has been arrested and is being questioned by the French police.

I calculated from what Marguerite had told me that the article had been written about six months after she had left Veillard, a year and a half after Adeline was born.

The next piece was from the same newspaper, dated November 1995, some two and a half years later.

The French National Assembly has established a Parliamentary Commission on Cults in France (Commission Parlementaire sur les Sectes en France) following the acquittal of Alain Veillard and his two co-accused of the murder of sixteen cult members last year. The French Prime Minister has stressed the necessity for ongoing vigilance in the war against cults and the dangers associated with such organizations.

The Damascans' move to Norway was beginning to make sense. France had clearly become a less than welcoming place for Veillard's group of followers. I continued my trawl through the net. Typing again Veillard's name into the search engine, I discovered that there were literally hundreds of websites relating to the Damascans.

I opened the first one – called xdamascans.com. It seemed to contain some kind of a discussion forum, set up by ex-members of the Damascans. Many of the contributors had been children who were either born into the cult or who had been brought into it by their parents who were members. Most had left in their teens or early twenties although some had returned a number of times before leaving for good.

Gripped by a growing sense of horror, I began to read personal account after personal account of physical, psychological, and sexual abuse. I read accounts from children who had grown up in compounds patrolled by guards, children who were forced to be sexually active from the age of nine both with each other and with the adults who were supposed to be parenting them. This sexual activity was sold by the cult as a way of "spreading God's love." There were accounts from children who were beaten violently when they did not show sufficient fear of God, who were put in isolation units, or forced to remain silent for weeks on end, or have their heads shaved. Children who were forced to collect money for the cult by selling tapes and literature on the streets and not allowed to return home until they had reached a certain quota; children who were brainwashed constantly, being forced to listen to broadcastings of Alain Veillard's voice on a public address system in the centers for twelve hours a day, any indication of free will or personal opinion considered "an open door through which the devil could gain access", dealt with by way of public exorcism to purge the "evil spirits."

There were hundreds and hundreds of these accounts, on hundreds of sites. Not all related solely to the Damascan cult, but a quick scroll through them told me that many of them did. It seemed that Veillard had built the Children of Damascus into a huge operation after he left France. But what I was reading was a very different picture from the utopian one painted by the official website.

What struck me in particular was that many of those who had lived with the Damascans had experienced great difficulty in leading a normal life once they left the cult. Some of the sites gave advice to ex-members on getting support and many of them recommended what was called "exit counseling." The expression that Marguerite had used – *when the light came on* – appeared regularly. I wondered if she herself had had exit counseling at some stage. I wondered too if the strange behavior Phyllis had described was anything to do with the cult. From what Marguerite had said, it had been over twenty years since she had been a member, but what did I know about how long the effects of an experience like that might last?

I opened site after site and read account after account, each one more shocking than the last, completely unaware of the time passing until I was interrupted by Guinness padding into the room. The cat knew he was tempting fate, but it seemed curiosity and hunger had got the better of him. I stood up, stretched my arms and, rubbing the back of my aching neck, decided to call it a night. Turning off the laptop and lights, I put a disgruntled cat outside with a bowl of milk, locked the doors, and went to bed.

★   ★   ★

Three hours later I woke up, hyperventilating and in a cold sweat. As I came to, I realized that it hadn't been the brightest idea in the world to look through those websites just before going to bed. It had taken me forever to get to sleep and when I eventually succeeded, I dreamed about being locked in a dark cell with a red-haired man in a long cloak reading the Bible. I hauled myself out of bed and wandered sleepily into the kitchen to get a glass of water.

As I stood at the sink with the cold tap running, glass in hand, I stared vacantly at my dishevelled reflection in the darkness of the kitchen window. And a face looked back at me.

Not my own.

I screamed and dropped the glass, which shattered instantly. I forced myself to look back at the window, but the face had disappeared.

I gripped the counter-top with both hands and tried to steady myself, took my courage in both hands, and looked at the window again. No. There was definitely no one there now. Shaking, I stumbled to the table and sat down. What should I do? Go outside and investigate?

I listened intently but all I could hear was the wind and my heart pounding. My mobile phone was on the counter-top. I made a grab for it and only succeeded in knocking it on to the floor. Trembling, I knelt down and managed to extract it from the pool of water and broken glass. It was still working. Hands trembling, I dialed the number of the garda station. It seemed to take an age and a half before it was answered.

"Hello. Buncrana garda station."

When Glendara is unattended, the line is diverted to the garda station in the bigger town sixteen kilometers away. I didn't recognize the voice.

"This is Ben O'Keeffe in Malin town." My voice sounded a lot calmer than I felt. "I think there may be someone in my garden."

"Okay, Miss O'Keeffe. Sit tight and keep your door locked. We have a patrol car in the area. Someone will be with you in five minutes."

Relief flooded through me, and I heard a faint mewling at the door. For the first time in my life, I wished I had a cat flap. I've always resisted getting one because I associate them with batty old ladies – a bit too close for comfort. But Guinness was scratching at the bottom of the door. He had realized that I was up and about and, reasonably enough, didn't see why he should be outside in the circumstances. *God*, I thought, *I could do with his company*, but opening the kitchen door was most certainly not something I wanted to do right now.

With some difficulty I managed to drag the kitchen table over to the door until it was close enough to allow the door to be opened no more than twelve centimeters or so. I clambered up on the table, feeling a little stupid, but nevertheless took a deep breath and unlocked the door as quietly as I could. As I turned the knob and opened it a fraction, Guinness shot in beneath the table like a bullet out of a gun. I banged the door shut and locked it immediately and the cat leaped on to the table, clearly realizing that, this evening, the normal rules did not apply. I gathered him up in my arms, grateful for his comforting, warm furriness.

A few minutes later, Andy McFadden and a Buncrana guard I didn't know were at my door. They had the grace not to smile as I shoved the table away to let them in, but, of course, a thorough search of the house, shed, and garden turned up nothing. Whoever had been at the kitchen window was long gone.

But by the time they had accepted my offer of tea and left shortly afterwards, I was feeling much saner. I fell asleep quickly with a cat who couldn't believe his luck curled up on my bed.

Chapter 8

I TURNED OVER the events of the night before in my mind as I left the house the next morning. I was absolutely certain I hadn't imagined the face at the window, but it hadn't been clear enough for me to recognize who it was; it could have been anyone. So I decided to assume it was merely a drunk taking a shortcut home through my garden and shoved it to the back of my mind. I had more pressing matters to concern me this morning. I had to get to Letterkenny for my appointment at the hospital.

Within two hours, I realized I couldn't have chosen a worse day. A delegation from the County Council was visiting the hospital. I had to wait to get in to see my client, and when I finally did get to see him, the poor man didn't even recognize me. I spent about twenty minutes with him to see if things improved and then I went looking for the Matron.

I found her standing in a corridor talking to a thin man in a gray suit. She introduced me.

"Ben O'Keeffe, this is Aidan Doherty, one of our prominent County Councillors."

I shook Doherty's hand. Though a handsome man, he looked as if he should be in one of the beds, not pressing the flesh. His hair was sticking up as if he'd been combing his hands through it for hours and his shirt looked as if he'd slept in it. His shirt, hair, and face were various shades of gray.

No sooner had we shaken hands than another man in a suit appeared at the end of the corridor waving at him and calling his name. Doherty nodded a polite goodbye and left.

"Lovely man," the Matron remarked as she watched his departing figure.

"Is he? I don't know him at all."

"Not at all like your usual County Councillor. Always talks to the patients when he comes here. And, more importantly, he actually listens to them. I think he really seems to try his best to help." She lowered her voice. "Much nicer than the wife."

I hadn't time to get into one of those conversations. I smiled. "About . . ."

"Oh, yes. Sorry – of course. He's not so great today, is he? I'm sorry about that. You've probably had a wasted journey."

"Not at all. I was glad to be able to see him. But I'm certainly going to have to come back."

"Some days he is absolutely perfect, you know."

"I'm going to get Brendan Quinn the psychiatrist to see him," I said. "So maybe you would keep an eye on him for the next few days and let me know when he is having a good day?"

"Of course," she promised.

"Great. I can call Quinn to do an affidavit of mental capacity and I'll get up straight away then."

It may seem obvious, but in cases like this, will and lucidity have to coincide. For a hospital will this can mean that the logistics are pretty awkward. If there is any doubt about a person's capacity, you need an affidavit from a medical practitioner drawn up at the same time as the will.

★   ★   ★

An hour later I found myself sitting in a plush 1960s-style, low-backed leather armchair in the Buncrana waiting room of Dr. Brendan Quinn. An enormous fish tank filled with exotically colored tropical fish sat in the corner of the room. It occurred to me that maybe I should get some. Fish are supposed to be calming. I hadn't felt calm since Wednesday morning and probably not for a long time before that.

I was shown into an office even more plush than the waiting room, if that were possible. The walls were a soft forest green with dark wooden panelling and the room was dominated by a huge mahogany desk in front of a bay window which looked out over the sea.

"Nice pad," I said as I shook hands with the tanned, gray-haired man on the other side of the desk. Despite my dealings with Quinn over the years, I had never actually been in his office.

"Why thank you, Miss O'Keeffe." The doctor bowed his head in mock formality.

"Were you away? That's some color you have."

"Italy for two weeks, the Amalfi coast. Without the lads, for once. We just got back yesterday."

"So that's why you're working on a Saturday morning. I was surprised to see the light on."

"Oh, I'm back in at the deep end. I arranged some appointments for this morning before I left. Did I see that you left a message about an affidavit of mental capacity for a will?"

"Yes. I left the client's details with the message. He's in Letterkenny General. I'd be grateful if you'd see him whenever you get the chance. You know the procedure. I'll have to see him the same day, after you've examined him. As soon as possible if you can; he's not expected to last long."

Quinn took his diary from the drawer of his desk and made a note. "What's he like today?"

"Not great, I'm afraid. The Matron is going to call me when he's in better form, and I'll call you, if that's okay."

"That's fine. If I don't hear from you, I'll look in on him on Monday morning; I'm at the hospital anyway. I can give you a call after, let you know how I found him."

"Great."

Quinn sat back in his chair. "Now, what's the real reason you're here? You could have rung me about that. Or just waited for me to call you back."

I smiled. "You can't get anything past a shrink. I was wondering, what do you know about exit counseling – you know, cults and the like?"

He frowned. "Any particular reason?"

"A client of mine died during the week in rather odd circumstances. I'm pretty sure she was an ex-member of a cult called the Children of Damascus."

Something about the expression on Quinn's face made me wade in with both feet. "Her name was Marguerite Etienne."

Quinn paled visibly. *Jesus*, I thought, *he knew her.*

"She wasn't a patient of yours, was she?" I went on.

"You know I can't discuss that." *Yes, she was.*

I shook my head. "No, no, of course. I know that."

All of the color suddenly seemed to have drained from Quinn's face. His tan had faded to a yellowy-gray. "When did she die?"

"Tuesday night, they think."

"How?"

"She drowned. Her body was found on a beach close to Glendara. The guards are investigating her death but they seem to think it's most likely to be suicide. I'm not so sure."

His eyes narrowed. "What do you mean?"

"I just don't think she killed herself. I thought you might be able to give me some information about exit counseling and the longterm psychiatric effects of being a member of a cult like the Damascans."

Quinn looked down at his hands as if he wasn't sure who they belonged to.

"And whether someone like Marguerite would be likely to do something like that?" I added.

His face was unreadable. He started playing with his fingers.

"So, do you know anything about it?" I pressed. "Or can you put me in touch with someone who does?"

He looked up. "What exactly is your role in all this?"

I shifted uncomfortably in my seat. "None officially. Just concern, I suppose. She was my client."

Quinn looked for a few seconds as if he was struggling to come to a decision. When he spoke again, he appeared to have regained control. Cool professionalism had returned.

"Okay. Well, as you might imagine, cult membership is not a particularly big problem in Inishowen, so I'm not exactly an expert in the area. But if you want, I can give you a bit of general information about the whole theory behind exit counseling."

"Shoot. I'm all ears."

He leaned back. "Obviously, the ideal is that someone leaving a cult like the Damascans will obtain specialized counseling straight away. But if that doesn't happen, it's generally recognized that people who have been through a traumatic experience may not realize it consciously for years to come. Many people, and this is often true of ex-cult members, develop a coping mechanism called Dissociative Identity Disorder or DID, which effectively means burying memories. In the context of a cult which involves enforced thinking and behavior, often over a long period of time, these memories may not always be part of a person's everyday thinking. They may become buried after that person leaves the cult, and are never dealt with."

"Never?" I asked.

"Usually the memories resurface at some stage, triggered by something that reminds the person of their experiences or because they begin to feel safe with someone they can talk to. It is then that they find that they need to deal with their issues and should have exit counseling at that stage – even if it is years after they have left the cult."

Alain Veillard's death, I thought. That was Marguerite's trigger.

"I see. And how successful would counseling be at that stage?"

"It depends. There's no reason why it shouldn't be just as successful as if it had happened immediately after leaving the cult."

"So, if you had someone who had left, say, twenty years or so ago, and they were now getting counseling, would you say they would be a suicide risk?"

Quinn avoided my eye. "Unlikely, I would have thought, if they were getting treatment, if they were under the regular care of a psychiatrist."

At that point he began to examine a file on his desk with great interest. Disassociation was not only the preserve of the mentally ill, apparently.

Further questioning produced nothing. Dr. Quinn made it clear, as they say in Donegal, that I had *got my gettings*.

I was standing in the waiting room, just about to head out on to the street when something made me turn around and knock on the door of his office. Before Quinn had a chance to reply, I opened it and stuck my head in.

"The funeral's at twelve o'clock today. In Glendara."

He didn't respond.

Chapter 9

BY NOON THE sky had turned a deep blue, and the sun emerged for the first time in a week as Maeve and I made our way up the long steps to St Peter and Paul's parish church in Glendara. It felt like a strange day for a funeral. In Donegal funerals usually take place under gray skies and involve much standing about in the rain in a cold and windy graveyard. But the weather today seemed strangely unsympathetic. Even the seagulls appeared more active than usual, swooping and diving and calling out to each other high above us.

The huge church looked almost empty as we walked up the aisle, Hal McKinney standing to one side in his undertaker's black suit, hands clasped formally in front of him. Only the front three pews on either side were occupied. And they weren't full. Simon Howard and Phyllis were there, and I recognized one or two of the women from Marguerite's yoga class. I was glad too to see that Iggy McDaid, the man who had found her body, had also come to pay his respects.

One person I hadn't expected to see was Molloy. But there he was, sitting on the aisle side of the last pew to be occupied. He looked up as Maeve and I slipped in beside him and gave me a smile. *I must be forgiven*, I thought.

Sitting alone on the right at the front of the church was a slim, dark young woman I didn't recognize.

"Who's that?" I asked Molloy, behind my hand.

"The daughter," he whispered back. "We found an address for her in the house. She flew over this morning."

"Oh, right."

"Are you okay? I heard you had a bit of a fright last night." His eyes, when they met mine, were full of concern, and my stomach did a weird little flip.

I looked down. "Fine, yeah. It was nothing really."

The church fell silent as the service began, and I looked around me. There couldn't have been more than twelve people in the church. If a person's funeral was a reflection of how they had lived, then it was hard not to conclude that Marguerite had led a very lonely life. Had she really touched so few lives in the two years she had lived in Inishowen, her death largely unnoticed by the people she had lived amongst every day? Was that the inevitable fate of a blow-in who didn't have family in the area?

Later, standing with the little group around the grave as Marguerite's coffin was lowered in, it struck me as odd that Marguerite should be buried here, in the Catholic graveyard in Glendara. Her connection to Inishowen didn't seem that strong. Had she even been Catholic? I presumed she must have been if she was being buried here. Maybe she had returned to Catholicism after she left the Damascans.

I wondered who had arranged the funeral. Her daughter? But then why would she not want to take her mother's body back to Norway with her? Marguerite's daughter certainly wasn't a Catholic; that was one thing I did know.

When the rosary ended, I joined the little queue of people waiting to sympathise with her at the graveside.

"I'm so sorry about your mother, Adeline." I held out my hand to the elegant figure in the expensive black suit. Physically, she was her mother's daughter. The same striking coloring, smooth skin, black hair, dark eyes. She was exceptionally thin, immaculately turned out, formally polite. But her eyes were torpid, her expression ice cold.

"My name is Abra, but thank you," she replied, accepting my handshake unsmilingly.

"Oh, I'm sorry."

"Excuse me, but I don't know your name either. I don't know anyone here." Her English was good, but her accent was stronger than Marguerite's. It was different too, not so obviously French.

I introduced myself. "I'm Ben O'Keeffe. I was your mother's solicitor. If there's anything I can do . . ."

A cold interruption cut me off mid-sentence. "Thank you. You're very kind. But we have our own solicitors."

I flushed. She thought I was touting for business. Before I had a chance to clarify what I meant, she moved on to Phyllis and shook her hand. It couldn't have been clearer that I had been dismissed.

I walked over to stand beside Molloy while I waited for Maeve, who was still in the little queue.

"Not what you'd call warm, is she?" I muttered.

"No. But then, I'm sure this is all a bit weird for her. Being summoned to the funeral of a mother she hasn't seen for twenty years who has committed suicide."

"Suicide?" It was all I could do to keep my voice from being heard by everyone in the graveyard.

Molloy shepherded me towards the footpath leading back to the square. "Sorry. I meant to tell you before now, although the final decision was really only made this morning. We've closed our investigation."

"What?"

He sighed. "I knew you wouldn't be pleased. Look, Ben, as I told you on Thursday, the pathologist indicated that it's very difficult to distinguish between ante- and post-mortem injuries in drowning. It's because the blood is washed away. So the injury to her head could have happened before or after she died. The only reason we opened an investigation at all was because it wasn't clear cut; the pathologist could not be sure that the death was a suicide."

"So, what's changed?"

"A number of things. Firstly, there was no sign of an intruder or a struggle when we searched her house. Or on the beach where we found her clothes."

"That doesn't mean anything. It could have been someone she knew. She could have let them into her house, and they could have gone down to the beach together. Or she could have been taken by surprise on the beach."

Molloy disagreed. "Her clothes and shoes were on the shore with her house keys in the pocket of her jacket. And then, when we talked to the police in Norway to get help to track down the daughter, they filled us in on that strange sect she is a part of. I presume you knew all about that."

"I didn't, actually. Not till yesterday. Anyway, what did that have to do with your decision to give up the investigation?"

"Nothing directly. But when we discovered that Miss Etienne was also part of that cult when she was younger, I had a chat with a psychologist who does some work for the National

Bureau of Criminal Investigation. Just to get his view on it. And according to him, suicide rates amongst ex-cult members are very high. Even years after leaving the cult."

I frowned. "It wasn't Brendan Quinn, was it?"

"No. Why?"

"No reason. But what about the will?"

"Okay, that is a bit odd," Molloy conceded. "But it's not unheard of to have a suicide victim with unfinished business. Maybe it wasn't something she planned. Maybe she did it on impulse. She could also have thought her instructions to you were sufficient; she might not have realized she had to come back to sign something."

"No," I insisted. "She knew she wasn't finished with it. I told you that. She was coming back in the next day. We talked about it. I told you she was frightened, for God's sake. Doesn't that count for anything?"

Molloy looked exasperated. "There were a number of other reasons why we decided to close the file, most of which I can't tell you. The pathologist came back to us on one or two things I can't go into that also point towards suicide."

I shook my head in disbelief.

"We have nowhere else to go, Ben. We spoke to everyone in the area who knew her, and no one seemed to know anything. As a matter of fact, no one really seemed to know her very well at all."

"Oh come on, someone must know something."

"Not necessarily. We are aware that she kept to herself. She often walked on Lagg, apparently, and it seems this time she intended not to come back. Overall, there's no reason to doubt that it was anything other than suicide."

I was dumbfounded. So that's why Molloy had forgiven me. The guards didn't need me anymore. As far as they were concerned, the case was solved.

"So that's it. Case closed?"

"Well, yes. Insofar as there ever was a case. It was always far more likely to be suicide. But with the post-mortem results being inconclusive, we had to keep an open mind for a bit, see if anyone came forward."

"Four days? You kept it open for four days? You broke your hearts," I snapped.

"We just don't have the resources to pursue something like this, Ben. I can understand why you're upset. I know she was a client of yours but I'm afraid that's the way it is. It's a suicide."

"Tom. She was frightened."

Molloy sighed. "You're the only one pushing for this. I spoke to her daughter this morning, and she has no difficulty with the investigation being closed. She accepts what has happened. She told us that she was aware her mother was always a bit fragile."

Now I saw red. "Of course no one's pushing for it! Sure the woman was a blow-in, and nobody cares about a blow-in. And her daughter hardly knew her. If she was a local, you'd—"

Molloy interrupted me. "That's not fair, Ben."

Before I could argue further, Maeve and Simon Howard appeared suddenly together, and Molloy leaped at the opportunity to escape.

"I have to go. I need to get back to the garda station."

I glared at his departing back as he strode off towards the town, not realizing that Maeve was trying to get my attention. When I finally tore my eyes away from Molloy, she and Simon Howard were back chatting.

I forced a smile. "So you two know each other?"

"I look after Sable," Maeve said.

"Sable?" I queried.

"My son David's Great Dane," Simon said with a grin.

"Simon's just suggested lunch," Maeve said. "What do you think? There's not much point in me going back to the clinic now. It's nearly one. The Oak?"

"Okay," I replied. "Should we ask Phyllis to join us?"

Maeve glanced in the direction of the bookseller's large figure disappearing down the pathway to the square. "I did, but she didn't want to. She's pretty down. Said she'd rather be on her own."

"Okay. Order me something, would you – anything at all – and I'll follow you down in a minute. There's something I have to do first."

The graveyard was deserted by the time I made it back there so I headed into the church. It felt a little eerie. I'm not a fan of empty churches. My experiences with them to date haven't been exactly positive.

The priest was alone at the altar doing something with communion cups and a napkin. He looked up when I entered. "Can I help you?"

"I'm sorry to bother you but I was just wondering . . . the funeral that's just finished? I was Miss Etienne's solicitor and I really need to contact her daughter. I forgot to get her details before she left, and well . . . I wondered if you might know where she was staying?"

"Of course. I think it's the Atlantic Hotel in Ballyliffin."

"That's great, thanks. How long is she staying, do you know?"

He smiled. "I've no idea, I'm afraid. A few days, I presume. I imagine she'll have to wrap up her mother's affairs."

As I turned to leave, a thought occurred and I turned back. "You did very well arranging it all so quickly, Father." I decided I'd go with the title to see if it eased the flow of information.

It seemed to. He smiled again.

"I was glad to be able to help. Miss Etienne's daughter asked the sergeant how she should go about arranging things, and he put her in touch with me. I spoke to her on the phone; she told me to organise everything and said she would be happy with whatever I decided. It was a bit unusual but it made everything very straightforward. Hal did the rest."

"You knew Miss Etienne?"

"Not well. But she did come in here sometimes; she just used to sit here quietly. She told me once that she'd been born a Catholic but had lapsed a bit."

"She wasn't unusual in that."

"True." This time his smile was sad. "No. I suppose I was just glad we could give her some comfort."

By the time I got to the Oak, Maeve had settled herself at the table closest to the fire, while Simon was leaning on the bar chatting to Carole.

I joined Maeve and she shoved a plate across the table at me. "I got you a cheese sandwich."

"Thanks."

"Bit cold, wasn't it?" I knew Maeve wasn't referring to the weather, which had kept up its treacherous show of sunshine the whole way through the burial. "I think that must be the smallest funeral I've ever seen here."

"I suppose she didn't know very many people."

"Usually pretty large then, are they?" Simon appeared behind us with a tray of soup and bread, and Maeve moved to one
side to allow him in.

"You've seen the church. You should see the size of the wed-
dings." Maeve turned towards me. "What was that big confab
with your sergeant about?"

Simon grinned. "*Your* sergeant?"

"They've decided Marguerite's death was suicide," I said.
"They've closed the investigation."

Maeve's face fell. "God. That's really sad. Simon, you lived
next to her, didn't you?"

Simon nodded, spoon halfway to his mouth.

"Was she depressed, do you think?"

"No idea, to be honest," he said. "She was a little bit odd,
but no, I wouldn't have thought she was depressed."

I joined in the interrogation. "What do you mean *odd*?"

"A little strange sometimes. Almost other-worldly for want
of a better way of putting it. Erratic."

"How, exactly?" I leaned forward on one elbow.

Maeve raised an eyebrow, but I pretended I didn't see it.

"Oh, I don't know," Simon said. "It was just an impression
I formed. As I said, I didn't know her very well. It is bloody
tragic though, what happened."

"It's a wee bit better than the alternative, I suppose," Maeve
said with a sigh. "It would be horrible to think that someone
had something to do with her death. But God, the suicide rates
up here are too high."

"*The less said about life's sores the better,*" Simon said.

"Oscar Wilde?" I guessed.

"*The Picture of Dorian Gray,*" he confirmed, bowing in my
direction.

"Very impressive," Maeve said. "What was all that about the name, by the way? Did I hear the daughter tell you her name was *Abra*? I thought her name was Adeline. I'm sure someone told me that."

I nodded. "She did say Abra. Do you know her?" I asked Simon.

"Didn't even know she existed." He flashed Carole a smile as she delivered his coffee to the table. "Striking-looking girl though."

The barmaid flashed him an equally broad one and sashayed back to the bar.

Maeve grinned. "You're not having much bother settling in by the looks of things. I've never had anything delivered to me in my life here."

"I think you might be the wrong gender," Simon told her.

"Clearly. So how did you end up here, as a matter of interest?"

"What artist wouldn't want to work here? It's one of the most beautiful places in the world."

"Okay, that's fair enough. We'll accept that, won't we, Ben?" Maeve said.

Simon looked apologetic. "Actually it's a bit like Scotland, which is *the* most beautiful place in the world, I'm afraid. No, the truth is I needed a change of scenery for a while. And my son, he . . ." He stopped suddenly.

"The son I've met?" I prompted.

He looked at me as if confused for a second and then seemed to re-focus. "Yes. I only have the one, thank God. What I was going to say was that it was he who suggested we come here. He said he thought the place was beautiful. I was surprised by that: David doesn't like color; he cannot usually see beyond the gray. Not exactly painting with the full palette, the poor boy."

Maeve and I exchanged a look.

Simon bowed his head. "You're right. I'm being harsh. I actually thought it might be good for us to live together again. But it hasn't really worked out that way. Instead I've ended up having a Great Dane dumped on me, and David's away more than he's here." He smiled ruefully. "Anyway, more coffees?"

The next half hour passed with ease and Simon turned out to be engaging company. I was desperate to pursue the subject of Marguerite a bit further but I wasn't sure how, especially with Maeve's eyes boring into me every time I mentioned it. Instead, Simon talked about his own work, asked interested questions about Maeve's and my choice of career and what it was like to live and work in such a small town. And he managed to raise our spirits in a way we wouldn't have managed alone.

As we were getting up to leave, the door of the pub opened and David Howard stuck his head in. He nodded wordlessly at his father and closed the door again.

"Ah, the Prodigal Son." Simon pulled on his jacket. "By the way, I'm having an exhibition in the Beacon Hall and the opening is tomorrow night. Would either of you be interested in coming?"

"I can't, I'm afraid. I'm on call as usual," Maeve sighed.

"Benedicta?"

"Call me Ben."

"I thought Benedicta was the name on your brass plate?"

"It is, but . . ."

He shot me another one of his wolfish grins. "I like Benedicta. It's kind of prim."

Chapter 10

AFTER WE SEPARATED I felt at a bit of a loose end – the office wasn't open on Saturdays. Believe me, I was well aware of how sad that made me appear.

I called into Stoop's newsagents to pick up the Saturday papers. When I came out, I caught sight of Simon and David standing in the middle of the square with an elegant, black Great Dane leaning against Simon's legs – the famous Sable, I assumed. I stopped, opened the paper, and pretended to be engrossed in it for a minute or two.

As I watched them over the top of it, it occurred to me, yet again, that the son really was cut from a different cloth from his father. Where Simon was tall and broad-shouldered in an overtly masculine kind of way, David was narrow and slight, and somewhat effeminate. And from what I could see, although they were too far away for me to hear what they were saying, they were having a row. Simon gestured angrily while his son stood with his hands clasped in front of him, looking bored and disengaged.

Suddenly, he turned away in exasperation. But before he managed to look in my direction, I darted around the corner, walking quickly in the direction of my car.

★   ★   ★

Simon's ebullient company had kept my demons at bay over lunch, but they returned with a vengeance as I drove by the garda station on my way home. I still couldn't believe that Molloy had given up so easily. The suicide verdict was wrong, I was sure of it, but what could I do? I wondered if there was any point in driving out to Ballyliffin to see Marguerite's daughter. I had asked the priest where she was staying, thinking that maybe if I talked to her, I could convince her to push the guards into pursuing their inquiry. But now I wasn't so sure.

This was one problem I couldn't talk through with Molloy. So I drove past the garda station and pulled into the parking area in front of the veterinary clinic.

The door swung open easily but the reception area was deserted, so I called out, but there was no reply. I checked my watch. It was five to two; everyone would still be at lunch. I sat in one of the seats in the waiting area and tried to engross myself in a dog magazine. There must be someone about if the door was unlocked, I decided. After a few minutes, it occurred to me that Maeve might be out in the back area where they examined the bigger farm animals. I made it only as far as the back door before I collided with her, all boiler suited up, tugging at her boots.

"When did you appear? I never heard you." She leaned against the door for balance.

"A few minutes ago. Are you in the middle of something?"

"Just finished. For the minute, at any rate. Something up?"

"I fancied a chat."

She grinned. "Have we not just had one?"

"Without company."

"Right." Maeve shrugged off the boiler suit, stepped out of it and hung it on the back of the door. "More coffee?"

"Great."

I followed her into the back office, perched on her desk and tapped a pen against the desk distractedly as she switched on the kettle and spooned some instant coffee into two mugs.

When she had finished, she leaned back against the counter. "Okay. Stop tapping and spit it out."

"What do you think of Marguerite's death – honestly? Do you think it was suicide?"

"Why? What do you mean? I thought you said the guards . . ."

I nodded. "They did. But I'm not convinced."

She raised her eyebrows, just as she had when I had been quizzing Simon. I began to wonder if this was a mistake.

I picked up the pen again. "You did say you thought it was strange when you first heard about it."

Maeve crossed her arms. "I suppose I did. It was because she didn't seem the type. But it's never something you expect, is it? I mean, I hardly knew her really. Not personally. I wouldn't have known if she was depressed."

"No, I suppose not," I said noncommittally.

"Do you have any reason to think it wasn't suicide?"

I couldn't tell Maeve about Marguerite's visit to the office. Telling Molloy, a guard, was one thing, but telling Maeve would be a step too far. "Nothing definite, I suppose," I said. "Just a feeling I can't seem to shake off. I can't help but think that something doesn't quite fit, but I can't put my finger on it."

The kettle boiled and switched itself off.

"So what do you think it was, if it wasn't suicide? An accident?" Maeve asked as she poured boiling water into the two mugs.

I shrugged.

"Murder?" she said, looking incredulous. "Jesus, Ben, you'd want to be pretty sure of your ground before you start tossing that word around. Remember what happened the last time."

I stirred my coffee. "I know. But I wondered if maybe I should go and see the daughter before she goes back. What do you think?"

Maeve's eyes widened. "Why would you want to do that, for God's sake? She nearly took the nose off you at the funeral."

"I thought maybe she might be able to persuade Molloy . . ."

"Ben." Maeve waved her spoon at me. "Don't meddle. The guards know what they're doing. You're a solicitor, not a detective."

"Yeah, I know, I know. Forget I said anything. Look, are you going to this art exhibition tomorrow night?"

"No. I told you earlier – I'm on call. As always," Maeve grumbled.

"Ah, go on. Can't you swap with someone?"

She frowned. "Now why would you need me to go to an art exhibition with you? You're not going to start asking that sculptor guy more questions about Marguerite, are you? I wondered what you were up to at lunch."

"No," I responded indignantly. "I just thought we could do with a bit of culture, that's all."

Maeve's expression changed. A grin crept over her face. "You like him. You fancy the Scottish sculptor and you want me to ride shotgun."

I looked away. "Something like that."

She rubbed her hands together. "Excellent. Well, good on you. Still can't go, I'm afraid. You'll have to fly solo this time."

While Maeve went looking for biscuits, I gazed out the window, wondering what the hell I was getting myself into. Then something caught my eye in the corner of the yard. I looked closer, but my brain had difficulty processing what I was seeing for a second, it was so ludicrous. Sitting upright in a basin, with its forelegs sticking out in front, wearing a serene expression and a bright yellow bucket on its head, was a sheep. I laughed.

"What on earth are you doing to that poor creature out the back?"

She joined me at the window. "Oh, the ewe. She had lambs a couple of hours ago and the womb prolapsed. Couldn't get it back in, so she's sitting in a basin of disinfectant until the swelling goes down."

"And what's with the bucket? She looks like a man in a top hat waiting for a whiskey and soda."

She grinned. "That's to stop her moving. If you put something on their heads, they stay still."

I shook my head in disbelief. "Incredible. I'd never have known that."

It was impossible to miss the note of warning in her voice when she replied, "We all have to stick to what we're trained for, Ben."

Chapter 11

I LIFTED MY head gingerly off the pillow knowing that any sudden movement was going to hurt, opened my eyes a tiny fraction, and checked the time on my watch. It was ten to twelve. With a huge effort, I flipped the pillow over and laid my hot cheek down again on the cooler side. I stretched my arm out for the glass of water I had at least had the foresight to bring up the night before, and promptly knocked it over. God, just what I needed: a red wine hangover.

I dragged myself out of bed, picked up the glass from the floor, and shuffled to the bathroom to refill it. As I fell back into bed, I caught sight of a crumpled sheet of paper on my bedside table. I picked it up and smoothed it out, then sighed. It was one of my drunken lists. Across the top I had written the name *Marguerite*. Underneath I had added *1. Death certificate*. I hadn't made it as far as number two. I searched my addled memory for what, in my intoxicated state, I had meant — but no luck.

With a mammoth effort, I threw off the covers and I made my way across the landing towards the shower. A loud scratching noise at the window made me jump. I opened the window to let Guinness in.

"Well, hello. What have you been up to all night, eh?"

He jumped down from the windowsill, purring loudly as he weaved in between my legs, my lack of co-ordination allowing him to trip me up repeatedly as I stumbled towards the bathroom.

It came back to me while I was inhaling my third cup of coffee. Molloy had told me at the funeral that the post-mortem had turned up one or two things he couldn't tell me about, and last night — somewhere between my first and second bottle of wine — I had been trying to figure out how I could get a copy of that report. It was then that I remembered ordering a death certificate for a client in a probate case about a year beforehand and being surprised when the registrar sent me the certificate with the post-mortem report attached. I had wondered at the time if it had been a mistake, sent in error simply because the certificate was ordered by a solicitor. But maybe it could happen again? It was worth a try. I didn't see any ethical problem in ordering Marguerite's death certificate. Death certificates were documents of public record.

As I washed my cup, Molloy's words echoed in my mind. *"You're the only one pushing for this."* I had no doubt he was telling the truth. It did seem, as far as everyone else was concerned, that the whole episode was finished, conveniently dismissed as the unfortunate suicide of a disturbed woman with a tragic past. Marguerite's death had provoked some mild sympathy, but no one cared, not really. She was dead and buried now and would be forgotten about by this morning.

Well, maybe not by everybody. Phyllis cared, that had become clear over the past few days. And I'd spent enough time thinking about things. It was time to actually do something.

I drove the five miles along the coast road to Glendara in silence; a sore head prohibits radio, I've discovered. I rolled down the window to breathe in the salty air, and it helped. The day was gray and blustery, the sea was streaked with purple and green and there were lacy patches of white water visible in the distance.

I drove through Glendara and on out to Ballyliffen past the golf links and the Isle of Doagh where Marguerite had been found. I parked the car in front of the old Atlantic Hotel and battled through the wind to get to the front door.

My heart sank when I saw who was behind the reception desk.

"Hi, Jackie."

Jackie Breen, Carole-from-the-Oak's sister, looked up. She has always reminded me of a Persian cat – fluffy but spiteful. "Ben. What brings you out here?"

"I'm after one of your guests."

Her eyes narrowed with curiosity. "Sounds ominous."

I smiled. "Not really. I just wondered if I could have a word with her, if she's about. Adeline Veillard? Or Abra," I said as an afterthought.

The receptionist didn't even need to look. "You're out of luck. She's gone. Checked out this morning."

"Are you sure?"

"Aye. Was only ever booked in for the one night, and she left at the crack of dawn this morning. Didn't even have breakfast, I don't think. Can I . . . ?"

I cut her off before she could quiz me further. "No, it's fine, Jackie. Thanks anyway."

I left the hotel reeling. I had let Marguerite down all over again. And I had the same damn hangover as the last time.

★   ★   ★

I drove back into Glendara, made my way straight to the office, and quickly typed up a letter to the Registrar of Births,
Marriages and Deaths in Letterkenny. I took a stamp from the
drawer and dropped the envelope in the post box.

Standing on the footpath outside the post office, I realized
that I didn't feel like going back home. Maybe because she had
seemed to be one of the few people to be genuinely distressed
about Marguerite's death, I found myself propelled towards
Phyllis's book shop. She opened sometimes on a Sunday afternoon – completely dependent on her own whim, of course.

As I approached the shop, I noticed a group of teenagers
hanging around the wooden bench outside, chatting. One of
the boys waved at me and I smiled back. It was Hugh O'Connor.
He was sitting at the very center of the group, and even in the
few seconds that I watched, it was clear that he was the star of
the show. Although those on the periphery glanced briefly in
my direction to see who had gained his attention, they immediately transferred their gaze back to him, watching him
intently not only when he was speaking, but checking for his
response when others were. An acne-covered, gangly-looking
boy sitting beside him seemed particularly in awe of him. Hugh
O'Connor had something, there was no doubt about that. That
kind of charisma rarely leaves a person. If you don't have it
when you're eighteen, you'll never have it, and if you have it at
eighteen, you'll have it at eighty-five.

The doorbell jangled when I entered the shop and Phyllis
looked at me from behind her newspaper. Today she was wearing bright purple, from top to toe. The headline on the front
page read *council row on re-zoning.*

"Load of nonsense," she said, putting the paper down. "Ben, how are you?"

"Just in for a potter, if that's okay. And to see how you're doing."

She removed her glasses. "Oh, not that great, to be honest. Hard to believe someone so young could be here one day and gone the next. Just like that. I mean, she was here last Saturday, sitting on this very stool."

"I know. I'm sorry I didn't get to talk to you at the funeral."

"No, well, I wasn't really in the humor."

"She didn't seem to know many people, did she?"

"So you'd think. The church wasn't exactly packed, was it?" Phyllis pursed her lips. "I don't know. You'd think people would pay their respects at the end, no matter what went on during life."

"What do you mean?"

"Oh nothing, don't mind me."

Before I could probe any further, there was movement behind one of the bookshelves, and I jumped slightly as David Howard, Simon's son, emerged from one of the aisles and disappeared back down another. Despite the wooden floor, he had managed to move completely silently.

Phyllis leaned forward. "That boy gives me the willies."

"He doesn't say a lot," I conceded.

"No, I mean, he really gives me the willies. Do you mind staying with me till he leaves?"

"Seriously?" I was surprised; Phyllis is no shrinking violet.

She looked a little embarrassed. "Is that okay?"

"Sure. If you want me to."

After a few minutes, David came up to the counter with a couple of tatty-looking hardbacks. He gave me a nod of recognition, paid without a word, and left the shop. Phyllis looked relieved.

Before I could say anything further the door reopened and two women came in with what looked like school book-lists in their hands.

"I'll leave you to it," I said. "I'll go have a browse."

Phyllis pointed towards the stairs. "Browse away. There's some more new stock upstairs, if you're interested. It's that box I started unpacking when you were here last week. I never got around to finishing it. I'm not exactly motivated at the moment. It's still by the window."

Fifteen minutes later I staggered back down the stairs with my arms full of paperbacks. Never shop with a hangover; your judgement is shot.

Phyllis was standing at the window, arms crossed. When she heard my tread she turned.

She tut-tutted. "Ben, you're like me. You think you're going to live to be a million and be able to read everything you want to."

"I know." I dropped the books on the counter. "I think I'm developing a problem."

"And I never see any of them coming back," she said. "Not that I'm complaining. It's just that your cottage must be beginning to look like this shop."

Phyllis buys back many of the books she sells. It's no wonder the town doesn't have a library.

I walked over to join her by the window. Hugh and his gang were still outside.

Phyllis commented, "That boy is way too handsome for his own good."

Although there were at least six kids out there, there was no question as to who she was talking about.

"Good-looking boy, all right," I said.

She tapped her finger on the glass and Hugh looked up and waved. "Favorite spot for those kids lately, for some reason. Hugh seems to be always there, especially on a Saturday."

As we watched, Hugh got up from the bench and left with the gangly boy who had been sitting beside him. The other kids immediately dispersed too, their reason for being there having departed with the two lads.

Phyllis turned back towards the shop, and I followed her to the cash register.

"His mother was my best friend in school, you know. She was a stunner in her youth too. She had him so young though – her looks didn't last, I'm afraid. Think it's made her suffer a bit."

I poked about in my bag for my wallet while Phyllis checked each of the books.

"Three euro okay for each of these?" she said.

I left the bookshop with two bulging paper bags in my arms. It was all I could do not to drop them both on the pavement when a voice behind me made me jump.

"You're Ben."

I turned. David Howard was standing by the bench where the kids had been sitting.

"Oh, hi. David, isn't it? How are you?" I stumbled over my words. Had he been waiting for me?

"Fine."

I struggled to come up with something to say. "Em . . . I saw your dog in the square yesterday. Sable, isn't it? She's beautiful."

"I saw you with my father in the pub," he said.

"Yes. We went for lunch after the funeral."

"He doesn't usually go to the funerals of his women."

"I'm sorry?"

"Other than my mother's." David spoke as if he was talking to himself. "He went to hers."

"I'm sorry," I said uneasily, not entirely sure what I was sorry for.

"He has an appetite. He says it's an appetite for life but it's not. It's for people. He consumes people. And they don't even notice he's doing it, most of the time."

He spoke as if he were explaining something to someone exceedingly stupid – me, presumably. And when he had finished he looked at me expectantly, his father's eyes unblinking, waiting for me to flinch while my mind raced, searching for a way to respond.

But my mouth was still open when he walked away, leaving me standing on the footpath with two bags of books. Now I could see why Phyllis had said that he gave her the willies. What the hell had he meant; *the funerals of his women*? Was Marguerite one of *Simon's women*?

The car park of the Beacon Hall was almost full when I pulled into one of the last remaining spaces, locked the car and walked towards the main door. I wished Maeve was with me.

Once inside, I followed the sound of voices up the stairs towards the public hall. The room was packed but hushed; a speech was being made at the top. There was a desk to the right of the door with a very pretty girl handing out catalogues, and a long table with glasses of red and white wine. I took a brochure and helped myself to a glass of white.

Through the crowd I could see sculptures on low plinths placed at intervals along the walls. The collection seemed to be mostly figures, almost African in style. I made my way to the closest, a figure sitting on a block with its head in its hands and its elbows resting on its knees. It was impossible to tell whether the figure was male or female. It had long legs and tiny feet, no eyes, no features at all, in fact, apart from a rough impression of a nose, but it was very striking.

I searched the sea of faces for someone I knew and finally recognized a voice: one that was utterly incapable of a whisper. Liam McLaughlin was lurking behind one of the pieces chatting to a couple of people.

He greeted me with a grin. "Didn't know you were a patron of the arts. Or is it the artist?"

I retaliated. "I suppose there must be some tax relief in it, if you're here."

"Naturally."

"Not listening to the speeches?" I asked, nodding towards the front of the crowd as the people Liam had been talking to moved away.

"Nah. It's Aidan Doherty. A lot of nonsense about how well the Council are supporting the arts . . . heard it a hundred times before." Liam took a sip of his wine and made a face. "Although he looks bloody awful. He's lost a lot of weight."

I glanced up at the stage. Doherty was certainly very thin.

"So, what do you think?" Liam gestured towards the sculpture closest to him. "Is he any good?"

I looked. It was another figure with its head buried in its hands. Though again the face was not visible this one was clearly a woman and it spoke of utter despair; it was hard not to be genuinely moved, looking at it.

"He is."

"Not cheap."

"No, I expect not."

I heard a voice at my shoulder, and a familiar scent in my nostrils. "So you came."

I turned and Simon smiled broadly, a glass of red in his hand.

"And what do you think of my humble offerings?"

"Great — I mean — they're wonderful. Honestly."

"Why, thank you," he bowed. "No sign of your vet friend?"

"She's on call, unfortunately."

"Well, I'm very glad you came anyway."

"Simon?" The pretty girl from the desk appeared at his side and whispered into his ear.

"Better go. Prospective purchaser," he said with a wink, pushing his way back through the crowd.

For the next while I watched Simon work the room while I chatted with Liam. It was clear that his charm didn't hurt his sales. But two mineral waters later, I decided I'd had enough culture for one evening.

Before I reached the door, I felt a hand on my arm.

"Don't tell me you were going to leave without saying good-bye?" Simon made a sad clown face.

"You looked busy."

"I would far rather have been talking to you. To rectify things, how about you have dinner with me some evening? If you don't think I'm being too forward, that is."

I gave him one of my rabbit-in-the-headlights looks. Was it a good idea to spend the evening alone with him? I wasn't at all sure it was. But I did want to find out how close he really had been to Marguerite. Although God knows how I was going to broach it. *Was Marguerite one of your women? Oh, and by the way, do a lot of your women die?*

Aloud I said, "That would be nice. Thank you."

He bowed graciously. "I'll give you a call at the office."

And I fled.

Chapter 12

IT TOOK ME forever to get to sleep that night, and I was awake by six. Maybe it was that one glass of wine – I couldn't remember the last time I'd had only one – or maybe it was the fact that I had agreed to go out for dinner with Simon Howard.

I knew it made no sense but I couldn't help but feel that I was being disloyal to Molloy. Yes, we had had a moment, and yes, I was pretty sure it was the culmination of something that had been building between us for a long time. But that moment had happened nine months ago. Since then we had been friends and colleagues, nothing more. And he had never given me an explanation as to why he had pulled back. So why then did I feel I was betraying him by going out for dinner with another man?

It wasn't as if my intentions in doing so were romantic, whatever I had let Maeve think. Simon knew Marguerite far better than he was admitting. I was sure of it, and not just because of my encounter with David. I needed to work out why he was hiding it. Of course, I realized I was doing exactly what Maeve had warned me not to do: I was trying to play detective. But Molloy had left me no choice. If he had kept the investigation open, I would have no need to interfere.

Molloy had been a good friend to me during some of my toughest times in Inishowen. His pulling back from me romantically had not changed that. I had kept so much of my life from him for so long, he could have been hurt by that and it would have been justified. But instead, when I had finally broken down and told him the full story about my sister's death, he had stayed with me all night, watching over me from an armchair in my sitting room while I slept on the couch. And he had given me some very good advice, advice that had helped me to repair my relationship with my parents.

I owed him the same generosity of spirit that he had shown me. I knew that the decision to close the investigation into Marguerite's death hadn't been his, that it had been made elsewhere, which meant I probably owed him an apology for my behavior towards him at the funeral. So I decided to call in to the garda station on the way to the office. Also, I knew it was a long shot, but it did occur to me that if there had been a change of mind about the investigation into Marguerite's death, I wouldn't have to go to dinner with Simon after all.

McFadden was on his own at the desk.

"Morning, Andy. Is Molloy about?"

He shook his head. "He's away."

"Away? Where?"

"Dublin, I think. He went away on Saturday, said he'd be back today some time. No sign of him yet." He looked at his watch. "It's early though. I reckon he'll be back this afternoon."

"Okay. Thanks, Andy." I pulled at the handle of the door.

I heard a chuckle and turned back.

McFadden grinned. He placed his hand over his mouth in a mock whisper. "Between yourself and myself, I think there's a woman involved."

"You look wrecked," Leah greeted me cheerfully when I walked in the door of the office.

I couldn't return her smile. "Thanks. I actually had a very good night's sleep," I lied. "It's obviously not good for me."

"Your half nine appointment is here. It's Iggy McDaid. I'd swear he's pissed," she added in a low tone.

"Ah no. I'm applying for his driving licence back at the court on Wednesday. How the hell did he manage to get drunk at half nine in the morning?"

Leah grinned. "Maybe he never went to bed or maybe he just topped up last night's for breakfast. Rather you than me anyway. He stinks!'

I stuck my head into the waiting room and was greeted with an enthusiastic wave from the corner. "Five minutes, Iggy."

I returned to the desk. "God, you're right. He looks hammered."

"Didn't he find Marguerite's body?" Leah said.

I nodded and sighed. "Give me a few minutes to get myself organised."

My limbs felt heavy as I climbed the winding staircase to my office. I sat down, glanced through my list of appointments and looked despairingly at the stacks of files and correspondence on my desk. Although maybe it was no bad thing that I wouldn't get time to think today.

Five minutes later, I headed back down to reception to collect the post.

"I'll take Mr. McDaid up with me now," I said as I flicked through the envelopes.

Leah shook her head. "You can't. He's wandered off again. Probably too long for him to go without a drink."

"Oh, for God's sake."

"You've plenty of people to take his place though."

She was right. The waiting room was packed. "Who on earth are all those people?"

"It's the Concerned Parents Community Group. They have an appointment at ten."

"All of them? Do they all need to be here?"

"God knows. And," she said as she handed me a file, "Mr. Dolan and Mr. Gallagher want to have a quick word with you first."

It was hard to miss the two men I knew weren't part of any Concerned Parents committee standing by the door of the waiting room.

As I led them into the little front office, I remembered what Liam had said about Gallagher owning Marguerite's cottage. Had he bought the house after Seamus Tighe had died, picked it up for a song because no one else would buy it? Was that how these two men made their money: buying from desperate people at desperate times? I shook myself. I was being ridiculous. I had no reason to think that the Malin Head deal was anything other than a straight-up business transaction, with a willing buyer and a willing seller.

We didn't bother with seats. "Yes, gentlemen, what can I do for you? I'm still waiting for contracts, I'm afraid."

As usual it was Gallagher who spoke. "We're aware of that. But we're both going back to the States tomorrow for a few days, so we thought we'd better have a word with you before we go. Can you act as agent for us in signing if we're not in the country when they come in? We don't want to waste any time in getting the deal finalised."

"Certainly. As long as you authorise me properly in writing. I'll email you an authority to sign. I'll also have to go through the special conditions when the contract comes in before you commit yourselves to it, but we can do all that by email and phone."

"Any idea when that'll happen?"

"I'll see what I can find out." I reached for the phone on the desk.

The solicitor for the seller had a client with him so I left a message. When I hung up, I glanced at Dolan, and he looked at me expectantly as if I was some kind of performing seal he'd paid good money to see and was determined not to leave until he had seen at least one decent trick. His moustache was twitching.

"I'll call the auctioneer," I said.

Liam bellowed into the receiver as if he was using a megaphone to shout at me across the square. "McLaughlin and Son Auctioneers. Hello?"

"Liam, Ben here. Any news on that land in Malin Head? I'm still waiting on contracts. Any chance you can chase them up?"

"Aye. No bother. The old man who's selling wouldn't be the speediest mover in the world. I'll remind him to call in to his solicitor and give them instructions."

I replaced the receiver and smiled. "You probably got most of that."

"Yeah. That's okay," Gallagher said. "Let us know the minute you receive anything. We've lodged our planning application so we don't want the planning to issue until we have a water-tight agreement."

"Understood. It may take them a while to get maps, but I'll contact you immediately I get something in."

★ ★ ★

I worked through lunch and Leah brought a sandwich and some takeaway soup to my desk. She could tell I was distracted, but thankfully she didn't ask me why. At one point she had to lift my arm to pull my sleeve out of the soup and it was impossible not to notice the concerned glances and the extra cups of coffee that made their way to my desk during the course of the afternoon. By five o'clock my head was pounding.

At half past five I heard Leah's shouted goodbye up the stairs followed by the door slamming behind her, and I was alone. I'd dreaded this moment all day since my visit to the garda station that morning. I was alone with thoughts I didn't want to think and images that lurked like shadows at the edge of my consciousness. I was ashamed of how I'd allowed myself to come to rely on someone again. Ashamed of how I'd allowed my feelings for Molloy to go unchecked despite all evidence to the contrary.

There was a knock on the door. Reluctantly I went downstairs to open it. Molloy was standing on the doorstep. He looked odd, not himself, which didn't help the way I was feeling.

"Could we have a chat?" he said.

"Okay."

He followed me into reception. For some reason I remained standing and I didn't offer him a seat either. Maybe I wanted him to feel as uncomfortable as I did.

"What do you want to chat about?" I asked, knowing even as I heard myself say it, that the word *chat* was all wrong as a description of whatever was to come.

"Did you call into the station looking for me this morning?" Molloy asked.

"It doesn't matter." *Just say what you have to say and get it over with*, I thought.

He looked down.

"That's not what you've come to talk to me about, is it?"

"No, it's not." He paused.

I glanced at the stairs to my office. "I have work to do, Tom."

He sighed. "Okay. I'll just say it," he said. "I was in Dublin this weekend."

My tone was sharp. "I know. McFadden told me."

Molloy looked at me, his eyes pleading with me to understand. "I went to see Laura. Laura Callan . . ."

I didn't need a biography. I knew damn well who Laura was. Laura Callan was a forensic pathologist who had come to Inishowen to look at some bones that had been discovered some months before. And in a rather unpleasant coincidence, she had also been the pathologist who gave evidence at the trial for my sister's killing. Maybe not so much of a coincidence — it's not as if there are many pathologists in Ireland. When Marguerite's body had been found, it had crossed my mind that Dr. Callan might be about to reappear. When I had first spotted Laura Callan in Inishowen, she was one of the last people on earth I wanted to see again, but it was her presence that had prompted my opening up to Molloy — and so I had come to believe, in the long run, that her reappearance had been a good thing. At the time, Molloy had told me she was an old college friend of his.

"Go on," I said.

He examined my face. "Laura is my ex, Ben."

I felt my stomach turn over. "Ex-wife?"

He shook his head. "Ex-girlfriend. Ex-partner, I suppose. We were together for a few years a long time ago."

"I see."

"I'm sorry I didn't tell you that before. It just didn't seem . . ."

I cut across him. "You're back together."

"It's not quite as simple as that."

"Congratulations." My voice was ice.

"Ben, if you'd let me explain something . . ."

I picked up a stack of files from the reception desk, with no idea what they were or who they related to. "I'm sorry but I'm up to my tonsils here. I have a ton of work to get finished before I go home."

"Ben . . ."

"Look," I snapped. "I'm not entirely sure why you've singled me out especially to give me this good news. I mean, it's not as if I wouldn't have heard it eventually through the small-town grapevine. But I'm very happy for you."

Did I imagine the flash of hurt in his eyes or did I just wish for it? I walked towards the front door, files in hand, leaving Molloy no choice but to follow me, and I held it open for him. I just managed to close it behind him before the tears came.

Chapter 13

WHAT FOLLOWED WAS a night with even less sleep than the one before. Molloy's words played on a loop in my head and by early morning they had reduced to just two – *ex-girlfriend* – repeated over and over again like a seagull's piercing cry.

I woke at five after about two hours' sleep. At seven I gave up trying to fall back asleep, hauled myself out of bed and decided to do what I always do when I am feeling lousy – go for a swim. An icy four- or five-stroke sea swim was just what I needed to kickstart my body and mind and jolt me out of the well of self-pity in which I had spent the night.

The morning was bright and cold as I left Malin town and drove across the old bridge, much colder than it should have been in late September. I took the shore road towards Malin Head, making for Lagg Beach. After a few miles I slowed down to take the narrow road to the left leading down to the beach, but something stopped me. And after a moment's hesitation, I drove on.

The road began to incline, with wire fences and bracken on either side, and after about five hundred meters, I came to a brown signpost marked *Inis Eoghain 100* indicating a left turn up the hill. I took it, and ten minutes later, I came to the old cottage that Marguerite had described to me as hers.

I pulled in, thought for a minute, and then rooted in the glove compartment for the woolly hat and gloves I keep there all year round. The wind in Inishowen is like nowhere on earth – you learn that very quickly if you live here. I pulled on the gloves and hat, climbed out of the car and walked to the little gate.

The cottage was pretty, probably thatched at some stage, with small windows and a tiny front garden, slightly unkempt-looking. I walked up the path to the front door. Although I was sure I wouldn't get an answer, I took the precaution of using the doorknocker just in case – it wouldn't do for the local solicitor to be caught snooping if there were someone inside – but as expected, there was no response.

I peered through the front window. Through the dust, I could see what I presumed would have been Marguerite's sitting room. Except for a black iron fireplace on the inside wall and some newspapers on the floor, it was completely empty. Someone had cleared it out. I went around to the back of the house and peered through the other windows, into the kitchen and bedroom, but they were the same – empty apart from a few pieces of furniture, a table and chairs in the kitchen and a bed in the bedroom, the property of the owner Gallagher, presumably. It seemed that all of Marguerite's possessions had been taken away, all traces of her removed. She had died less than a week ago and now it was as if she had never even existed. I wondered who had done it. The daughter? Would she have had the time on her flying visit?

I turned away from the house. There was no garden at the back, only a small yard with a clothesline and a fuel shed. The yard led into a larger farmyard, but the two areas were separated by a heavy iron gate which was padlocked. I realized that this was the yard where Seamus Tighe had died. I shuddered, thoughts of Maeve trying to pull his body from the tank running through my head. And I stood for a moment with my hands on the gate, my view blocked by a rundown shed.

My usual route to Lagg was the road I had not taken on the way up. On my way back, I decided to drive a little further on to a lay-by from which you could also gain access to the sea – this time via a long pebbly stretch of shore leading back to Lagg Beach. Or Five Fingers Strand if you were talking to a tourist.

I grabbed my towel and swimming togs from the passenger seat, crossed the road, and clambered over the wall and down the rocks towards the sea. The wind was sharp, but the sky was a pale blue and the early morning light gave everything a fresh new aspect. Black cormorants hopped along the edge of the water calling out to each other, making their *pip pip* sound, and I felt that peppery feeling in my nose that comes with really icy temperatures. My swim was going to be bracing.

I walked through clumps of seaweed like heaps of brown string scattered along the water's edge and thought about Marguerite's final hours. Had she really been so full of despair that she felt she had no other choice than to take her own life? I just wasn't convinced. Marguerite had been frightened of something or someone when she came to see me, I was sure of it. And there were people who knew her better than they were admitting. I wasn't prepared to accept that she had been as lonely and isolated as she appeared, whatever Molloy said. The thought of Molloy caused a stab, but I pushed it away before it took hold.

Marguerite's funeral had been small certainly, but maybe I had been wrong. Maybe the public farewell is not always an accurate reflection of a life lived. Sometimes people left behind have their reasons for staying away from the public farewell.

I couldn't believe that what had happened to her had been an accident either. You didn't have to live in Inishowen to know that the currents were lethal in Trawbreaga Bay; treacherous, in fact. There were warning signs at regular intervals all along Lagg Beach and the road leading down to it; you'd have to be blind to miss them. Yes, I swam here, but my swims were medicinal, not athletic. I swam no more than four or five strokes at a time and hauled myself out immediately. Even that was probably a risk.

But if it hadn't been suicide and it hadn't been an accident, the inescapable and horrible conclusion was that Marguerite had been killed, which meant that the last time she was on this beautiful beach she had been afraid, afraid of the person she knew was about to kill her. The notion turned my blood cold.

I stopped suddenly at a pyramid-shaped sand dune covered in marram grass above a ridge of stones where the shore turned inwards, and I realized with a jolt that this must have been where Marguerite's clothes were found. Molloy's words came back to me. *You know that stony section just before you turn the corner to come on to the main beach?*

This morning the tide was in, and between the first and the second beach, the second being Lagg, the tide had created a high stone circle filled with water, making a sort of pool enclosed on three sides. A grim thought occurred: because of the sound of the waves, no one walking along the main beach would be able to see or hear anything that happened here, albeit being only meters away. What a lonely place to die, I thought.

I walked down on to the rocks and looked to my right. A mile of golden sand stretched out in front of me with the craggy headland behind it. Lagg Beach. One of my favorite places on earth. I stopped for a moment to gaze out at the waves as the morning sun cast a silvery hue over the dark hulk of Glashedy Island.

I walked a little further, heading northwards along the beach, and was just about to drop my towel on the sand and start to undress when I noticed a figure coming towards me from about twenty meters away. Male, I thought. He waved as if he recognized me and I waved back, refolded my towel and kept walking. I prefer to swim without an audience.

As the figure came into view, I saw that it was Simon Howard. I wasn't sure I was ready for him, especially this morning.

"Out for an early morning walk?" he called. He was wearing a red and gray striped scarf, his hands shoved into the pockets of a khaki jacket.

"Something like that. Needed to blow away some cobwebs."

When he reached me, his eyes dropped to my hands. "Is that a towel I'm looking at?"

I smiled. "It may be. But I think I've changed my mind."

"I'm not surprised. Do you usually swim all year round?"

"I'm not sure you'd call it swimming."

His eyes widened. "Bloody hell, you're game. Fancy a cup of coffee then if you're not going to swim? My cottage isn't far. You look like you could do with some thawing out as it is."

"Okay. Thanks."

He strode back down the way he had come, and I trotted along beside him, battling against the wind. He sighed. "Just look at the texture of the grass on those cliffs."

I followed his gaze to the rocky giants looming over the water.

He breathed in. "It's like velvet. Wonderful."

It was true. In the early morning light the headland looked as if it had been swathed in emerald velvet, before being scattered with Velcro sheep. "Knockamany Bends," I said.

"Sorry?"

"The cliffs. They're called Knockamany Bends."

He grinned. "What a great name. I can't believe I've never asked."

We reached the end of the beach and I followed him back up on to the road where he had parked his car.

It hadn't occurred to me when I accepted Simon's offer of coffee that we would have to drive to his house, but of course we did. I hesitated, but he promised to drop me back down to my car in time for me to get back to the office.

Marguerite had described Simon's house as being next to hers, and although technically it was the cottage next door, there was actually about a quarter of a mile between them, Simon's being further on. As we approached, I could see that Simon's was considerably larger than Marguerite's and more recently built, but it had the same little gate and pathway that led up through a small front garden.

"I noticed Marguerite's cottage has been cleared out," I said.

"Has it?" he asked vaguely.

"You don't know who did it?"

"No idea." He unlocked the front door and led me through the hallway into a big, bright kitchen at the back of the house. It was warm and cosy with high stools and a modern counter-top on one side of the room and an old squishy couch and armchairs in front of a dying fire on the other. Also a large bean bag full of dog hairs.

I perched on one of the stools while Simon poked at the glowing embers and threw on some extra sods of turf. Thankfully, there didn't seem to be any sign of David.

"Now, Benedicta," Simon held up two pottery mugs with a camp expression on his face, "what's it to be? Coffee, tea, or me?"

I laughed. "Coffee, please."

He rooted in the cupboard and produced a coffee grinder and percolator before taking out a bag of beans and placing them on the counter.

"There's something stuck to the bottom of that bag," I said.

He lifted it up to take a look and peeled what looked like a tea bag from the bottom. He sniffed it and made a face.

"Peppermint tea. Foul stuff. Must be Marguerite's."

"Really?"

"I expect so. I certainly wouldn't touch those." He tossed it in the bin. A perfect shot.

I tried to sound uninterested. "She kept her own tea here?"

"Well, I'm not sure I'd say *kept*. I seem to remember her bringing some here once – she wouldn't drink coffee. This one must have escaped."

It was all I could do to stop myself from dashing to the bin and fishing the bag back out. There seemed to be so little left of Marguerite now, I wanted to preserve it somehow.

Simon ground the coffee beans, the noise preventing any further conversation for a minute or two. When he had finished, I spoke again.

"I was just thinking about Marguerite while I was on the beach."

"Oh?"

"You know, her clothes were found close to the spot where I ran into you."

"Were they?"

"Did she spend much time down there – on Lagg?"

"No idea." He filled the kettle and switched it on to boil. "Would you like to see my studio? While the kettle's boiling?"

"Sure."

I followed him out of the back door where we crossed a small yard full of what looked like scrap metal. At the end of the yard was a stone building not unlike a small chapel. Simon took a key from above the doorframe, unlocked the door, and we entered a large room with a high ceiling filled with light. The room was much bigger than it appeared from the outside; it had been extended further back.

One piece dominated the room. It was a sculpture of a woman standing about two meters high, clearly unfinished, for there were a number of chisels laid out on a bench beside it. Three more pieces of a similar size were concealed beneath tarpaulin covers. The walls were spread with shelves containing smaller sculptures, some completed and some not, and there were tools everywhere, and bags of clay. Eerily, there was also a plastic skeleton hanging in the corner alongside a poster showing organs and muscle groups.

Simon looked at me, awaiting a response, but I wasn't sure what to say. The place smelled much like a builder's yard and in contrast to the house, it was utterly freezing. But that wasn't the problem. There was something about the room that gave me the creeps.

"It's a great space," I said.

"Go on," he urged. "Have a look around."

Obediently, I walked from piece to piece and offered some fairly inane comments.

"Have you given any thought to taking up art again your-self?" he asked.

I shook my head.

"I could always give you some lessons," he grinned. "Just to loosen you up again."

After a few minutes I came across some sketchpads of vary-ing sizes leaning against a wall. I looked up, but Simon had moved to doing something with tools at the sink so I picked up the first one and started to flick through it. It contained a number of pencil drawings, full figures and various anatomi-cal studies of hands, feet, noses, ears. No eyes, I noticed; none of Simon's pieces seemed to have eyes. When I had finished, I replaced it and picked up a second pad, a smaller one. The first drawing caused my breath to catch. Simon looked up and came over, peering over my shoulder.

I could hardly get the words out. "Is that . . . ?"

"Marguerite? Yes. Do you know I'd forgotten about those?" He took the sketchpad from my hand.

"I thought you said you didn't know her very well?"

"I didn't."

"But she modeled for you. Didn't she?" I asked. "Or did you do them from memory?"

He smiled. "No, she modeled for me. But it doesn't mean I knew her. Lots of people model for me. I don't get to know my models; it doesn't work for me, if I do."

"I don't understand." I realized my hands were shaking slightly so I shoved them into the pockets of my jeans.

"My models can't become real to me. If they do, it breaks the spell."

"Ah, come on."

"I don't know how else to explain it," he said. "I need to be able to make them what I want them to be, so I can't get to know them."

He replaced the sketchpad against the wall. "It's the way I work. Every artist is different."

"Were these drawings for a sculpture?"

"Yes."

"And did you sculpt her?" I looked around me as if I expected a life-size sculpture of Marguerite to appear in front of me.

"No. It never happened, as a matter of fact. Can't think why now. Anyway, I reckon the kettle must be boiled by now, don't you?"

In the kitchen I warmed my hands on the steaming mug, still chilled from the studio. At least I wanted to believe that was why they were trembling. But I couldn't let it drop.

"Did you ask her to model for you?"

"Marguerite? I presume so. I can't remember now. Why?"

"I'm just surprised, that's all. She seemed such a private sort of person."

"I suppose she needed the money. I do pay my models," he explained.

"Oh. I see." I digested this for a minute.

He took a deep breath. "If I'm honest, I feel a bit guilty about her. She would call in here sometimes – not often, just the odd time – but if I was working, I used to pretend I wasn't in. I park my car round the back, so you can't tell from the front of the house if there is anyone here. It's only now that I realize she must have been lonely."

I stared into my mug, my own guilt starting to seep back in.

He interrupted my thoughts with an attack from left field. "So, what about this dinner you agreed to have with me? Or had you forgotten?"

"No."

"I could cook? I do a mean risotto." He twirled a tea towel like a magic wand.

"Let's go to Caffrey's," I said, naming the tiny bistro that had just opened in Malin town.

"Thursday night?"

I heard myself agreeing. *To hell with Molloy*, I thought.

Chapter 14

THAT AFTERNOON, I stuck my head through the door of the waiting room to see a large female figure draped in a canary yellow shawl, with a cardboard box on her knee.

"Phyllis? Are you okay?"

She looked up. "I was wondering if you had five minutes? It's not urgent or anything." But the anxiety in her brown eyes belied her words.

"Sure. Of course. Come on into the front."

She followed me into the front office still carrying the cardboard box, nudging the door closed behind her with her large rump. She placed the box on the desk.

"Look," she said breathlessly. "Tell me where to go if you like, but you were the first person I thought of. These are Marguerite's things from the shop."

"I see."

"She was desperate for leaving things lying around, personal things – keys, bills, that sort of thing – so I gave her a drawer. And I only got around to clearing it out this morning. There's not much, but I hadn't the foggiest idea who to give the contents to. I mean, I'd give them to the guards but I've heard they're not investigating her death any longer."

"No. That's true," I said. "Although I'm sure they could still help."

"Maybe," she said doubtfully. She looked crestfallen.

"Her belongings should really go to her daughter," I said. "Did you try to contact her?"

"I did. She was staying at the Atlantic, so I rang them on Saturday, but she had already checked out. She left straight after the funeral, apparently. She's gone home, wherever that is."

"Yes, I heard. She didn't stay very long."

"No. That's what I thought. And well . . ." she said sheepishly, "I sort of overheard you saying at the funeral that you were Marguerite's solicitor."

I stood by the window with my arms crossed. "I see."

"So I decided you might be the next best person to give them to. I thought at least you would know what to do, or who should have them."

I did, I knew exactly what I should do: I should pass Marguerite's possessions on to the guards because I certainly had no right to hold on to them. But I knew, too, that if I did that, then all they would do was contact her daughter and destroy the items if she didn't want them, which more than likely she wouldn't. I suspected that Phyllis knew that too, so I suppressed my conscience and followed my gut. Somewhere in this box there might be a clue as to why Marguerite had died.

"Okay, Phyllis," I heard myself saying. "Leave them with me, and I'll see if I can contact her daughter."

Phyllis's expression lightened considerably. "Oh, thanks, Ben, that's such a relief. I'll let you know if I find anything else."

As she turned to leave, I called her back. "Before you go, do you mind if I ask you something?"

"Go ahead."

"Do you remember the other day, when you said you thought that people should pay their respects in death no matter what happened in life?"

She looked away, avoided my gaze.

"What did you mean by that?" I said.

She seemed to hesitate, and for a second, I thought she was going to tell me . . . but the moment passed.

"Oh, nothing really." She smiled guiltily. "I have to learn not to gossip."

When I returned to the reception area with the cardboard box in tow, Leah was on the phone. She beckoned me over and put the call on hold.

"It's Brendan Quinn. Can you have a quick word with him before you see Iggy McDaid?"

"Iggy McDaid?"

She grinned. "He's back. Want me to handcuff him to the seat?"

"Don't rule it out," I said. I put the box on the reception desk and took the handset. "Brendan, how are you? Did you get to see my client?"

"I did," he replied. "I saw him first thing this morning and he was perfect. Like a twenty year old. So I suggest that if you want to see him, that you do so as soon as possible today, and I can complete an affidavit for you."

"That's great, Brendan. Thanks a million. I just have one person to see now and then I can head down straight away. I'll talk to you soon."

I was just about to hang up when I heard him clear his throat. "Em . . . just one other thing."

"Yep?"

"That matter we were talking about the other day – the exit counseling? I've done a bit of looking into that. If you're interested, we could meet up and discuss it."

"That would be great." I couldn't hide my surprise. "When suits you?"

"As it happens I have to be in Glendara to see some patients at the hospital on Thursday, so I could call up to your office then, if you'd like?"

Glendara has a small community hospital full of long-term geriatric patients – although I had been there myself after a mishap a few months before.

"Sure. That's great, Brendan. I appreciate it."

I hung up, deep in thought. My last conversation with Brendan Quinn had been like pulling teeth. So why had he changed his mind about talking to me all of a sudden? I placed the box Phyllis had given me on top of one of the filing cabinets. My curiosity about both would have to wait. I had a client to see.

When I had finished seeing Iggy I made the trip to Letterkenny – and this time I managed to get the will drafted and signed. My first opportunity to examine the contents of the box Phyllis had left in my care came that evening. After I had eaten, I evicted an indignant Guinness from the armchair in front of the fire and deposited him firmly on the sofa, poured a glass of wine, and settled myself in his place with the cardboard box on the coffee table in front of me.

Opening the top flaps, I immediately felt a stab of conscience: I was about to invade Marguerite's privacy in a way that she might not have been happy about. But I could not ignore this

box. It was as if fate had delivered it into my hands. I had convinced myself that my duty to Marguerite extended beyond
her death. And since I had failed her in life, I was going to try
my damnedest not to fail her now.

I peered inside the box. A sapphire-blue scarf was strewn on
top and from it a light fragrance drifted towards me. I took it
out and placed it on the table. Underneath was a selection of paperbacks – autobiographies mostly, all with their prices pencilled
in Phyllis's handwriting inside the front flap. I took them out of
the box one by one and placed them on the table with the scarf.
When I had done that, the box seemed almost empty, although
a variety of small items remained scattered across the bottom.

I picked up a pack of Gauloise cigarettes, half full. I didn't
think I'd ever seen Marguerite smoke. I sniffed them; they
were slightly stale. I wondered where she would have been able
to buy such an exotic brand of cigarettes in Glendara, until I
saw the duty-free label on the side of the pack. I placed them
to one side.

I removed the remaining items and laid them out in front
of me, then put the box under the table. They consisted of a
medium-sized cosmetics bag, a tiny desk clock, a box of herbal
tea bags – peppermint – and some pens and pencils. That was
it. Not much to go on. The fact that there didn't seem to be
anything of any great value lessened the guilt I felt at not handing everything over to the guards, at least for the moment. But
as I picked up the cosmetics bag, my discomfort returned. It
seemed so personal, such an invasion to go through its contents. But I suppressed my doubts, unzipped the main compartment, and emptied everything out on to the table. There
wasn't much – a brown mascara, a lipstick, a compact with a
mirror, and some charcoal-gray eyeshadow.

But with all of its contents now removed, the bag was still bulky. I turned it over in my hands – there seemed to be something in the zip compartment at the side. I unzipped it and with some difficulty pulled out a bundle of envelopes that were held together with a rubber band.

Immediately the rubber band snapped in my hand, and the bundle fell apart, scattering the envelopes on to the carpet. I picked one up. It was a letter, the address handwritten. I recognized Marguerite's handwriting from the slip of paper she had given me in the office. The address was the same:

It was a letter to her daughter. I turned the envelope over; it was sealed. I looked at the front again. To the left of the address was an inked stamp. I fetched my laptop and turned on Google Translate. *Not known at this address. Return to sender.*

I gathered up the other envelopes. Most of them were similar; sealed and with the same addressee, with postmarks stretching back a year or so. All were marked *not known at this address*, or *return to sender* or both. I couldn't bring myself to open any of them. That seemed a step too far.

There were three other envelopes, opened envelopes this time and addressed to Marguerite. They were bills, by the look of them: a mobile phone bill, an electricity bill, and a credit card bill. I opened the credit card bill first. It was for the month of June and it contained only two items – a charge to Aer Lingus for €149 and another to a hotel booking website for €250. This must have been the holiday Phyllis had talked about, I thought. But where had Marguerite gone? To see her daughter?

I withdrew three sheets from the next envelope – it was Marguerite's mobile phone bill for July, a long itemised bill. So long, in fact, that the sum due seemed rather low, until I realized the charges related mostly to texts. I scanned through the list; there were over a thousand of them, sent at all hours of the day and night. It didn't take me long to work out that one number came up more often than any other.

I sat back and stared into the fire, the bill in my hand. The most likely scenario for such regular and consistent texts was a lover. I had been there, I knew. But if I was right, then who was Marguerite's lover? David Howard's words came flooding back to me: *He doesn't usually go to the funerals of his women.* Could it have been Simon? Should I ring the number and find out? What would I do if he answered?

I searched for my mobile phone until I remembered I'd left it at the office. But I had Simon's number at the office too — he'd given it to me when he'd come by, so I didn't need to call, after all. I could just compare the one he'd given me with the number on the bill. I pulled Guinness on to my knee where he curled up contentedly. Had Simon been lying to me about how well he knew Marguerite?

Chapter 15

A PANICKED PHONE call from a client meant that I had to go straight to court the next morning without going to the office, so I couldn't compare numbers until later.

The rain pelted down as solicitors, guards, and punters crowded their way up the steep stone steps into the old courthouse. I was waylaid in the aisle by Molloy. To my embarrassment, I flushed.

"Are you acting for Iggy McDaid?" he said.

I was relieved. Apparently we had returned to professional formality.

"I'm applying to get his driving licence back. Why?"

Molloy lowered his tone. "He's ossified, that's why."

"Oh, for God's sake. Where is he?"

Molloy pointed towards the door. "Under the stairs. Mouthing off to anyone who'll listen, making a right nuisance of himself. Just thought you should know."

"Thanks. I'll have a word with him."

Sighing, I fought my way back out of the courtroom to the foyer, which by now was packed full of steaming people, with the usual collection of smokers hanging around the doorway. It smelled like wet sheep. I found Iggy slouching against the rickety stairway leading to the gallery above the courtroom, hands in his pockets, singing quietly to himself. He stopped when he saw me.

"How are ye doin', solicitor?" he slurred in recognition. "Am I up?"

I held my breath. The stale booze from his breath and stale sweat from the rest of him was a fairly lethal combination.

"Not yet, Iggy. I think we might have to adjourn it. What do you think?"

"What for?"

"I just think it might be the wisest."

"But . . ." As he withdrew his left hand from his pocket to steady himself for a proper protest, a filthy handkerchief came with it and fell to the ground. It fell hard, as if there was something wrapped in it.

I leaned forward to pick it up, but Iggy put his hand out to stop me, and with a mammoth effort, he bent down, grabbed the handkerchief, and pulled himself back up to his full height. As he did so, whatever was wrapped inside the cloth slipped out. I caught a brief glimpse of something black and metal before he grabbed it again and rammed it back into his pocket. Luckily, the whole procedure seemed to exhaust him and he offered no resistance when I explained to him that his chances of having his driving licence restored right after a drunken appearance before the judge were pretty slim.

I returned to the courtroom just in time; the judge had already started on the licensing list. I was relieved to see it was Judge Barney Power, a pragmatic sort, as I took my place on the practitioners' bench in front of the clerk. Molloy was at the far end with a stack of files in front of him; he prosecutes the garda cases for the state. I gave him a nod of thanks and he smiled.

Auctioneers' licences, pub licences, and removals of disqualification orders — most of them for the offence of drunken driving — all are called before the criminal list. Iggy was in the final category. When his name was called by the clerk, I stood up.

"I appear for that applicant, Judge. I wonder if you might adjourn that matter until next month?"

As I spoke, I heard a disturbance at the back of the court and in my peripheral vision I saw someone push their way up through the packed courtroom. My heart sank. Somehow I managed to keep my eyes firmly fixed on the judge as Iggy staggered up into the witness box and stood there, hands clasped behind his back, swaying regally. Through some miracle the judge didn't notice him or, I suspect, chose not to. As he checked with his registrar for the adjournment date, I saw Molloy nod at one of the guards who removed Iggy and bundled him to the back of the court.

Adjournment granted, I sat down in relief. I had barely done so when I felt a tap on my shoulder and turned to see Hugh O'Connor kneeling behind me, his face so close to mine I could smell his toothpaste.

"That was some performance, eh?"

I was noncommittal. "Mmm."

He grinned. "Iggy McDaid, the only man in Inishowen who can sing and hum at the same time."

I suppressed the urge to smile and he saw it. Was clearly pleased by it.

"Do you need me yet?" he asked.

"Not yet. Might be this afternoon before it's reached."

"That's grand. I'm not going anywhere. Just wanted to let you know I'm here." He winked.

After he left I leaned across to whisper to Molloy: "Hugh O'Connor. First time in the list. I'll be looking for copy statements."

He nodded. "I want to have a word with you about that one."

The judge rose at one and the court cleared till two o'clock. I sat in beside Molloy.

"You wanted to talk to me about O'Connor?"

"Yes." He leafed through the stack of court files in front of him until he found the right one, opened it, and glanced through it. "We have no statements as yet on that one, only garda statements. We're waiting on the farmer to come in and make one. You'll have it as soon as we do."

I took a note. "What's the allegation? I know there's a dangerous driving charge in there."

Molloy read the inside cover of the file. "There sure is. Crazy driving, apparently. Ended up in a field in Moville — God knows how he walked away from it. Managed to drive away, as a matter of fact. Then he came back the next day all sweetness and light with a present of a bottle of whiskey, and flowers for the missus."

"You're kidding." This time I couldn't help but smile.

Molloy didn't. "I'm not. Anyway, the farmer reported it, despite the whiskey and flowers, and we arrested your boy the next day. He was released on station bail and bailed out by his mother." He closed the file. "You know who that kid is, of course?"

"Leah said he's Hugh O'Connor's grandson."

Molloy nodded.

"Is the old man still alive, by the way?" I had been meaning to ask Leah. "He seems to have been out of the news for a long time."

"Died about ten years ago. Your client's mother was O'Connor's only daughter."

By half past two, Hugh O'Connor's case had been adjourned for two weeks, and I was finished in court. I headed back to the office, anxious not to put off any longer the task of comparing the number on Marguerite's phone bill with the number Simon had given me.

I dumped my court files on the reception desk, took the bundle of Marguerite's envelopes from my briefcase, and ran upstairs, where I opened the top drawer of the filing cabinet and pulled out the file tagged *Miscellaneous Contact Details*.

I quickly found Simon Howard's number and compared it to the one on the bill, checking and rechecking with the precision of a lottery winner comparing numbers on a winning ticket, but they did not match. And a quick scan through the text numbers showed that Simon Howard's number did not appear anywhere on the bill at all. Maybe he had been telling the truth. Maybe he hadn't known Marguerite very well. I put the letters and the bills in the file. With a mammoth effort I then put the file aside and forced myself to focus on work.

Half an hour later, having re-calculated the same sum on some messy probate papers for the third time, I conceded it wasn't working; *I* wasn't working. No matter how hard I tried, my discoveries of the night before kept intruding on my thoughts. So I threw the papers I'd been working on into the shredder, snatched up my coat, and headed down the stairs.

"Just going out for a bit," I called to a startled Leah as I ran out the door. But I didn't wait for a response.

As I drove out on the Ballyliffin road, I became aware that it was exactly a week since I had last made this journey to the

Isle of Doagh. It seemed much longer. Today the beach was deserted — not surprising for a Wednesday afternoon in September, but I was pleased. I always feel the sea is company enough when you need it. I parked my car on the grass above the beach just where I had parked it that morning, locked it and went down on to the sand and towards the rocks where Marguerite's body had been found.

Before I reached them, I stopped to gaze across the sea towards Lagg. The sky was an eerie yellow and gray as if there was a storm brewing, but visibility was surprisingly clear. I could see Marguerite and Simon's cottages across the bay, like tiny white dots in the green patch above the beach.

As I walked slowly along the shore, I tried to work out what was bothering me so much. I had a panicky sense that Marguerite was disappearing from view too fast. She had no ancestors in the area, no parents or grandparents. It was almost as if she hadn't been here long enough for her existence to be real, and memories are short. Soon, I was afraid there would be no trace left of her at all. She was like a footstep in the sand, washed away by the next tide.

I needed to find some way to use the little bits of information that had fallen into my lap; to find out the truth of what had happened to Marguerite before she was gone completely. The first thing was to find out who she had been ringing and texting so obsessively. I took her phone bill from my pocket, changed my mobile phone setting to number withheld, and dialed the number. But before I could press call, the phone vibrated in my hand. It made me jump.

It was Leah. She sounded breathless. "Ben, I don't know where you are, but I thought I'd better remind you about your four o'clock appointment in case you'd forgotten. They're here."

"Oh, Christ. Tell them I'm sorry, I got delayed. I'll be there in ten minutes." I dashed up the hill towards my car.

The road from Ballyliffin to Glendara is hilly and full of blind bends, but as I entered the long straight stretch leading into the town, I began to relax. *Nearly there*, I thought as I glanced at my watch. My clients had been early to begin with so I calculated I'd only be five minutes late.

I saw a flash of silver in the distance. The road was wide but still, I slowed down, just to be safe. Suddenly, out of nowhere, a car was coming towards me, swerving dangerously across the white line. *Jesus*, I thought, *that driver is drunk.*

As the car came closer, it seemed to increase its speed. My heart pounding, I glanced frantically to my left and right, but there was nowhere for me to pull in. I held my breath and tried to concentrate on the road. It was no good. Literally meters away from me, the other car swerved right into the center of the road, forcing me off the tarmac completely. Somehow I managed to keep my hands on the steering wheel as I desperately tried to keep control. The Mini bumped wildly along the grass verge as I frantically braked and braked again. It seemed like minutes, but must have only been seconds until finally the car slowed down and came to an abrupt halt. Immediately, the outer wheels lost their grip, and I felt the car lurch violently to one side as it slid into the ditch. I was thrown towards the passenger seat and pulled back again as the seatbelt tautened and caught me in its grasp.

I opened my eyes with no idea when I'd closed them and looked down, terrified of what I might see. There was broken glass on my knees, and my hands were bleeding, but somehow I managed to unbuckle the seatbelt and found I could move my arms and legs. I pushed down the door handle, my hands shaking violently. The door creaked loudly as I tried to push it open. I felt weak, my whole body trembling, but I succeeded in opening it wide enough to be able to climb out and fall on to my knees on the grass verge. I tried to stand up, but my legs gave way again.

I was just about to make another attempt to stand when I felt a firm pair of arms lift me up, and help me away from the car. I don't think I've ever been so grateful to hear Liam McLaughlin's voice.

"You're all right, pet, you'll be all right."

He put his arm around me and walked me a couple of meters down the road before easing me gently into the front seat of his car.

Close to tears, I struggled to speak. "The other car . . . what happened to the other car?"

"I don't know, pet, I never saw another car. I just came up behind you and saw you in the ditch," he said. I tried to tell him what had happened, but his phone was already against his ear. "Hush now, I'm going to call an ambulance."

Within minutes the ambulance from Glendara arrived, and I was taken to the hospital. After a thorough examination and a few bandages for the cuts on my hands, I was told that nothing was broken and I was free to go if I had someone to collect me and bring me home.

Sitting in the hospital waiting room feeling more than a little self-conscious, I finally rang Leah and told her what had happened. I was just about to ring Maeve to ask her if she could come and collect me when Molloy stormed into the room with a face like thunder.

"Christ, Ben. Are you okay?"

"I'm fine."

"Are you sure?"

"A few scratches. No bones broken."

He sat down heavily in the seat beside me. "God knows how. Your car is a mess. What the hell happened?"

"I don't know. I was driving back from Ballyliffin, when I met a car. It swerved on to my side and pushed me off the road. That's all I can tell you."

"There was no sign of any other car when we arrived."

"Well, that's what happened," I said belligerently.

"Did I say I didn't believe you? We know there was another car. We found skidmarks that weren't yours."

"Sorry."

"What make was the other car?"

"Big. Silver."

Molloy shook his head. "Great. Silver and big. Should take us no time to track that one down." He shot me a half-smile.

My eyes welled; I wasn't sure whether I wanted to cry or laugh. "Don't be mean to me. I'm sore."

The bit about being sore was true. I was beginning to ache all over and my neck and shoulders in particular were in agony.

Molloy's face softened. "I'm sorry. I'm just worried about you. You gave me a fright. Come on, I'll take you home. I have all your things. We arranged for Hal McKinney to collect your poor old Mini. He has it in the garage – says he might be able to rescue it."

He reached for my hand, but I shoved it into the pocket of my jacket. If he held it, I knew I would cry.

Four hours later I woke up, still aching all over. I sat up slowly. My neck and shoulders remained painful, but it was more of a dull ache than it had been earlier, and the area on my chest where the seatbelt had caught me was really tender when I touched it. I was going to have some impressive bruises in the morning. Sitting on the bedside locker were the remains of the tea, toast, and soup that Maeve had brought up to me a couple of hours previously, before I had fallen asleep. It occurred to me that if I hadn't been feeling so lousy, I would have laughed at the idea of being nursed by a vet.

I looked at the clock. It was twenty past nine. I decided I should try and get up for a few hours, so I would be more likely to sleep tonight. So I struggled out of bed, pulled on a dressing gown, and went into the kitchen to make myself a cup of tea. Immediately Guinness appeared at the window, and I let him in, pathetically glad of the company.

"How are you, my old mate? Did the vet feed you?"

The cat wound himself around my legs, purring loudly. I took my tea into the sitting room and curled up on the sofa with him stretched out on my knee. And as I sipped the tea, my eyes fell on the pile of items Molloy had taken from my car. Marguerite's mobile phone bill was lying on top. I wondered if he had noticed it. My own phone was there too.

I picked it up, checked that the setting on my phone was still number withheld, and dialed the number from the bill. It went straight through to voicemail.

Hello. This is Councillor Aidan Doherty. I am unable to take your call right now. Please leave a message after the tone or call me at my office.

Chapter 16

I took a taxi to work the next morning, a little achy but generally okay. My Mini was in much worse shape; I caught a glimpse of her on Hal's ramp as I walked past the garage on the way to get a paper. He said he could fix her; it would take at least a week but he promised me a car on loan in a couple of days when he had one to spare. It was going to be awkward for me to survive without a car, but it did occur to me that at least it was Hal's garage business I was availing myself of, rather than the undertakers.

At the office, I set about tackling the post. I was determined to get some work done this morning, since yesterday had been a complete write-off. I opened a large brown hand-delivered envelope first and was relieved to see it contained the contracts for the land in Malin Head for Dolan and Gallagher. I buzzed Leah.

"Dolan and Gallagher's contracts are here. Can you ring the States and tell them that I'll get back to them when I've had a chance to go through them properly?"

"Thank God. They're driving me bonkers. Gallagher rang again yesterday afternoon. I know they think I'm lying to them, that I have them hidden away somewhere. I'll ring them at nine a.m. their time."

I moved on to the next envelope. The top right corner bore the stamp of the Registry of Births, Marriages and Deaths. I sat back. This had to be Marguerite's death certificate – so much for concentrating on work. I stared at the envelope for a few seconds, willing it to contain what I wanted it to before I tore it open and withdrew the four sheets inside. Just as I had hoped, the Registrar had sent me a copy of the post-mortem report with the certificate.

I scanned through the death cert first. As expected it listed the cause of death as drowning, and I noted that Marguerite's age was forty-two. I turned my attention to the post-mortem report. On the first page, Marguerite's height and weight and time of death were recorded; the pathologist had estimated a time between seven p.m. and midnight on Tuesday, September 12, 2015. As I scanned the rest of the page, much of the language I didn't understand, but there was mention of bruising to the back of the skull with the words *post- or ante-mortem undetermined* and at the bottom was a section marked *Identification Features* where the strange tattoo was mentioned and described.

I turned to the next page, where my eyes were irresistibly drawn to a section for *Additional Remarks*, just before the signature of the pathologist. There were only two.

1. *Traces of clonazepam found in the stomach.*
2. *Deceased was approximately eight weeks' pregnant at death.*

My breath caught as I read it again. I walked over to the window clutching the report to my chest. *Marguerite was pregnant.* My mind began to race. Who was the father? Aidan Doherty? Was he the man she had been seeing? I had a vague memory of the Matron in Letterkenny Hospital saying something about his wife. Was that why he hadn't been at the funeral – because he was married? And was that what Phyllis had meant about paying your respects at the end no matter what went on during life?

The questions just kept coming. But my thoughts were interrupted when my phone buzzed. Dr. Brendan Quinn was waiting for me downstairs. I had forgotten he was due this morning. I asked Leah to make some coffee and send him up.

I was taken aback when I saw him. He was much changed. He was paler than I had ever seen him, his holiday tan long gone, and the dark shadows under his eyes made him look as if he hadn't slept since our last conversation. He sat heavily on the seat I offered him.

When he spoke, it was as if he had been holding his breath for a long time. "I want to talk to you about Marguerite Etienne. I think I may need some advice."

"Okay," I said cautiously.

He clarified his words. "Professional advice. Which means this conversation must be completely confidential. I'm relying on solicitor-client confidentiality."

"Of course."

"Good." He looked relieved. There was a pause.

"I'm listening," I said.

He swallowed. "Marguerite Etienne came to see me about a year ago, in my professional capacity. I suspect you may have guessed that from our conversation the other day."

He waited for a reaction, but I didn't give him one.

"She wanted to talk to me about her experiences with the Damascan cult. She wished to deal with them, finally. Alain, her ex-partner . . . I presume you know about him?"

I nodded. I noticed his eyes were bloodshot. Was he drinking, I wondered.

He smiled weakly. "Yes. I got the impression you had done your research. Anyway, Alain had just died, and I think she finally felt she was free in some fashion – free to deal with what had happened to her and get back in contact with her daughter." He sighed. "So I helped her. Helped her come to terms with her experiences in the cult. Marguerite was a very damaged person. She had coped over the years by suppressing memories, by building up walls and never letting anyone close to her."

He stopped. Suddenly I had a horrible feeling I could see where this was going.

"And?" I said.

"We became close."

"How close?"

Quinn stared at the desk, an expression of utter misery on his face. "We had a relationship. A sexual relationship."

I didn't speak for a few seconds. Eventually I blurted out the obvious. "Is that not a breach of your professional code?"

"Of course it is," he snapped. "Not to mention my marriage vows. What I want to know is what I should do about it. Professionally speaking."

I was incredulous. "You're worried about that now? When the only person who could make a complaint about it is dead?"

He didn't reply, but guilt was etched across his face.

"Did you know she was pregnant when she died?" I said.

He looked up, paled even further. "No, I didn't."

"Two months."

"Two months?" He looked confused. "Are you sure?"

"Positive. It's in the autopsy report. I got it this morning."

"In that case, the baby wasn't mine," he said in an odd voice. "Our affair ended six months ago. She must have been involved with somebody else."

"Who?" I said.

"I have no idea." The pain on his face was unmistakable. He was telling the truth.

"What happened?" I asked. "This doesn't seem like you, Brendan."

He shrugged. "I fell in love with her. That's the honest truth. I didn't set out to."

"Did you continue to see her after?" I asked. "As her therapist, I mean?"

"Yes," he said. "I suppose I shouldn't have, but . . . well, she wanted me to and I guess I wanted to as well. That was until about two months ago, when she telephoned me and said that she couldn't see me any more."

"Did she say why?"

"No. She was a bit strange about it. I got the impression that someone was pushing her into it. Pushing her into breaking off contact with me." He looked down again. "Maybe it was the person she was seeing."

Realization dawned. "So you did know she was seeing someone else. Or at least you suspected she was."

"No, I . . ."

"You think that person knew about your affair with her, don't you? And might still make a complaint about you. That's why you're coming to me for advice." I couldn't keep the anger out of my voice. "All you care about is saving your own skin."

"No," he protested. "That's not true. I was worried about her when she stopped seeing me. Marguerite was dealing with serious issues she had suppressed for a very long time. With my support she was coping well. She was ready again for a relationship with her daughter, and she finally seemed to be happy in

Inishowen. Obviously, she hadn't told me that she was in a new relationship, but I suppose that's understandable given our history. But she was in a good place. I would have been anxious for that to continue."

"When was the last time you saw her?"

"About six weeks ago. I saw her once more after that phone call."

"How did she seem?"

"Edgy, slightly defensive. I assumed it was because she was uncomfortable about leaving therapy."

Suddenly I remembered the other item on the *Additional Remarks* section of the post-mortem report. "Was Marguerite on any medication?"

Quinn shook his head. "Not that I was aware of. I certainly didn't prescribe any for her. I think it's unlikely. She wasn't keen on the idea of drugs of any kind."

I looked out the window. "So why *are* you telling me about this now – honestly? If it's not your own skin you're worried about?"

"Honestly? I can't stop thinking about her. Whatever you may believe, I know no one is going to report me at this stage. Marguerite wouldn't have told anyone about our affair, she wouldn't want me reported. But after what happened to her, I needed to talk to someone."

"And you know I can't pass on what you say, if you tell me as a client," I added sourly.

"Well, of course I couldn't tell just anyone," he conceded. "But I feel so guilty. I know the guards have decided it was suicide and I can't stand the idea that I might in some way be responsible for that."

He looked so pathetic that I softened.

"But then if she was in a new relationship . . ." he said hopefully.

"Maybe you're off the hook?"

"That's not what I meant." He looked wretched. "Could it have been an accident?" he asked feebly.

I was late to meet Maeve at the Oak for lunch, but after Quinn left, I ran a quick search for clonazepam, the drug that had been found in Marguerite's stomach. I discovered that it was a benzodiazepine; one that was regularly prescribed for the treatment of epilepsy or panic attacks. Which opened up a whole new set of questions. Had Marguerite suffered from epilepsy?

My mind was still reeling when I opened the pub door and my heart sank when I saw who Maeve was talking to at the bar; it was Jackie from the Atlantic Hotel. They were with a taller blond woman who was familiar but whom I couldn't place. I approached with caution.

Maeve spotted me first. "Oh hi. The girls here have suggested organising a new yoga class. Carole knows another teacher."

Of course. It was at Marguerite's yoga class that I'd seen the taller woman. She and Jackie usually arrived together. I couldn't remember seeing either of them at the funeral.

"Sure, why not?" I shrugged. "It's a whole week since the last one died."

Maeve reddened "Maybe it is a bit soon." She was the only one who looked uncomfortable, which made me feel mean.

"Not at all," the tall woman insisted. "Sure it'll take a few weeks to organise anyway. Let's make a list of who would be interested. You two grab a table, have a think about it, and we'll be down in a wee minute. Anyone got a pen?"

Maeve looked apologetically at me as she produced a chewed-up red biro from her pocket. I ordered a sandwich and coffee from Carole and headed over to the big table in the corner of the pub. Maeve followed me.

"God, I'm sorry about that," I said as I dumped my bag on a seat. "Bad morning."

"Don't worry about it. I think you're right, it is too soon. I should have said something myself. How are you feeling, by the way? I thought you'd take a couple of days off work."

"Can't afford to. I'm drowning in paperwork. But I'm grand really. Thanks for looking after me yesterday." I nodded in the direction of the blond woman. "Who's that one?"

Maeve followed my gaze. "Clodagh O'Connor. You've met her before, haven't you?"

"Not properly. I remember her face from the class."

Maeve smiled cheekily as she took off her jacket. "Oh – what with your accident I forgot to ask. How did your cultural expedition on Sunday night go?"

For a second, I didn't know what she meant. Then I felt a jolt of panic. "God, I'd forgotten. I have a date tonight."

"You're kidding. That was quick work. This happened at the exhibition?"

"No, well – yes, sort of. I ran into him again on Tuesday on Lagg."

"Excellent. I want all the gory details."

Just then, the two women arrived at the table with mugs of coffee.

"Well?" Clodagh demanded. "Who have you come up with?"

The woman was beginning to get under my skin, so I responded by ignoring her completely. I turned to Jackie. "Who's this new teacher?"

"Some woman from Derry. She teaches in Magee."

"God, no one told me that!" Clodagh exclaimed. "A Derry wan? Can we not get someone of our own?"

"Derry is only twenty miles up the road," I said.

"Different jurisdiction. Is there no one from around here who will do it?"

"Our food's ready," Maeve told me, glancing over at the bar. The two women were deep in conversation when we returned, Jackie's words sounding sympathetic, but the edge was hard to miss. "Sad though, your woman drowning herself like that. All that yoga and meditation didn't do her much good, did it?"

"I think she was a nervy kind of person beneath all that stuff." Clodagh's red nails tapped her coffee mug.

"Why do you say that?" I said.

"Jackie?" Clodagh deferred to her friend like a managing director to a secretary at a board meeting.

Jackie leaned forward conspiratorially. "My Damian was out with her a few weeks back, putting extra locks on her door, and he said she was a bit skitterish."

"Did he tell the guards that?" I said sharply.

Jackie seemed surprised. "Why would he?"

"Because they were looking for information, that's why."

"But sure that wasn't serious." Jackie looked at Clodagh for reassurance. "The guards were just keeping themselves right. Sure they knew she killed herself, didn't they?"

"Jackie's right," Clodagh said. "What would be the point of Damian telling anybody? That was weeks before she died. Anyway, they know what happened to her – she was unbalanced."

I could feel Maeve willing me to keep quiet so I bit my tongue.

"I didn't much like him going out there, anyway." Jackie's lips were pursed.

There was a limit to my self-control. "What do you mean by that?"

"Single woman like her . . . things were said about her."

My patience snapped. "Jesus Christ, Jackie, your Damian's not exactly George Clooney, for God's sake. I'm sure she could have resisted him."

Jackie glared at me as Clodagh said self-righteously, "This is a family area. The French have a different way of doing things. It's not our way."

Maeve walked me back to the office.

"God, Ben, what's wrong with you? You're chewing the head off everybody at the moment."

"Ah, that Jackie made me see red. Does she really think someone like Marguerite would have been interested in her husband?"

Maeve grinned. "You know the way it is – single women are always a threat. Just as well you have that sculptor."

But I wasn't in the mood to be humored. "And who on earth is that Clodagh O'Connor woman? I'm sorry, I know you know her."

"I'm no fan either, to be honest," Maeve admitted. "They say the softest thing about her is her teeth."

I laughed despite myself as we turned the corner. Brendan Quinn's gold Volvo was still parked outside the office. He must have decided to walk up to the hospital, I thought.

Maeve stopped dead in her tracks. She whistled. "That's some car."

"I know. Hard to miss, isn't it?"

"It's not that. I've seen it somewhere recently, I'm sure of it."

"Where?" I asked.

She thought for a minute. "That's weird. At Lagg – down by the beach. The night Marguerite died."

Chapter 17

MOLLOY WAS STANDING outside the office. Maeve took off as soon as she saw him, assuming we had business to discuss.

"I was just calling in to see how you are," he said. "Heard you were back at work this morning." He looked uncomfortable, as if I'd caught him lurking somewhere he shouldn't. It was only the second time I had seen him look like that; the first being at my office three days before.

"No keeping secrets from you, is there?" I said tetchily.

He smiled. "Small town. You should be used to it by now. You sure you're okay?"

"I'm fine."

"I wanted to talk to you. We're trying to track down that silver car . . ."

I cut across him. "I got Marguerite's death certificate."

"Oh, did you now?" He raised one eyebrow.

"With the post-mortem report."

"Ah."

"I suppose you knew she was pregnant?"

"Well, yes. We had the results the day she was found."

"Why didn't you tell me?"

"I couldn't. It was confidential. Anyway, I don't remember you being overly helpful yourself."

Molloy's annoyance made him look more like his old self; reversion to our old battleground had removed his discomfort. Part of me was relieved. I wasn't comfortable with Molloy's care for me at the moment. It made me want to rely on him again – and that was dangerous.

But I had heard that word *confidential* one too many times today.

"I had no choice. You know that," I said. "But how could you have just dismissed her death as suicide if you knew she was pregnant?"

"Ben, she was forty-two and single. It was hardly likely to be a happy event."

"You think she killed herself out of despair over an unwanted pregnancy? That's a bit simplistic, isn't it?"

He sighed. "We found a letter she had written to her daughter. That's how we managed to get in touch with her so quickly. The letter was clearly a goodbye. It read like a suicide note."

"Well, maybe it was a goodbye. But that doesn't mean it was a suicide note. Her daughter didn't seem to be interested in being in contact with her. Isn't it possible she was giving up trying to have a relationship with her daughter if she had another baby on the way?"

Molloy paused. "What do you know about her relationship with her daughter?"

I could have kicked myself. The only reason I knew that Marguerite had been trying to get in touch with her daughter was from the letters Phyllis had given me, the letters I had no right to have.

I looked away. "I have an uneasy feeling about it, you know I have. About the whole thing."

Molloy looked troubled. "You don't think you're uneasy about it because of . . . ? Maybe it's bringing back some things?" He looked at me, his eyes full of concern, and suddenly I found it difficult to speak.

"No," I said, "it's not about my sister."

He looked at the pavement for a second before speaking again. "Ben. Marguerite Etienne was forty-two, pregnant, and very much alone from what we could make out. No one came forward with information following the appeal. Not one single person. The only people who spoke to us were the people we approached. And very few of them knew her. She wrote a last letter to her daughter who seems to have barely known her either, and she died a couple of hours later."

"How do you know that?"

Molloy marked the times off on his fingers. "She was at your office till twenty past six and she died between seven and midnight the same night, according to the pathologist. The letter was dated the sixteenth of September. The same night."

"But the will . . ."

"The will also points to suicide. She puts her affairs in order, writes what is effectively a suicide note, and walks into the sea."

"But I keep telling you! She *hadn't* put her affairs in order."

"I know, Ben, but she must have thought she had," he said patiently. "Everything else points to suicide."

I bit my tongue.

"And then there's her history." He shook his head. "You seem to think we've done nothing, just taken the easy way out. But we've spoken to the French and Norwegian police at length about the cult of which she was a member. People come out of that organization pretty damaged. It seems very likely that Marguerite was fragile, mentally. If you read the post-mortem report, you would have seen that she had benzo-diazepines in her system when she died."

"Yes. Clonazepam. Used for the treatment of epilepsy."

He looked at me curiously. "So you've done your home-work. Well, if you've read up on it, you'll also have seen that it is regularly used *recreationally*. It's a commonly abused benzodi-azepine. We've checked with all of the local doctors and none of them wrote a prescription for clonazepam for Marguerite."

"She could have gone to a doctor somewhere else."

"True, but if she *was* taking it without a prescription, then who knows what kind of dosage she was taking. One of the possible side effects of clonazepam is suicidal ideation."

"So, that's it then?"

"What do you want me to do? There's absolutely no reason to reopen the investigation." Molloy spread his palms out in a gesture of helplessness.

"Of course there isn't," I said as I turned on my heel and went into the office.

Oh, it wasn't Molloy's fault, I knew that. The guards' con-clusion was perfectly reasonable, considering the information they had. It wasn't his fault that no one had come forward in response to the appeal either. I was taking my frustration out on him for more than one reason, I was aware of that, too.

But there were people who knew Marguerite better than they were admitting; Brendan Quinn and Aidan Doherty for a start. She was pregnant, for God's sake; it hadn't been the Immaculate Conception. Quinn had made some admissions, but what was his car doing at the beach the night she died if he hadn't seen her for six weeks?

I couldn't blame the guards for closing the investigation, but Molloy's theory about Marguerite's despair was wrong. I truly doubted that she would have committed suicide over a pregnancy. She wasn't some frightened fifteen year old; she was a mother already. It was far more likely that she wanted to keep the child, and that someone else didn't want her to.

I picked up the post-mortem report again. I had been so shocked when I discovered that Marguerite was pregnant when she died that everything else had taken second place. But something else had jarred when I read through it the first time, something at the back of my memory like an itch I couldn't reach to scratch. Molloy had reminded me of it when he mentioned clonazepam, the drug found in her system. There was an inconsistency there somewhere: I just had to remember what it was.

Finally it came back to me. It was something that Phyllis had said — *She wouldn't even take an aspirin. She didn't take any medication.* Surely the fact that Marguerite was being careful about medication implied that she had known she was pregnant? And if she was being careful, did that not also imply that she wanted the baby, that she was going to keep it?

I did a more detailed search for clonazepam on the net. I discovered that it was a benzodiazepine with *anxiolytic, anticonvulsant, muscle relaxant, amnestic, sedative and hypnotic qualities.* Molloy was right — possible side effects were suicidal ideation along with sedation, apathy, fatigue, dizziness, difficulty with co-ordination, slow reactions, poor concentration — all things Phyllis had mentioned. I moved on to have a look at some chat sites. Comments online by people who had taken the drug said that it tasted minty, like menthol. And significantly — it was dangerous to take in pregnancy. So why would

Marguerite have willingly taken clonazepam if she knew she was pregnant?

I thought about calling Molloy and telling him what I'd remembered. But was it enough to change anything? After the conversation we'd just had, I wasn't convinced. I needed more.

I glanced out the window of the office; Quinn's car was still there. He would have to come back for it sooner or later, but I couldn't stand guard at the window all afternoon to catch him. I rang his mobile and left a message for him to call me as soon as possible. Before I hung up, Leah buzzed from downstairs.

"Hugh O'Connor's father is here to see you. He wants to have a word with you about Hugh."

"Is Hugh with him?"

"Nope."

"Hmm. Okay then. Send him up."

A tall thin man in an ill-fitting suit walked into my office. He smiled in recognition when he saw me. "So, we've met before. I hadn't made the connection."

The man standing in front of me was Aidan Doherty. I hoped my expression didn't give anything away – the night before, I had been dialing his number.

He offered his hand. "It was at the hospital, wasn't it?" He had a kind smile that brightened his eyes. I could see that at one time he had been handsome, but he seemed worn.

"Yes, that's right. You have a good memory. I guess it's a requirement of the job," I said, offering him a seat. I hesitated. "Leah said you were Hugh's father?"

He nodded. "I know – the name. It's a bit confusing. Hugh decided to take his mother's maiden name. He adored his grandfather."

"Oh yes . . . the famous grandfather." I sat down. "What can I do for you, Mr. Doherty?"

"I'm here about Hugh. I know he's got himself into a spot of bother."

"Hugh's over eighteen, Mr. Doherty, so I can't discuss his business with you without his consent, I'm afraid."

"Aidan, please. I know that. But he is aware that I'm here. You can ring him, if you like."

He scrolled through his list of contacts and handed me his mobile with his son's number highlighted. I realized that what I was holding was probably the very phone Marguerite had been dialling and texting so obsessively. Hugh answered on the third ring.

"Hugh, it's Ben O'Keeffe here. I have your father with me. He wants to talk to me about your case. Is that okay with you?"

I could hear a laugh on the other end of the phone. "Aye. Let him away on. Whatever makes him happy."

"Are you sure?"

"Aye. It's no bother to me. It'll make no difference."

"Okay, Hugh. I'll let you know when the statements come in." I handed Aidan back his phone. "Well, you were right, he has no problem with it. What do you want to know?"

"I just wondered if there was anything I could do."

"What do you mean?"

He looked anxious. "Well, would it help if I spoke to the guards myself? Hugh's been having something of a rough time over the past couple of years. Family difficulties. He has a bit of a temper sometimes, too. But then things haven't always been easy for him. His mother and I . . ." He trailed off.

I waited for him to continue, but he didn't.

"You can try – but I doubt it would help. It's a serious enough charge. And it's already on Pulse," I said, referring to the garda records system.

"I'm too late, then?"

"I suspect so."

Aidan sighed. "He only told me about it last night. His mother bailed him out. She didn't tell me either, unfortunately." He added apologetically, "I'm just concerned for him. His mother is very protective of him."

"You said you and his mother . . . ?"

Aidan glanced at the floor for a second, then seemed to come to a decision. "As a matter of fact, would you mind if I asked your advice about something – for myself? There should be no conflict with Hugh."

"Sure. Go ahead."

"And it would be completely confidential?"

There seemed to be a lot of concern about confidentiality today. "Of course."

He clasped his hands in his lap and took a deep breath. "Look, I know it sounds a bit far-fetched, but I'm being blackmailed."

"I see. Do you want to tell me about it?"

"Well, I don't really want to go into any details. But the bottom line is, I had an affair. I'm not proud of it and it's over now, but the information has made its way into the wrong hands. And it's being used against me." He ran his fingers through his hair.

"How?"

"The individuals I'm dealing with seem to think that my political career will suffer if the story comes out. I'm not sure that's the case, frankly, but I don't know what to do about it. I don't want my family to be hurt."

It was all I could do to stop myself from asking him who he had been having the affair with.

"Have you spoken to the guards?" I asked.

"I haven't, no." He looked fearful. "Not yet."

"With all due respect, Mr. Doherty, that is what you should be talking to the guards about. Not Hugh. Blackmail is a serious criminal offence. I'm sure they could be discreet."

"I'll think about it," he said in that way people do when you know it's the last thing they would consider. It was clear I hadn't given him the advice he wanted, and immediately, I wished I could take it back, but it was too late. Within minutes he had thanked me and left.

I watched him from the window as he crossed the street, shoulders hunched as if he were carrying a great weight. Was he the father of Marguerite's child? A baby would certainly have hurt his family and probably his career too. How far would he have been willing to go, to stop that happening?

I was beginning to see why Marguerite might not have been so popular with the women of Inishowen. Two lovers, both married, within the space of a year. Was Simon a third?

I went downstairs to quiz Leah.

"What's the story with the family name? That was pretty confusing at the start."

"Doherty and O'Connor? Sorry, I should have told you. Hugh took his mother's name."

"So I gathered. Isn't that a bit unusual?"

"My sister says he's obsessed with his grandfather. Wants to be just like him. Follow in his footsteps. Remember what he said to you about running for election?"

"Oh yes. What about his father though? Aidan Doherty is a pretty successful politician too, isn't he?"

Leah smiled. "Not in the same league. Doesn't have the same killer instinct. Doherty's credentials all come from his marriage."

"To Hugh's mother?"

"Clodagh."

I put two and two together. "Oh God, Clodagh O'Connor! *That's* Hugh's mother?"

"Yep. Tough woman."

"So I gather. I just met her at lunchtime."

"Actually, I'm surprised Doherty didn't take the wife's name himself," Leah said wryly. "I'd say if he hadn't married her, he'd still be shoeing horses. But that wasn't going to be enough for Clodagh O'Connor, coming from a big political dynasty like that."

"That's what he did?"

She nodded. "Blacksmith. There was a bit more to him than the horses though; he started making jewelry. Nice stuff, actually. Iron cuffs, pendants, that sort of thing. They say he only went into politics under pressure from the wife."

A flashback of Marguerite fidgeting with a bracelet came into my head. Had Aidan given it to her? I wondered what had happened to it. She hadn't been wearing it when she died – I was sure I would have noticed it if I had seen it on her body.

Chapter 18

WE WERE INTERRUPTED by the phone. Leah passed the receiver over to me.

Liam McLaughlin sounded upbeat. "I hear the contracts are in."

"You're quick off the mark. Have you a spy in my filing cabinet or something?"

"Have you had a look at them yet?"

"Give me a chance. They only came in this morning. I'll do them this afternoon."

"Grand." He paused. "How are you feeling after yesterday?"

"Fine. Thanks for rescuing me."

"God, I got some fright when I saw your poor little Mini in the ditch."

"You and me both."

"So, if you're back at work, does that mean you're fit to come to the Wax Auction tonight?" I could tell he was grinning on the other end of the phone.

I groaned. "Do I have to?"

"You'll be missed, if you don't. I have you down as one of the sponsors. It's at six."

★ ★ ★

The pub was heaving when I walked into the Oak at half past six. A band was playing at one end on a makeshift stage and an overpowering smell of burning wax filled the air. Three massage beds had been erected in one corner of the pub, and three women in bright yellow T-shirts bearing the words *Brid's Beauticians* were enthusiastically applying strips of hot wax to their victims' legs and chests, much to the enjoyment of the crowd that had formed around each one. Every yelp provoked a loud cheer.

Andy McFadden was on one bed; he must be the garda representative, I thought. Clearly they hadn't persuaded Molloy to take part or maybe he was otherwise engaged. I decided not to think about that. Hal McKinney was on a second bed, and on the third, playing up to the crowd and lapping up the attention was Simon Howard.

"Need a ticket?" A grinning Hugh O'Connor was seated at a table with a Scottish shortbread biscuit tin full of cash.

"No, thanks. I've already been stung for sponsorship."

"Great. I have something for you to sign." The boy handed me a list of names on a clipboard and directed me to mine.

"How did you get roped into this?" I asked.

"I'm going to be Captain of the Under Twenties next year," he smiled.

"Ah."

"Got to have pride in your own town. That's what it's all about, isn't it? No one else is going to do it for us."

"I suppose that's true."

He took the clipboard back. "Donegal is the forgotten county and Inishowen is the forgotten part of Donegal. That's what my grandfather used to say. It's up to us to look after our own."

"You were close to your grandfather?"

"I was only a wee fella when he died, but I've read all his speeches in the Dail. They're on the net." His eyes narrowed. "You should have a look yourself. If you're going to stay around here, you should read up on a bit of local history."

I was about to say something noncommittal when I heard Liam's voice at my shoulder. "So you came, then?"

"As I remember it, you didn't give me much choice."

"And you've met our Hugh, I see. Wouldn't have been able to do it without this young fella. Carted all the stuff over from Brid's with his young mate over there." He nodded in the direction of the acne-faced youth I had seen with Hugh at the weekend, standing uncomfortably by the window. "Gained yourself a few fans in the process too, eh?"

He winked. "Just what we need – a bit of community-mindedness in the youth. Future Taoiseach in the making, aren't you?"

A shout came from the waxing corner. "Liam, you're up!"

Liam headed back over. I was just about to follow him to see what was happening when Hugh grabbed me by the arm.

"I hope Aidan didn't cause you any bother earlier on."

"Not at all. It's fine. I was just concerned that you knew he was talking to me about your case."

"I wouldn't pay any heed to him," the boy said dismissively. "No one does."

One positive side effect of going to the Wax Auction was that I didn't have time to think about dinner with Simon Howard. Since I had agreed to it, I had come close to losing my nerve and canceling any number of times. But I was more determined than ever to find out what I could about his relationship with Marguerite, and so it was too good an opportunity to

turn down. And let's face it, my own ego needed a little mas-
saging after what had happened with Molloy. Was I playing a
dangerous game? Perhaps.

As Liam had so kindly pointed out, it might have been a
while, but apparently I was still capable of carrying out the
pre-date ritual. After trying on at least six different outfits and
leaving them strewn across the bedroom, watched all the while
by a bemused Guinness sitting in the doorway, I finally settled on a simple short black dress which I wore with a silver
perfume-bottle pendant my parents had given me for my thir-
tieth. At half past eight, I put on my coat, lured Guinness out
the door with some left-over chicken and walked across the
green to Caffrey's on the other side of the village.

I was about to open the door to the restaurant when my
phone beeped. A text. *Damn it*, I thought. *After all that, he's
going to be late or, worse, cancel entirely.* But it was from Maeve.
Have fun. Break a leg!

Simon was sitting in one of the old armchairs by the fire in
the little pre-dinner drinks area, sipping a glass of wine and
flicking through one of the books piled up on the table beside
him, looking utterly at ease. He stood up when he saw me. I
could smell his aftershave as he kissed me on the cheek.

"You look lovely."

"Thank you. So do you. After your earlier trauma."

He gave me a quizzical look before laughing when he figured out what I meant. "Oh, the Oak. I thought I saw you
there. It was good fun. I'm a bit raw though, I can tell you.
Those girls are rough." He gestured towards his glass. "I hope
you don't mind but I ordered us a bottle of Chablis. If you don't
like it, we can order something else."

"I'm sure it's lovely."

The waiter, a boy racer I had defended on a charge of careless driving at the last court, looking angelic in white shirt
and black trousers, took my coat and handed us menus while
Simon poured me a glass of wine. We ordered food and made
small talk while we waited for our table and after ten minutes
we moved to a secluded table in the corner of the restaurant.
And eventually I began to relax, probably because of the wine.
But I still hadn't worked out how I was going to introduce
Marguerite into the conversation.

"Where is your Mini?" Simon asked. "I didn't notice it outside your house."

Oddly, I found it a little unnerving that he knew where I
lived, although it wasn't exactly a state secret. But I told him
about my accident.

He looked horrified. "That sounds bloody awful. Are you
okay now?"

"Oh, sure. I was a bit shaken up but I wasn't really hurt."

He reached out to place his hand on mine across the table. I
wasn't sure whether I liked it or not. It crossed my mind that
I must be seriously starved of physical affection if I couldn't
tell the difference – and the thought was so ludicrous it
made me want to laugh. I reddened and picked up my wine
glass.

"It's a bad area for car accidents around here, isn't it?" he said.
"I was reading some fairly disturbing statistics in the *Journal*."

I smiled. "The *Journal*. Listen to you! A few achs, ayes, and
wees and you'll soon be talking like a local."

"I have them already," he teased. "I'm Scottish, remember?"

I asked him about his life in Scotland and he told me he
was a widower, that his wife had died a few years previously
from cancer.

"I'm sorry. I suppose that's why you and your son are so close."

"Are we?" he asked quietly. "I'm not so sure. He was very attached to his mother. I did think that we might live together here but I sometimes wonder if the only reason he even visits is to see the damn dog."

"What does he do for a living?"

"Oh, God knows. Something to do with money. Accountancy? Something soulless anyway."

"You're quite different, aren't you?" I said.

"Oh, I think he and I have very little in common. To be honest, I suspect if it wasn't for that dog, we'd never see each other. Might be easier. I didn't mean that," he added quickly.

"I had a rather odd conversation with him actually. On Sunday."

"Oh?"

"He seemed to be almost warning me off."

Simon's eyes narrowed. "Warning you off what, exactly?"

"I wasn't entirely sure. He seemed to be implying that you — how shall I put it? — like women."

Simon laughed. "Well, he's not wrong there. There's no law against that though, is there?"

"Well, no . . ."

"As I said, he and his mother were very close. He was an only child, of course, and he had some medical problems when he was younger which meant he was a bit clingier than other kids. When she died, he was only seventeen. I've always got the feeling that he would be happier if I stayed celibate for the rest of my life."

"Ah. I see."

"Unfortunately, that's not in my nature." Simon smiled as he poured me another glass of wine.

"It must have been pretty traumatic for him all the same, losing his mother to cancer when he was still so young."

"I suppose. He took off for a few years traveling."

"After she died? On his own?" It struck me as an odd thing to do, or to be allowed to do, more to the point, at seventeen, immediately after losing your mother.

"Aye. Just made up his mind to go for it. Seemed to do him some good. Frankly, he's always been a wee bit 'different' for want of a better way of putting it, but he came back a bit more together. Had a job and everything."

"The job he's doing now? That he travels for?"

"I think so," Simon said vaguely.

"He seemed upset when I was talking to him." Something stopped me from telling him what David had said about Marguerite. I thought I'd leave that for later.

Simon waved his hand dismissively. "Don't mind him, seriously. He's just lacking in a few social skills."

We ordered a second bottle of wine after the main course, which meant we were the last two in the restaurant at half past eleven when the staff began to drop hints about closing up. Simon suggested we go to the pub next door for a last drink. As we left the restaurant, he placed his hand briefly on my back in a gentle, protective gesture.

As I watched him order two brandies at the bar, I realized how much I had enjoyed the evening. He had disarmed me. But I still hadn't managed to bring up the subject of Marguerite; there just hadn't been an opportunity to do it without seeming as if I was interviewing him. And part of me hadn't wanted to. Part of me wanted to pretend this was nothing more than dinner with a man to whom I was attracted. Which, I had to admit, I was.

"Let's do it again," he said, as he raised his glass a few minutes later.

Perfect, I thought. *I'll get another opportunity. It'll come much more naturally if I know him a bit better.*

"I had fun. Thank you," I said. "Think I might have a bit of a hangover in the morning though."

"Oh, but worth it, surely?" He laughed, leaned over, and kissed me briefly on the lips, taking me completely by surprise.

Chapter 19

THE NEXT MORNING I opened my eyes just as my phone beeped on the bedside locker. Sleepily, I reached out to pick it up, knocking over the alarm clock and the glass of water with one swipe. This was becoming a bit of a habit. I read the text.

Dinner again, or am I pushing my luck? Simon X.

I texted him back. *Bit early, isn't it?*

The reply came a few seconds later. *Play hard to get if you like! I'll try again later.*

I leaned out of bed to pick up the clock and glass from the floor and replace them on the bedside locker, then buried myself back beneath the covers, replaying the night before in my head. Miraculously, I had no hangover. We'd only had the one drink in the pub before Simon had walked me back to my gate, kissing me again on the cheek before making sure I got in safely: the perfect gentleman. Away from his company, I was annoyed with myself that I hadn't managed to ask him about Marguerite, but I consoled myself with the fact that it looked as if I would get another opportunity.

I found myself singing in the shower; I felt lighter than I had in a while, as if a dark cloud had finally shifted. Downstairs, I fried up some French toast, made a pot of tea and settled down at the kitchen table with the previous day's paper, knowing that my first appointment wasn't till eleven.

An article on the front page caught my eye. It was a follow-up to the one Phyllis had been reading on Saturday about the Council row on re-zoning.

A County Council vote on re-zoning for Inishowen required by the new Donegal County Development Plan has proven to be more controversial than expected. A stalemate has arisen with regard to the re-zoning of certain areas of the peninsula, with unnamed lobbyists attempting to gain support across party lines for the status quo to remain. A final vote is expected in the next fortnight.

As I opened the paper to read further, I wondered which "areas of the peninsula" were at issue. They weren't specified in the piece. Would the Council vote affect Gallagher and Dolan's purchase? If Malin Head were affected, there was a possibility it could delay the issue of planning permission or even scupper it completely. That wouldn't make them too happy.

A short taxi-ride to Glendara later, I called in to Hal's to check on my car before I went to the office. My poor old Mini looked pretty sad with her left wing still bashed in, but Hal assured me that she would be ready by Monday and he gave me a black Golf to see me through the weekend. It was an old diesel car and it sounded like a tractor, but I was relieved to have some sort of wheels again.

I made it to the office by half past ten and checked my messages. Quinn still hadn't called me back so I tried his office number again, but it was engaged. His mobile was engaged too.

While I waited to call again, I did a quick Google search to find out more about the conduct and ethics of medical practitioners and their patients. It confirmed my feeling that medical practitioners should never form any kind of personal relationship with patients, their partners, or their close relatives.

I checked my diary; the following Tuesday was the first day of the new legal year. The Circuit Court was sitting in Letterkenny, and I had to be there for some settlement meetings at lunchtime. So I dialed Quinn's mobile again and this time reached his voicemail. I left a message for him to meet me at the courthouse at two. I hoped my tone indicated I wasn't giving him a choice.

I was settling into some work at my desk when Leah buzzed.

"Phone call for you, Ben. It's that sculptor friend of Marguerite's. He won't tell me what he wants."

I hadn't yet told Leah about my dinner with Simon. "That's okay. Put him through."

He sounded cheerful. "Benedicta, I'm ringing to see how you feel about Antrim."

"Antrim? Any particular reason?"

"I was wondering if you'd like to spend the weekend with me – in Antrim, in case I wasn't making myself clear."

"Which weekend?"

"This one."

I felt my panic level rising. "Today is Friday."

"I meant tomorrow night," he said, as if that made a damn bit of difference. "I'm in Belfast tonight for an exhibition, but I could meet you tomorrow evening about halfway – there's a little place I have in mind. If you take the ferry from Greencastle across to Magilligan Point, it should only take you an hour or so."

I stalled. "Can I think about it?"

"Nope. I have to ring them back straight away. They have another booking waiting if I don't get back to them in ten minutes. Go on," he urged. "Live a little. There are two bedrooms."

I could hear the grin in his voice. Now I was embarrassed.

I screwed my eyes shut while I gave him my answer. "Okay. But you'd better give me some more details if you expect me to actually get there."

"Will do. I'll send you a text."

He rang off, leaving me feeling dizzy. Neat technique if you want something, I thought – just don't give the other person a chance to turn you down. I should have tried that with Quinn, if he had actually answered his phone.

But I had just agreed to spend the night with a man I barely knew in an unknown location. How wise was that?

On my way to lunch I called in to the book shop to find Phyllis dressed in bright orange and green, and balanced precariously on a stepladder shelving books. She looked like an enormous piece of fruit.

I held the ladder for her, although it felt as if something considerably sturdier than me was needed to keep it steady. I scanned the shop and lowered my voice. "Are you on your own?"

The bookseller eyed me curiously from above. She nodded.

"Would you mind if I asked you some more questions about Marguerite?"

"No, of course not. Tea?"

I shook my head. "No, thanks. I don't have long."

She struggled down from the ladder, breathing heavily when she got to the bottom. "To be honest, I haven't been able to get her out of my head either. What do you want to know?"

I had decided to simply come straight out with it. "Was she having an affair?"

Phyllis sat down on the footstool at the base of the ladder with a sigh. "Yes, I think so."

"With Aidan Doherty, the County Councillor?"

"Yes. I didn't want to say anything to you before. Anyway, I thought you might have heard the rumours."

"Did she tell you about it?"

"God, no. But it was fairly obvious. He used to come in here a lot. In fact, this is where she met him, I think."

"Is that why you said you blamed yourself?"

"Partly," Phyllis said sadly.

"What happened?"

She shrugged. "I'm not sure. It seemed to end badly, as these things often do. They were found out, or guilt got the better of him. One or the other, I suspect. I was very conflicted about it."

"Why?"

She sighed again. "Because Clodagh was my friend."

My expression must have betrayed my surprise. I couldn't imagine two more different people than Clodagh and Phyllis.

"It was a long time ago now," Phyllis explained. "We haven't been close in years. Poor girl. She didn't have it easy."

"I thought Clodagh's background was pretty privileged?"

"Wealthy, yes. But that father of hers was a complete bastard. The famous *Big Hugh O'Connor*." Phyllis spat the name out. "It was never spoken about openly, of course, but he was a misogynist – cheated on his wife constantly. Clodagh's mother had a terrible time with him."

I raised my eyebrows. "Sounds as if her daughter didn't fare much better."

"I'm sure most people would think that," Phyllis agreed. "That Clodagh married a man like her father, that Aidan cheating on her was history repeating itself. But it didn't seem like that to me."

"Why not?"

"Aidan is a very different kind of man to Clodagh's father. I'm no fan of cheaters, mind. If you don't want to stay with someone, then have some balls and tell them, is my view. But with Aidan and Marguerite . . ." She broke off suddenly.

"What?" I said curiously.

She frowned. "I've just realized it's rather a strange coincidence – who he decided to cheat with. Funny, I hadn't thought of that before . . . that house again."

"What house?"

"Clodagh used to go out with Seamus Tighe. The man who lived in Marguerite's cottage before she did."

"Really? The man who drowned?"

"Yes. Seamus was Clodagh's boyfriend when they were teenagers. He lived in that cottage with his mother, just the two of them. God, Aidan having an affair with Marguerite seems even more like fate playing a cruel trick now. But Clodagh is a tough woman."

"So I believe."

"She's had to be. Her upbringing did that to her." Phyllis tried to explain. "She and Aidan got married when they were still teenagers. I always thought she was on the rebound, that she married him with a broken heart. Sometimes I even wondered if she ever really loved Aidan. She could be pretty cruel to him. He seemed rather diminished around her."

"And Marguerite?"

"Marguerite seemed a diminished kind of person too, some-how. When she met Aidan it was as if they recognized some-thing in each other. Marguerite was a different person when she became close to Aidan — more outgoing, brighter. For a while at least. They were a kind of balm for each other."

"Do you think people knew about it — the affair?"

"Oh God, aye. There was definitely talk. Clodagh knew herself. I don't know if Aidan told her or she found out, but she came into the shop to let Marguerite have it one day and that seemed to end things. If they weren't over before that."

"You're sure it ended?"

Phyllis gave this a few seconds' thought. "Well, I can't be a hundred percent sure. But I can tell you that he used to come in here regularly and after that scene with Clodagh and Mar-guerite, he never came in again."

"When was that?"

"Maybe six weeks before she died? That was when Margue-rite started to act rather strangely. I thought it was because she was upset at the end of the affair, but it was more than that. She started rambling, saying strange things."

"What sort of strange things?"

"Prayers, they sounded like. I saw her coming out of the church a couple of times. I'm not one for religion, you know that, Ben, but I thought, *Well, if it's giving her some comfort, where's the harm?* It was better than seeing her taken advantage of by some creep. But it didn't seem to — give her much comfort, that is."

"By creep, do you mean Aidan?"

Phillis shook her head vehemently. "No, I don't mean Aidan. He was kind to her. I think they genuinely loved each other. But she was disturbed about something."

"Have you any idea what it was?"

"After she died, when I heard about that cult she used to be in, I thought it might have to do with that. Memories resurfacing, flashbacks, that kind of thing. But she started going on and on about the importance of family. Of knowing where you came from. She'd talk to customers about it, people who came in the shop. I even saw her talking to the kids out there on the bench one day. I'm sure they all thought she was batty.

"Then when I heard about her daughter after she died, I thought that explained it: the lack of contact with the daughter. I thought she just missed her, maybe more so when her affair with Aidan Doherty ended."

"It's a possibility, I suppose." I wondered instead if Marguerite's obsession with family might be connected with her pregnancy, and the possibility the child might never know its father because he was married to somebody else.

Phyllis stood up with a groan, rubbing her back. "Anyway, I've been going over it in my mind since she died. And she really was behaving very strangely. Almost as if . . ."

"As if what?"

"Well, I know this sounds odd, particularly to me because I know she wouldn't even take an aspirin, but she was behaving almost as if she were drugged. If I didn't know better, I'd have sworn she was taking something those last few weeks, after she came back from her holiday . . ."

I lowered my voice even though we were alone in the shop. "You know they found a benzodiazepine in her system when she died?"

Phyllis's eyes widened. "You can't be serious. Valium?"

"No. It's one that's used for the treatment of epilepsy."

She looked crestfallen. "Really? Did Marguerite have epilepsy?"

"I don't know. But keep that to yourself."

Phyllis said wearily, "I'm amazed, after her reaction to the aspirin I offered her. But then I suppose that's why the guards took no notice of me when I told them about her strange behavior. It just backed up what they already knew – that she was taking this drug, whatever it's called . . ."

"Clonazepam."

Something else didn't add up, I realized as I walked back to the office after lunch. I knew now that Marguerite had been having an affair with Aidan Doherty, but Clodagh had known about it. In fact, if the comments I'd been hearing since Marguerite's death were anything to go by, it sounded as if the whole town knew. But if that were the case, then why was Aidan being blackmailed? What would he have to lose if the details came out? Even if those details included a pregnancy.

And what of Marguerite's odd behavior in her last few weeks? Was it to do with the cult or the drug that was found in her system when she died?

When I got back to the office I did yet another search on the Children of Damascus. I wasn't sure what I hoped to find this time – maybe some prayers or chants, words that Phyllis might find familiar. Instead I found myself back at the site for ex-members of the Damascans, xdamascans.com. This time I noticed a link to a *Contact Us* page, where I found a list of telephone numbers for over ten countries. I scrolled down and to my amazement there was one for Ireland. On checking the code, I discovered that it was a Monaghan number; only two hours away by car.

Without hesitation, I dialed the number. I reached a voice message and left my name and phone number and by the time I had made it down the stairs to reception to collect some typing five minutes later, the call had been returned.

"There's a Michaela somebody for you on line one," Leah whispered, her hand over the receiver. "I didn't catch her surname, and she wouldn't tell me what it was about, just said she was returning your call. Do you want to talk to her?"

"Thanks, Leah, I'll take it." I took the phone from her hand. "Hello, Michaela?"

A softly-spoken woman replied. "Hi. Is that Ben O'Keeffe?"

"Yes."

"I'm Michaela Reddy from the survivors group. You called earlier?"

"Yes. Thanks a million for ringing me back. I was wondering if it would be possible to meet at some stage to have a chat. I'm trying to find out some information and I think you might be able to help me."

"What kind of information?" The tone was wary.

"I'm trying to help someone who used to be in the Children of Damascus," I said. Not strictly true, but I would tell all when we met.

"Okay. You're in Donegal, is that correct?"

"Yes, Inishowen."

"Meet me at Annie's Café in Aughnacloy at eleven o'clock on Monday."

"What do you look like?"

"It's all right. I'll find you. Does that suit?"

"That's great. Thanks. I'll see you then."

The second line was blinking as I hung up the receiver. Leah was busy at the photocopier by that stage so I pressed the button and answered the call myself.

"Hello. O'Keeffe and Company Solicitors."

The voice was silky. "Answering our own phone now, are we? Haven't we gone down in the world."

I froze, every nerve in my body signalling fear. *It couldn't be.* My shoulders tensed, like a board.

"Who is this?"

"Don't play coy with me. You know exactly who it is."

I gripped the counter as the room started to spin. Leah glanced up from the photocopier. She mouthed the words *Are you okay?* I nodded.

"How did you get this number?" I realized I was about to throw up.

"How do you think? Phone book, baby. Phone book. You're public property now."

"Leave me alone. Do not contact me again, do you hear me?"

"Oh come on, baby, I'm thinking of paying you a visit. Thought I'd come up to your neck of the woods. It's been too long."

I slammed down the phone.

Chapter 20

I SLEPT BADLY that night. I stared at the wall for hours, my heart racing as if I'd drunk too many cups of coffee, that smooth voice playing over and over again in my head.

The fact that Luke Kirby had managed to get hold of a mobile phone in prison, that was no huge surprise; Luke had an ability to get hold of anything he wanted. But how the hell did he know where I was? I had been so careful to change my name, using my mother's maiden name and my own second name. And what the hell was he doing calling me after all of this time? I was sure in some sick way it amused him. Playing with people was something he had always derived pleasure from; playing with the cruelty of a cat with a dying bird. I hoped to God that was all it was.

About four a.m. the thought occurred – had the silent calls been from him, too?

I was woken by the shrieks of children playing ball on the green so I must have dozed off at some stage, and when I checked the time, it was ten o'clock. As I stared at the ceiling I realized that yesterday's call meant that I would now have to tell Leah about Luke – and that meant telling her about my sister's killing and the trial. The thought of it exhausted me. To

date, the only people who knew about my sister's death were
Molloy and Maeve. And I preferred it that way. I had come to
Inishowen to escape, to try and forget, even leaving my name
behind so I wouldn't be associated with the trial. The latter had
been a media circus – the public fascinated by the notion of a
lawyer like Luke Kirby on trial for murder, and all of the sala-
cious details that went with it.

I tried to put him out of my mind. Maybe he wouldn't call
back. Luke tired easily of that which he initially found amusing, I knew that too. Maybe it would have been enough for
him to call me from prison and to hear the fear in my voice.

I dragged a bag from underneath the bed and started to pack.
Whatever doubts I had about Simon, suddenly it suited me
very much to be out of Inishowen for the weekend. I badly
needed a distraction. I threw in a fleece, some combats, a pair
of hiking boots and a dress, and after a quick shower, I pulled
on a pair of jeans and a sweater. Simon had given me no idea
what kind of a place we were staying in or what we would be
doing, so all I could do was to try to cover all bases.

After breakfast I left some food and water out for Guinness
and opened the top window over the kitchen sink so he could
clamber in and out, locked the front door, and set off.

Driving through Glendara I spotted a familiar figure coming
out of the veterinary clinic. It was David Howard, carrying a
big bag of dog food. After a brief hesitation, I slowed down and
pulled in. I climbed out of the car and walked across his path
as if I were heading in to see Maeve.

"Here for the weekend?" I smiled and he didn't and it felt
like a mistake already.

"My father is away," he replied.

I wondered if Simon had told him who he was spending the weekend with. If he hadn't, I certainly wasn't going to volunteer it.

"Have you a minute?" I asked.

He didn't respond, but he did put the dog food on the ground so I took that to be an assent.

"I wanted to ask you something. What did you mean, the last time we spoke – what you said about your dad?"

He stared at me in that unnerving way of his, his eyes betraying nothing. But I couldn't back down now.

"About your dad and Marguerite," I prompted.

"Why do you want to know?"

"Marguerite was my friend."

He tilted his head to one side. "Why are you so interested in my father?"

"I'm not, I just . . ."

"If you're asking for my advice, I suggest you stay away from him." He picked up the dog food and started to move away.

I followed him. "Why? Why should I stay away from him? David!"

He turned slightly. "Because my father doesn't care what he breaks. Who he destroys."

"Are you talking about your mother?"

He kept walking.

"Who else did he destroy? Do you mean Marguerite?" I persisted. "David, please."

He spun around, his eyes flashed. "Marguerite was weak. What happened to her was entirely of her own doing."

And he walked away.

★   ★   ★

The short journey up the peninsula towards Greencastle took me much longer than it should have; twice I pulled in to gather my thoughts and once I turned the car back towards Glendara, only to carry out a second U-turn five minutes later. At one point not far from Greencastle, I nearly collided with McFadden in the squad car. He wagged his finger good-naturedly at me and drove on.

Was it David who was unbalanced and strange, or was his father the one not to be trusted? Phyllis's view was the former, and in my experience, Phyllis was a fair judge of character. David had good cause to be odd, I supposed, having lost his mother while he was still a teenager. But was his father partly responsible for that? I had thought at times that Simon could be a little callous about his son. Maybe David had reasons for disliking his father.

So was David telling the truth? Was Simon, the man with whom I was about to spend the weekend, a cruel and heartless man beneath his gregarious exterior? Was he even dangerous?

Somehow I made it as far as Greencastle where I drove past the Maritime Museum and down the steep incline towards the pier. The fifteen-minute crossing to Magilligan Point leaves every hour on the hour. The ferry looked full. I think if it had been, I would have simply turned the car around and driven back to Glendara and not waited for the next one. But instead of being waved away, I was directed to drive on by a man in a fluorescent green jacket standing at the gate and the barrier came down almost immediately. I had taken the last remaining place.

Although the waterway separates two jurisdictions – Northern Ireland and the Republic of Ireland – the crossing is only a mile or so long. Today the sea was choppy and the waves glistened in the precarious autumn sunshine while the wind hustled the clouds across the sky like a renegade dog worrying sheep. It reflected the way I was feeling inside: uneasy.

My phone buzzed. It was a text from Simon. Three words only.

Drive to Bushmills.

I had a sudden urge to call Molloy, but I knew I couldn't. What the hell was I doing traveling to an unknown destination to spend the night with a man I barely knew?

A knock on the car window interrupted my thoughts, and I wound down the window and rummaged in my bag for some money to pay for my ticket. As I handed it over, the man taking it gave me a wide grin.

"Hey, solicitor."

I almost didn't recognize him sober. "Iggy! How are you doing?"

He surveyed the Golf with disdain. "Where's the wee Mini?"

"It's in the garage."

"Nothing serious, I hope. That's a grand wee car, your Mini."

"Should have it back next week. I didn't know you were working here."

"Aye. Only since yesterday. Just to keep me going till I get me licence back. I have it now for the next few weeks." He handed me my change and my ticket. "There you go."

"That's great, Iggy. Good luck with it."

I rolled the window back up and watched him for a while as he chatted to the other drivers, producing a sweet for a kid in the back of the car in front. When I couldn't see him any longer, I buried myself in the paper I had nabbed from the waiting room in an attempt to calm down my insides.

★   ★   ★

An hour later, having stopped off briefly to pick up a few bottles of wine, I pulled in by the side of the road and dialed Simon's number.

"Where are you?" he said.

"Bushmills, as per your instructions. I'm on the main street, I think, just in front of the police station."

"Great. You're almost here. Take the road for Ballymoney and drive along it for about three kilometers until you see a turn to the left. Take that turn."

I was scribbling all of this down. *Ballymoney*, I wrote.

"Drive on for about a kilometer or so."

"And then?"

"Then there'll be a man standing in the middle of the road with a bottle of wine."

Ten minutes later, I was driving along a bumpy country lane, meandering erratically past fields of sheep. After about a kilometer or two, I turned a particularly sharp corkscrew bend and as I came out of it, I saw Simon perched on a wall about fifty meters ahead on the left. I took a deep breath and resolved to relax and see where the weekend took me. I hadn't much choice now.

He waved and climbed down to meet me. I rolled down the window.

"I thought you said there'd be a man standing in the middle of the road with a bottle of wine?"

"Bloody lawyers." He gave me a kiss on the cheek through the open window. "So pedantic. Well, Benedicta?" he asked, gesturing towards the little ivy-covered gate lodge behind the wall that he'd been perched on. "What do you think? It's a pretty thing, isn't it?" he said, mimicking Bing Crosby from *The Little Drummer Boy*.

He was right. It was pretty.

"You can park round the front."

I drove after him through the rather grand, pillared entrance which must once have led to a large main house and parked on the graveled area beside the lodge. I climbed out of the driver's seat, stretching my stiffened limbs.

Simon took my bag and motioned me into the house. "Wait till you see the inside."

A glass corridor connected the main part of the lodge to a kitchen and bathroom extension. I stood for a minute before Simon took my hand and led me into the original part of the house – a perfectly round sitting room with armchairs and a fire crackling gently in the grate.

He then led me up a winding staircase. "I have to confess, I did tell you one little white lie."

Wild flowers were strewn across the stairs leading to a double bedroom, perfectly circular just like the room below, dominated by a huge old mahogany bed with a crisp white duvet and over-stuffed pillows. On the top step was a bottle of champagne. It didn't take a genius to work out what the lie was.

On the dressing table was a small sculpture, just like the one I had admired at Simon's exhibition in Glendara. I gave him an enquiring look.

"For you," he said.

I picked it up. It was heavier than it looked; a female figure, face down, seated with her arms wrapped around her legs. It was beautiful.

"It's lovely. But you shouldn't have done that. It's too much." I put it back on the table.

"I wanted to." He smiled at me. "You're someone who will appreciate it."

"Well, thank you. It's really lovely. Honestly."

He shot me a mischievous look. "Anyway, it's one that didn't sell."

I laughed.

"You're not annoyed about the room?" he asked.

"No, of course not. I assume you're sleeping downstairs."

Simon had been telling the truth about one thing; he was an impressively good cook. The Spanish omelette and salads he prepared were laden with garlic just the way I liked them and the wine was even better. A couple of hours later I sat curled up in one of the armchairs in front of the fire in the sitting room with a glass of red. Nina Simone was playing on the CD player and the remaining washing-up was being finished by Simon at his insistence in the kitchen. I was beginning to feel very mellow. I wouldn't say my conversation with David had left my mind entirely, but let's say it was dormant. And Luke Kirby seemed very far away.

As I looked around for somewhere to rest my glass, I noticed a newspaper on the coffee table, open at the Arts section. I picked it up. There was a review of Simon's exhibition in Belfast. It was a well-known gallery; Simon was clearly a rated sculptor. The review was good too. There were photographs of some of the pieces I had seen the previous weekend and – my breath caught – one of the drawings of Marguerite I had seen in Simon's studio.

I stared at the photograph. Why on earth would he still have used those pictures after what had happened?

I heard a noise from the kitchen and put the paper back where I had found it. Seconds later, Simon came shuffling along the glass corridor in his socked feet, wine bottle in hand. He drained the bottle into our two glasses, sat down in the other armchair and stretched his long legs out in front of him.

"So, what would you like to do now?" he asked. "Would you like to go out? We could take a trip into Bushmills. It looked as if there were some nice little pubs there."

"No. Let's stay here. It would be a shame to waste the fire. Anyway, I'm pretty sure you're over the limit already."

"Okay. Fine by me." He settled back into his chair. "You all right? You sound a bit odd."

I hesitated for a second and then reached over for the newspaper. I held it up.

He grinned. "Good review, wasn't it?"

"I see you're exhibiting those drawings you did of Marguerite."

"Yes. The gallery in Belfast were looking for a bit of variety – they wanted to know if I had anything other than sculpture. What's wrong?"

I dropped the paper again. "Nothing. Forget it."

"No. What were you going to say?"

"Doesn't it bother you? Exhibiting them after what happened?"

"Not really, no. They're bloody good if I do say so myself."

I was quiet. Sipped my wine.

"Do you play chess?" he asked, pointing to a stack of board games under the sideboard. "I noticed those earlier on."

"I used to, but it's been years."

"Fancy a game?" he suggested. "I'll be gentle."

"Okay."

He dragged up a little coffee table, placed it between us, and we sat facing each other on the sheepskin rug in front of the fire. I was lousy. He took a bishop, a rook, and three pawns from me in the first ten minutes.

"You're not concentrating," he said. He frowned. "There's something on your mind. I can tell."

"Do you remember saying that Marguerite's behavior was a bit erratic, when we were in the Oak after the funeral?"

"Yes."

"What did you mean by that?"

"Why?"

I shrugged. "I just wondered."

"You ask a lot of questions about Marguerite."

"Do I? Sorry. It's just that you said you didn't know her very well, but yet she modeled for you. I suppose I find that difficult to understand."

"You think there's something I'm not telling you."

"No, I . . ."

He sighed. "Well, you're right. There is something. If you really want to know, I'll tell you."

"Tell me. Please."

He sat forward in his chair. "I don't feel good about this – it seems unfair to tell tales on someone who is gone, but I can see you're not going to relax until I do, and it might explain why my feelings towards Marguerite may seem a little contradictory."

"Go on."

He breathed in. "As you know, Marguerite did a little modeling for me – she needed the money and I needed a model. All very straightforward. Nothing complicated. Sometime after that, she appeared at my door. It was late at night and she looked upset. She'd been crying; she wouldn't tell me what was wrong, but she wanted to come in. I left her in the sitting room while I went to make her a cup of that disgusting tea she drank. When I came back into the room, she wasn't there." He stopped. "Are you sure you want to know this? Because I feel really uncomfortable telling you."

"Please," I urged.

"Okay. I went looking for her, and I found her. In my bedroom." He hesitated. "Lying on my bed. Naked."

"Naked?"

"Completely. I don't know whether she meant to seduce me or what, but I asked her to get dressed, gave her the tea, and she left."

"When was this?"

"A couple of weeks before she died."

"And when she modeled for you . . . ?"

He smiled. "She was fully dressed."

"Did it ever happen again?"

"Never. As a matter of fact, I didn't see much of her after that. I avoided her. I thought a bit of distance was probably necessary. That was, until she called in on the night she died. I was so surprised that she wanted to appoint me her executor. I thought she'd be embarrassed. But it was almost as if she didn't remember it."

"She never mentioned it?"

"She never mentioned it. And neither did I. It seemed unfair to do so."

"Does David know about this?" I asked.

Simon seemed taken aback. "No, I don't think so. Why would you ask that?"

"I think he might be under the impression that there was something going on between you and Marguerite."

Simon laughed dismissively. "I doubt he thinks that. David has his own problems. He had no interest in Marguerite whatsoever." He leaned towards me. "Now can we please talk about something else?"

The next morning I awoke to find him sitting on the bed smiling at me, a breakfast tray with freshly squeezed orange juice, toast, and coffee on the bedside locker.

"You're pulling out all the stops, aren't you?" I said as I propped myself up on the pillows.

"I have no idea what you mean. I'm always like this." He poured us both some coffee and started buttering toast.

"How was the couch?" I asked.

"Let's just say I was hoping for an upgrade," he grinned. "So what do you fancy doing today? We could do the walk along the cliffs from the Giant's Causeway. It's supposed to be stunning."

"Sure. Sounds great," I said, chewing on a piece of toast. "I brought hiking boots," I announced proudly.

"We could even take a picnic."

"Grand."

"That's this afternoon's activities sorted then." He took the toast from my hand. "So what on earth will we do between now and then . . . ?"

I snatched it back from him. "Hey, I'm hungry."

He let out a heavy stage sigh and picked up another piece.

I arrived back in Malin late that night – later than I should have. The ferry crossing had been canceled, and I had had to drive all the way around the inlet to get home.

As I turned the key in the lock, I felt a mixture of frustration and relief. I had managed to keep Simon at bay all weekend;

I can't say I wasn't tempted, but something kept stopping me. The scenario he had described with Marguerite explained the ambiguity surrounding his relationship with her, but I still wasn't convinced he was telling me the whole story. The ease with which he seemed always to be able to provide an utterly plausible explanation and then immediately change the subject made me decidedly uneasy. I wasn't at all sure I trusted him yet, although a large part of me wanted to.

However, my reluctance to sleep with him didn't seem to have put him off. If anything, he appeared to find the whole thing highly amusing and was pushing for us to meet up later in the week. I sensed he was a man who liked the chase.

Guinness wound his tail around my ankles as I walked into the hallway; he'd been sitting on the doorstep when I pulled up. But as soon as I entered the house, I could sense that something wasn't right. I dumped my bags on the floor of the kitchen, switched on the lights, and looked around me. At first glance everything seemed to be where it should be.

I made my way into the sitting room and switched on the lamp. Everything seemed okay in there too. Then I remembered something. I knelt down to check underneath the coffee table where I had left the box with Marguerite's things. My shoulders tensed. It was gone. Someone had taken it. Someone had been in my house. They must have come in through the window I had left open for Guinness. How could I have been so stupid?

I looked around me, but nothing else seemed to have been taken; the television was still there and so was my laptop. Whoever had broken in had been after something very specific, and it looked as if they had found it. But what on earth would anyone want with Marguerite's things?

I tried to remember what had been in the box. Tea bags, cosmetics bag . . . I was like a contestant on one of those television game shows. *God — the letters!* Where the hell had I left them? I raced back through the hall and out the front door, climbed back into my car, still warm from the drive home, and drove to Glendara and the office. Once inside, I dashed upstairs and made a beeline for the filing cabinet, fished out Marguerite's file and opened it, my hands still shaking. The bills and letters were still there, just where I had left them when I had brought them in to check for Simon's number.

Chapter 21

It turned out that a break-in wasn't my only unpleasant welcome-home present. I could tell by Leah's face on Monday morning that something else was very wrong.

"What is it?" I asked, ignoring the sense of dread I felt.

Her eyes welled. "Iggy McDaid is dead."

"*No!* What happened?" I was breathless with shock.

"He fell off the Greencastle ferry, drunk on Saturday night."

"You can't be serious. I was just talking to him on the ferry on Friday evening." Then it hit me. "Oh no — *that's* why the ferry wasn't running yesterday. I had to come back by Derry. I just assumed it was the rough weather."

"It's awful, isn't it? Two drownings in less than two weeks."

"It's weird, that's what it is."

Leah shook her head. "Poor old Iggy never had it easy. He's been a martyr to the drink all his life."

"I was just thinking when I saw him on Friday that he was looking good. He was completely sober, and he seemed to be getting a kick out of the new job."

Leah looked up. "That's what everyone's been saying; that he'd been sober since the court last week. And that was a long time for Iggy."

"I'll bet."

"He was only fifty-five too. I know he had a bit of a mouth on him when he was drunk, but when he was sober, he was the best in the world. When my grandad died, he used to go around to my grandmother's every week and chop up firewood for her. All because my grandad pulled him out of the ditch one time and drove him home. If anyone did him a good turn, Iggy would spend his life trying to pay them back."

"Poor man."

She handed me the post. "But then I suppose working on a ferry wasn't the best job for a man who couldn't stay sober. The wake's tonight and tomorrow. I'm going tonight if you want to come with me?"

"That's okay, Leah. I'll get there myself in the morning probably."

I started going through the envelopes and opening them at the reception desk, not really concentrating on the contents. Iggy had been the one who had found Marguerite's body and now he was dead, too. Was there a connection? Because it was a hell of a coincidence if there wasn't.

Leah cleared her throat, and I looked down at her. She glanced at the clock. "Don't you have to get going? Haven't you a meeting this morning?"

Of course, Aughnacloy. I needed to be in Aughnacloy by eleven. I dropped the post on the counter and ran.

The day was dry and bright as I drove down along the peninsula, crossed the border into Northern Ireland at Muff, and headed through the North via Derry, bypassing the busy towns of Strabane and Omagh. I accelerated past the Ulster American Folk Park so beloved of primary school outings at about

quarter past ten and arrived in the small County Tyrone town
of Aughnacloy at ten to eleven.

I had had plenty of time to think on the way there – not
that I came up with any answers. In the end, I decided to concentrate on the task in hand and resolved just to be honest. If I
wanted to get the information I needed, I had no choice but to
trust this Michaela woman and hoped that she in turn would
trust me enough to help.

It wasn't easy to find parking; the town was busy. Eventually
I pulled in nose first, in front of a large hardware shop, and set
off walking up the wide main street to look for Annie's Café.
It wasn't difficult to find – it was in a prime position. Taking a
deep breath, I pushed open the door.

About half of the dozen or so tables in Annie's Café were
occupied, mostly by women. I was a few minutes early so I
ordered a tea and sat down to wait, willing myself to stop looking up every time the door opened. By ten past eleven, I was
trying to decide how long I'd wait before giving up, when a
woman came in the door, ordered a Diet Coke at the counter
and walked straight over to my table.

"Ben O'Keeffe?"

I stood up. "Yes."

She smiled and held out her hand. "I'm Michaela. Sorry I'm
late."

She spoke in a strong Tyrone accent. For some reason I
hadn't been expecting that; it hadn't seemed so noticeable on
the phone. She sat down, popped open the can, and poured her
drink. She was late twenties, I guessed, although it was impossible to tell since she was shockingly overweight; she was what
would be described in Donegal as "four square."

"No difficulty spotting me, then?" I said.

"Didn't even need a description. I know everyone else in here," she smiled. There was real warmth in the smile.

"You're a local, then?"

"My grandparents live here. I came back here myself about ten years ago."

"Thanks for meeting me. I'm very grateful."

"That's okay. Are you going to tell me what this is about?"

I gave her a brief account of what had happened over the past few weeks. I told her that a client of mine had died in rather odd circumstances and that she had had a connection with Alain Veillard and the Children of Damascus. Michaela's face betrayed nothing; she listened attentively, taking periodic sips from her Coke.

When I had finished, she said, "And you want to find out more about the Damascans?"

"Yes. I thought it might help if I could talk to someone who had actually been in the group."

"Well, you've come to the right place. Or person."

"You were in the Damascans?"

"I was brought up in the Damascans. My parents are still members."

"Oh," I said, slightly taken aback.

"I'm not a member anymore. Haven't been for ten years. What do you want to know?"

"Well, firstly, is there any chance you actually knew my client? I know they're a big organization."

"What was the name?"

"Marguerite Etienne."

Michaela looked surprised. "I know the name, surely. Everyone knew that name. To be honest, I thought she had died a long time ago. I'm pretty sure that's what we were told."

"She died two weeks ago."

"Oh. I never met her. But I did know her daughter, Abra."

"Marguerite called her Adeline."

"I never knew her as anything other than Abra. Veillard must have renamed her – he did that sometimes. She and I spent some time together in one of the camps. She was a good few years younger than me, but she wasn't someone you could avoid noticing since she was the Teacher's daughter."

"Camps?"

Michaela smiled. "How much do you know about the Damascans?"

"Not much really. Just what I've been able to read on the net."

"Maybe I should start by telling you my own story?"

"If you wouldn't mind, that would be great."

She took a sip of her Coke. "When I was about a year old my parents bought a farm in the South of France. They wanted to move away from Northern Ireland and start a new life and so we moved there, the three of us. From what my grandparents tell me, Alain Veillard just appeared on our doorstep one day preaching love and Jesus, and within a matter of weeks, my parents were hooked. Hooked enough to sell their farm and move lock, stock, and barrel into the 'community,' taking me with them. And they never left."

"But you did?"

"Yes. As I said, I left about ten years ago and came back here."

"Why?"

"Because I had started to question the way things were, and that wasn't permitted." She looked up. "Ben, I could spend all day talking to you about the Damascans and I still wouldn't have covered everything. Do you want a bit of a crash course?"

I nodded. "Please."

"The Children of Damascus are a Christian Doomsday Cult. They preach the Bible, interpret it strictly – puritanically, I guess you'd say – follow arcane Christian rituals. They live together in compounds, or communities, donate all their assets and contribute all their income to the organization and follow the rigid code of ethics established by Veillard, who founded the cult in 1980. They home-school their children to eliminate outside influences and preach in the community to convert new members."

"Doomsday?"

"Essentially a name given to a cult which believes in a coming apocalypse that only a chosen few will survive," she explained. "Veillard convinced his followers that the end of the world was imminent due to environmental catastrophe and that they alone would make the transition to another life. He told them that death was an illusion, a journey they had to take through which they would be reborn on another plane; he told them that they alone were noble travelers who had been chosen to return to their spiritual home."

There was no mention of this on their website, I recalled.

Michaela smiled again. "Sounds bonkers, I know. But it's a powerful message. The Damascans still believe this even though Veillard is dead."

"I read about some other deaths. Wasn't Veillard tried for murder at some stage?"

She nodded. "It seems that Veillard persuaded a number of the members that their mission on earth was at an end and that it was time for them to make their death voyage. They had done their duty and their reward awaited them on the other side."

"When was this?"

She looked at the wall to think. "1993?"

I did some quick calculations in my head. "That would have been a year or so after his daughter was born?"

"Possibly. Yes, that sounds about right. Sixteen members of the Damascans were found dead in a swimming pool at a remote farmhouse about an hour outside Toulouse. It belonged to a man called François Dumain. It appeared to be a murder-suicide pact. Some of them had also been drugged; they had taken Valium."

My hand jerked suddenly and I knocked my cup over. Luckily it was empty.

Michaela gave me an odd look. "Valium was Veillard's drug of choice. Many people came out of the Damascans still addicted. It was one of his ways of controlling people."

I leaned over to pick up my cup. "How old were you when this happened?"

"I must have been about seven. But I have no memory of it. My parents kept it from me, obviously. There were six children among the dead. Shortly afterwards, Veillard was arrested, charged, and put on trial. It was a complete media circus. Every day his followers turned up to support him. They packed the courtroom, my parents included. I've seen photographs of them in old newspaper articles."

"And he was acquitted?"

"Yes. Veillard claimed he was being persecuted for his religious beliefs and that the prosecutors had failed to establish a link between him and the deaths. The Judge seemed satisfied that two council members had killed the others and then killed themselves, but wasn't convinced that Veillard himself was responsible."

"So he got off?"

"He did. He even inherited the farmhouse where the bodies were found. Can you believe that? Dumain left a will leaving everything he had to the Damascans."

"Jesus," I said.

"Two years later, the French National Assembly set up a Parliamentary Commission on Cults in France to deal with the problem of dangerous cults, and suddenly the environment wasn't so friendly for people like Veillard and his followers any more. Shortly afterwards, Veillard left France, taking all of his followers with him. He decided to move his organization to what he felt was a more liberal society."

"Norway."

"Yes, Norway. The Norwegian Constitution was amended in 1964 to allow freedom of religion; religions operate freely there. Norwegians keep to themselves and I suppose that means they don't interfere. There doesn't appear to be the same fear of cults as there is in France." Michaela gave me a wry smile. "Also, the sea must have fitted in very neatly with Veillard's plan."

"What do you mean?"

"He believed that the route to the next life was by drowning. You had to die by drowning to get to your reward. Hence the swimming pool deaths."

"Marguerite died by drowning," I said quietly.

Michaela raised her eyebrows.

"And she had clonazepam in her system when she died," I added. "It's not Valium but it is another benzodiazepine."

At that she whistled softly. "That's some coincidence."

"Isn't it," I agreed.

"How did she drown? Was it an accident?"

"The guards think it was suicide."

"Did she go back to the Damascans? After Veillard died, maybe?" Michaela asked.

"Not that I'm aware of." I paused. "What happened to your own family?"

"We moved to Norway with the cult; my parents would have followed Veillard to the end of the earth if he'd asked them to. They're still there, from what I can tell. I haven't seen them since I left the cult. They've never forgiven me for deserting the 'family.'"

"I'm sorry."

She smiled sadly. "It's okay. We all have freedom of choice."

"You said you knew Adeline – I mean Abra?"

"Yes. I was older than her, but all of us kids were thrown together for much of the time while the adults worked. We were home-schooled. Everyone knew Abra, she was the 'Child of Destiny.' She was being groomed to take over from Veillard from the moment she was born."

I whistled. "Some responsibility."

Michaela nodded. "True. And she was a shy little thing too. It wasn't something she'd have sought out, I suspect, if she hadn't been shoved into the limelight."

"What did she know about her mother?"

"Her mother was talked about in hushed tones. Veillard saw himself as a reincarnation of Jesus Christ and Abra's mother a female Judas who had betrayed him. It must have been hard for Abra."

"Marguerite betrayed Veillard by leaving the cult?"

"Yes, but it was also said that she had been promiscuous with other men. The Damascans preach monogamy. Anything outside of that is seen as the work of the Devil. For the followers, at any rate."

"I read some pretty awful stories about the sexualization of children on the exit websites."

Michaela's expression darkened. "I've heard those stories too, although I never experienced it directly. Outwardly, strict monogamy was preached for adults, other than for the Teacher himself. But it was said that Abra's mother had the Devil in her, that she was motivated by sex, and that she chose the pleasures of the body over her child – and that was why she left the cult and her baby."

"Do you think she did have affairs?"

"I think it would have been very difficult for Marguerite to betray Veillard like that. The Damascans were a completely pa-triarchal organization. Women were utterly powerless within it. It seems to me, if Marguerite was unfaithful to Veillard then she was taken advantage of by one of his lieutenants."

"But her daughter was led to believe that her mother was some kind of Jezebel?"

"We all were. Marguerite was held up as a figure of hate, a symbol of all that was evil about the outside world."

"God."

My head was buzzing; I needed a break. I offered Michaela another drink and she accepted.

When I came back down with the tray, I asked, "And what about you? Why did you leave? Or how?"

"An impulse really. I was sixteen, beginning to rebel, and one day I just took an opportunity that didn't come up very often and did a runner."

I couldn't help but laugh. *Doing a runner* didn't seem to fit the image.

She responded with a grin. "We were all down in the local village one day handing out leaflets when I got talking to a truck driver heading to the ferry with a load of fish. I hitched a lift with him; I think he felt sorry for me hanging out with a bunch of religious nutters. And I made my way to Scotland. Got myself a job in a café and eventually managed to track down a phone number for my grandparents. As soon as they heard my voice, they dropped everything and came over and got me. They hadn't seen me since I was two."

"And you never went back?"

"Never. I might have, but the grandparents wouldn't let me. They were so grateful to see me, they weren't going to let go of me too easily. I think they thought if they did, they'd never see me again."

"God, that's some story."

"It's only since then that I've realized what a lucky escape I had. I wasn't aware at all during my childhood or teenage years of the Doomsday element of the Damascans. The adults keep that from the kids. All I was doing when I ran away was rebelling against the strict regime I was living under, just like any ordinary teenager. I had no idea there was anything unusual about the way I was living; it was all I had known. It was only when people started contacting me after I left, people who had also left, that I came to see what an evil organization it was, what an evil man Veillard was. So I set up the Survivors' group and the website."

"And Veillard himself only died last year?"

"Yes. But from what I can tell, the group hasn't changed very much. It's an international organization now; Veillard was nothing if not a self-promoter and businessman. His estate must have been enormous when he died."

I hadn't thought about that — the vast wealth that a cult like that could accumulate.

"His daughter has taken over," Michaela said, "but I can't imagine it's too easy for her. Her father's lieutenants are probably running the show in the background. All those men were misogynistic bastards, just like her father. She'll definitely be looking over her shoulder."

"I was hoping to be able to get in touch with her. Do you have any contacts still in the cult?"

"People only contact me after they leave, I'm afraid. Most of them need some kind of help. They're pretty fragile to begin with."

"Actually while we're on that subject, I hope you don't mind my asking, but . . ."

Michaela grinned. "How come I'm so sane having spent sixteen years in a religious cult? I credit my grandparents with my recovery. It makes a hell of a difference to have a strong support mechanism waiting for you when you come out."

"I've been told that. Sadly, Marguerite wouldn't have had that kind of support. Her family were all dead."

"Apart from her daughter," Michaela pointed out.

"Apart from her daughter."

Chapter 22

ON THE DRIVE back up to Glendara I couldn't get Marguerite's daughter out of my head. She had been brought up to think that her mother had left her when she was a baby, that the woman had chosen her vices over her own child. How Adeline must have despised her. But yet she had traveled to Ireland to attend her mother's funeral. I wondered if it would have been possible for her to do that if her father had still been alive.

Adeline must barely have remembered her mother, if at all. And in Inishowen where Marguerite had lived, her memory was fading fast, barely two weeks after her death. No one should be forgotten so quickly. Living on through our descendants, leaving our genetic imprint on the generations to come, is something that we value. But we should be allowed a genetic *and* an emotional connection. Marguerite had lost out on the emotional connection with her daughter through no fault of her own.

Her daughter had suffered that same loss, and her loss was continuing. I thought about all of those returned, unopened letters. Who had returned them, I wondered. Was it Adeline herself, or was it someone else? If the latter, Adeline may never have known that her mother was trying to contact her, never have known that her mother had been thinking about her right up until the day that she died. And if the guards had given Adeline that last letter Molloy had mentioned, then all she would have seen was a goodbye.

Suddenly, I knew with absolute clarity that it was up to me to try and fix that. If I had drafted Marguerite's will on the spot as she had wanted, then Adeline would have known that her mother loved her. But I hadn't, and no matter how much I tortured myself with professional guilt, I couldn't change that now. But what I could do was tell her. And more importantly, I could ensure she received her mother's letters. What was to stop me from delivering them to her myself?

I arrived back at the office at twenty past two and saw from the appointments diary that I had a meeting with the two developers at half past two to sign the contract for the land in Malin Head. So I had ten minutes. I switched on my computer.

Firstly, I checked the location of the Damascans' headquarters. It was about eighty kilometers inland just north of the city of Bergen. A search showed that although there was an airport in Bergen, it was difficult to get a direct flight. It looked as if I might have to fly to Oslo. I had just opened the Aer Lingus website to check flights when Leah buzzed. I had run out of time.

"Your half two appointment is here."

"Okay. Send them up."

I was on my guard the second Dolan and Gallagher walked into the room. Something about their expressions made me uneasy.

There was a curt nod from Dolan, but as usual, it was Gallagher who spoke. "Afternoon, Miss O'Keeffe."

"Afternoon, gentlemen. Have a seat." I directed them to the two chairs on the other side of the desk. "I've gone through the contracts and the title documents and it all seems fine. I'll just take you through the special conditions."

I handed them a copy and directed them to the appropriate section. "You'll see I've put in the special condition in relation to the planning permission that you wanted. The purchase of the land is subject to you obtaining planning permission for a hotel on the site within six months. That's what you instructed, isn't it?"

The two men nodded.

"That seems very fast for a development of this kind. Are you sure you will get it within that time?"

Gallagher answered. "We are."

I didn't mention the piece I had read in the newspaper about the re-zoning. The planning application was none of my concern; I was happy to leave that to their architect.

Instead, I went through the title documents and maps and the remaining terms and conditions. Gallagher told me that copy maps had already been sent out and checked by their architect.

"So what happens next?" he said.

"Well, once you sign the contract now and pay your deposit, I'll return the contracts to the seller's solicitor for the seller to sign. Once he signs we have a binding contract."

Gallagher frowned. "You mean until he signs, he doesn't have to sell us the land?"

"Correct. But you're still waiting for your planning permission. He has plenty of time."

Gallagher pulled himself up to his full height in the seat. "We will have our planning permission very soon, Miss O'Keeffe. Do not rely on that to delay things."

"Okay," I said slowly. His voice had acquired an edge I didn't like.

"If a situation arises where there is valuable planning permission attaching to this land and we have no contract in place," he went on, "we will hold you entirely responsible."

"Mr. Gallagher, the law says that a contract for sale is only binding on the seller once he signs it. When he signs is entirely up to him. I can put pressure on his solicitor, but ultimately it is something over which I have absolutely no control."

Gallagher glared at me. "That's not good enough. We instructed you to act for us in this transaction. We did not expect it to take this long."

I struggled to keep my temper in check. "The contract was drafted by the seller's solicitor, not by me. That is standard practice. As soon as I received it, I read the title. You are now signing and it will go back to the seller for him to sign. Your conveyance is proceeding at a perfectly normal pace. If anything, it is proceeding rather rapidly."

"The procedure does not concern us. That is your job, Miss O'Keeffe. We expect you to do it."

Gallagher pulled the two copies of the contract over to his side of the desk, scrawled his signature on both, watched Dolan do the same, and shoved them back towards me. I witnessed both and immediately the two men got up to leave.

"We'll be in touch," Gallagher said.

I felt slightly shaken after the two men left the office. When I heard the front door shut and was sure they had left the building, I went downstairs.

"Delightful, aren't they?" Leah said after I told her what had happened. "That's what I had to put up with last week when they were in America waiting for the contracts to arrive."

"I'm sorry about that. I hadn't realized they were so bad."

"Unpleasant men."

"I think they might actually have been threatening me."

"They were the same with me."

I handed her the file. "If I have one more session with them like that, I'll tell them to go elsewhere, big deal or not. In the meantime, I suppose you'd better get the contracts back."

A soupy fog enveloped the town as I drove through the square and out onto the Malin road that evening. My head was splitting and I was tired and worried. My lousy encounter with Dolan and Gallagher had turned out to be the high point of the afternoon and it was all downhill after that. I had to concede that some of it was my own fault; I hadn't been giving as much attention to the practice lately as I should have been.

Suddenly the prospect of going home to an empty house wasn't as appealing as it had been the night before. It crossed my mind that it would be good to have someone to talk to – not about work, I was always limited in what I could discuss about work – just someone to turn to after a lousy day. The person I really wanted to see was Molloy. That door had closed, I had to accept that. But I missed him. Apart from the pang I felt when I allowed him into my thoughts, I was beginning to realize how much I had come to value his opinion, and how much a part of my life he had become.

I found myself driving through Malin past my house and out towards Malin Head in the direction of Simon's cottage. There was no fog here. The sun was beginning to set and the sea was that wonderful purple and orange color I loved. The tide was on its way out and a long golden sandbar in the center of the bay was visible from the road. It always amazes me how a sandbar can appear within fifteen minutes and disappear just as quickly. I felt my spirits lift. Simon was right. It was the perfect place for an artist to live.

I drove past the entrance to Lagg, turned left up the hill past Marguerite's old cottage, and pulled in at Simon's house. There was no car outside, but I remembered what he had said about avoiding Marguerite by parking at the back. I rang the doorbell at the front, but there was no answer. He must be working, I thought. If he was in his studio at the back, he probably couldn't hear the front door. I went around to the back of the house. Sure enough, his car was there.

After a brief hesitation I knocked on the door of his studio and was rewarded with the sound of barking followed by scratching at the inside of the door.

Suddenly the door was pulled open with some force and standing there with an angry scowl on his face, his hair matted with clay and a Great Dane leaning against his thigh was Simon. He didn't speak, just glared at me as if he didn't even recognize me.

"Hello," I said. "I just thought I'd . . ."

Before I could finish my sentence, he slammed the door in my face. Then I heard a key turn in the lock. Shaken, I stood on the doorstep while I pulled myself together, and after a few seconds, I left.

When I got back into the car, I dialed the number of the veterinary clinic. Maeve answered the phone above another din of barking dog.

"You on call tonight?" I asked.

"No, why?"

"Fancy a drink later?"

"Absolutely."

★ ★ ★

Back at my cottage, I took a paracetemol, made some tea, and opened my laptop. I tried my best to ignore the sculpture sitting on the dresser. What I really wanted to do was to dump it in the bin.

After a search, I discovered that yes, the closest city to the cult's headquarters was the port city of Bergen, known as the "Capital of the Fjords." But neither Aer Lingus nor Ryanair flew there at this time of year; Wednesday was the first of October. It looked as if I'd have to fly to Oslo and drive, or take a train up. On the plus side, the flight to Oslo was only an hour and a half so I would be able to go for the weekend. Before I could change my mind, I booked myself on to a flight to Oslo for Thursday night and a return flight for the Saturday. Leah would just have to postpone my Friday appointments until Monday. Had Marguerite made the same journey, I wondered.

An hour later, I was sitting with Maeve in a pub on the way out of Glendara that we rarely visited, being grilled mercilessly about the weekend. There was a band playing in the Oak so we had decided to give it a wide berth.

"Hey, this isn't bad. We should come in here more often." Maeve curled her feet up underneath her as she settled herself on the faded velvet bench. "It's nice to get a seat."

I laughed. "We're getting old."

"Back to your weekend. I need more information. I'm married – I have to get my excitement from somewhere," she persisted.

"He's very nice."

"Nice?"

"Very charming, engaging, witty. Good company. That do you?"

"Not really."

"I didn't sleep with him, if that's what you're wondering."

"Why, for God's sake?"

"Saving myself," I said piously as Maeve spluttered out her drink.

"I had David in with me on Friday," she said as she wiped her jeans with a napkin.

"I know. I saw him coming out of the clinic. I had another strange conversation with him. What do you think of him?"

"Quiet. I never really get a whole lot out of him. Maybe he's a bit overshadowed by his father."

"Maybe. Anyway, I don't think that's going to go anywhere if tonight's experience is anything to go by."

I related my earlier altercation with Simon, but Maeve didn't attach too much weight to it; she put it down to artistic temperament.

Suddenly, she gave me a nudge and nodded in the direction of the bar. "Jesus, look at Aidan Doherty. Talk about worse for wear."

I looked up. A group of men in suits were standing at the bar. I hadn't noticed them earlier, they must have just come in. They looked like the fall-out from a political drinking session – a gaggle of party cronies all slapping each other on the back and making asses of themselves. The drunkest of the lot was Aidan Doherty. He was unshaven, his tie was askew, and he was leaning on the bar for support; the personification of the clichéd Irish drunk. But I saw his face when he thought no one was looking, when one of his colleagues moved to one side, and he looked utterly desolate.

"Looks a bit pathetic, doesn't he?" Maeve said.

We watched silently as he stumbled his way to the toilets, touching the wall for balance. It felt voyeuristic to be watching him in such a state.

Maeve shuddered, already half out of her seat. "Same again?"

"Sure. Thanks."

While Maeve made her way up to the bar, I grabbed my opportunity and headed down the back of the pub towards the toilets. I couldn't have choreographed it better. Aidan was just coming out the door of the gents as I approached. I put myself directly in his path and greeted him with a big, friendly smile.

"Hello, Aidan. How are you?"

He looked at me with glazed red eyes and no hint of recognition.

"It's Ben. Benedicta O'Keeffe."

Still nothing. He reached out his hand to steady himself against the wall. He looked confused.

"The solicitor," I prompted.

This time it registered. Aidan opened his eyes wide with the slow, exaggerated movement of the very drunk.

I checked to make sure there was no one within earshot. "Did you get around to going to the guards about what we were talking about?"

"It's all fine," he slurred. "Everything's fine."

"What do you mean?" I asked.

"I've taken care of everything. I always take care of things." He looked down at his shoes.

"How have you taken care of things?"

There was no response, he just kept staring at the ground.

"Aidan?"

Suddenly, he leaned forward as if mesmerised by the pattern on the carpet. Afraid he would fall, I pushed his shoulder back against the wall, and he seemed to regain his balance.

I tried again, my tone lower. "Who was blackmailing you, Aidan? Was it about Marguerite?"

He looked up at the mention of her name. His eyes, completely bloodshot, began to water. *Oh, God,* I thought, *he's going to cry. Please don't let him cry.* I realized I needed to pull back. I looked around for help to get him back up to the bar.

When I turned, his eyes were closed as if in pain.

"How can love destroy your life? Just like that. Before I met her . . ." His voice broke. "It's my fault she's gone. It's all my fault."

A voice behind me made me jump. "Well, Aidey boy? Havin' a wee moment?" It was one of the men who had been with him up at the bar. The man nodded at me. "Sorry about this. I think this man needs to go home."

He linked Aidan arm-in-arm and took him back into the main part of the pub while I went back to my seat. I watched with Maeve as Aidan meekly allowed himself to be led out to a taxi.

"They're coming from Iggy McDaid's corp-house, apparently," Maeve said, pushing a fresh drink towards me. "After some big Council meeting. I must get there myself in the morning. To the corp-house, not the Council."

"Did Aidan know Iggy McDaid?" I asked. "Or is it just the political show of going to every wake and funeral?"

"Oh, they knew each other surely. Iggy used to be a black-smith — one of his many jobs. Didn't you know that?"

I shook my head. "No. I knew Aidan was."

"Aye, they worked together. At least, Aidan worked. Iggy was usually drunk. Aidan got him out of more than a few scrapes. Offered him a job when no one else would touch him, took him to dry out more times than you could count. Iggy owed him a lot."

Chapter 23

MY PHONE VIBRATED at the same time as my alarm clock the next morning. It was Simon apologizing for the night before. By text. I didn't reply. I didn't need the hassle this morning. Instead, I opened the curtains to let Guinness in through the window and climbed back into bed convincing myself that I could afford five more minutes. But the cat had different ideas; he padded out of the room and sat where I could see him at the top of the stairs, staring back at me reproachfully.

"Okay, okay, I'm coming," I said as I pulled on a pair of tracksuit bottoms and a fleece and headed downstairs to serve the cat his breakfast, before dragging myself towards the shower.

The heavy fog from the night before had cleared and the morning was bright and crisp when I pulled into a parking space behind the County Council office. I was taking the keys out of the ignition when a knock on the driver's window made me jump. It was Aidan Doherty.

I wound down the window. He looked awful – worse, if that were possible, than the night before. His eyes were pink and his skin had a waxy sheen.

"Can I have a quick word?" he said.

He smelled even worse than he looked. Though he had clearly showered, the combination of toothpaste and stale alcohol through the open window was hard to ignore. But I did my best.

"Of course. Do you want to sit in?"

"No, thanks. It won't take long. I just wanted to apologize for last night."

Two apologies from two different men, and both about their behavior last night, I thought.

"It's okay. There's no need. I've forgotten about it."

He gave me a watery smile. "So have I, unfortunately. Can't hold my drink, I'm afraid. Made a bit of a fool of myself. What was I talking about?"

I gave him a wry smile. "You told me about love destroying your life."

Aidan groaned. "Did we talk about . . . ?"

"I mentioned Marguerite," I conceded.

"You knew her?"

"Yes."

He looked at his watch. "Maybe I will sit in for a bit. I have a meeting in ten minutes." He walked over to the passenger side of the car, opened the door, and sat down.

"So you know," he said flatly.

"About you and Marguerite? Yes."

He shook his head. "I'm sorry. I know you're acting for Hugh. That's where my priority should be. I shouldn't have been talking to you. I was just feeling sorry for myself."

"No, it's fine. It was my fault, to be honest. I started it – but you appeared upset."

"I was. I am. Look, I know solicitor–client confidentiality shouldn't really extend to the pub, but would you mind keeping anything I said to yourself? It's not something I want gossiped about. I have to take care of my family."

"Of course." I paused. "Can I ask you something, too? In confidence, too, of course."

He seemed to relax a little and he nodded.

"You said last night that it was your fault Marguerite was gone. What did you mean?"

He sighed. "I shouldn't have had an affair with her. That was wrong. I realized that and ended the relationship. But I'm afraid I hurt her very badly."

"When did you end it?"

"About a month ago, maybe six weeks?" He looked down, the picture of misery. "What's so awful is that she asked me for help the night she died. She rang me, upset."

"What was she upset about?"

"She wouldn't tell me over the phone," he said sadly. "She wanted me to come and see her, but for once, I decided to do the right thing. I told her I couldn't see her and I locked myself in my study with a bottle of whiskey."

"I can relate to that one," I told him.

"If I hadn't, maybe she wouldn't have taken her own life."

"You don't know that. We don't know what happened."

"It's the truth. She needed me and I let her down."

"You can't possibly think like that," I said gently. "It'll destroy you."

He looked up at me; his eyes were bloodshot. "Don't waste your sympathy on me. If you knew some of the things I've done . . ."

"I'm sure that's not true," I protested. But if I was honest, I didn't know.

With an effort he seemed to pull himself together. "I'm sorry, Ben. Ignore me, I'm talking nonsense." He gave me a watery smile. "Put it down to the hangover. I just wanted you to know that I'm determined to make my marriage work. Keep my family together. Or else it's all been for nothing. I just hope Clodagh knows that. And Hugh."

He opened the car door and without saying goodbye, he climbed out. I watched him walk off in the direction of the church, still carrying his terrible, invisible weight.

I locked the car. Why had Marguerite wanted to talk to Aidan on the night she died, I wondered. Was it to tell him about the pregnancy? And what or who was she afraid of? Jealousy was a hell of a motive for murder.

Before going to the office, I dropped briefly in to Iggy Mc-Daid's wake. Iggy had lived with his mother in the same terraced house down a narrow laneway off the Derry road all his life. The house was quiet when I called in; Iggy's mother and his three nephews in the room with the coffin and a couple of neighbors making tea and sandwiches in the kitchen. Old Mrs. McDaid sat by the coffin, clutching a set of rosary beads, looking utterly shocked and bereft. I was reminded that you are always a child to your parents, even in your fifties. I exchanged a few words with her, offered my condolences, and left to call in to the office and collect some files before driving to Letterkenny.

And to check whether Brendan Quinn had returned my call. Which he hadn't.

Letterkenny courthouse is a fine old Georgian building used for the District Court, Circuit Court, and the High Court when it comes on circuit twice a year. This morning, both the District and Circuit courts were sitting, and the foyer was teeming with solicitors and barristers, insurance company representatives, and punters. I had no cases listed for hearing this

morning, but I had arranged to meet a solicitor for an insurance company to agree figures in two personal injury cases,
and I needed to see the State Prosecutor in a burglary case
to exchange papers, so I made my way downstairs to the bar
room at the back of the building to seek them out. The room
was deserted so I sat down to wait, taking advantage of the
extra few minutes to call Brendan Quinn again. His secretary
put me straight though.

I dispensed with any pleasantries. "Brendan, you never called
me back. Can you meet me today or not?"

"Yes." He sounded cornered.

"Two o'clock in An Grianán?"

"I'll be there."

At a quarter past two I walked into the café of the theatre
building in Letterkenny. Quinn was waiting for me at a table
by the window, an untouched black coffee going cold in front
of him.

He looked up. "You're not going to let this drop, are you?"

Quinn looked almost as miserable as Aidan Doherty had
earlier. I was beginning to revise my opinion about Marguerite's death passing unnoticed.

"I can't, Brendan. It wasn't an accident. Either she killed
herself or someone else killed her and made it look like suicide.
Her clothes and shoes were found on the shore opposite the Isle
of Doagh – that stony section just at the end of Lagg? Do you
know where I'm talking about?"

He shook his head. "I know Lagg but not well. I have no
reason to be up that part of the peninsula."

I looked him straight in the eye. "That's odd because your
car was seen there the night she died. Down at the beach."

He paled. "What?"

"You heard me."

"Seen by whom?"

"I'm not going to tell you that. But yours is a pretty unmistakable car, wouldn't you agree?"

"I swear, I never visited Marguerite's house!" he said vehemently. "We only ever met in Letterkenny or Buncrana. And I was still away on holidays the night she died. I told you that!"

I wondered if there was any way of confirming that. In the meantime, I changed direction. "The first time I spoke to you about this, you said it was unlikely Marguerite would have committed suicide."

"Yes, but . . . I didn't think that someone might have killed her." He seemed appalled.

"So, you were thinking accident?"

"Yes, I was. But I didn't know the details at that stage. I didn't even know she was dead until you told me."

"And now?"

He ran a hand through his hair. "As I told you, I hadn't seen her for over a month when she died, but I wouldn't have considered her at risk at that stage. As a matter of fact, from the time I started treating her, I never considered her a suicide risk. Her concern was always for her daughter. She was desperate to re-establish contact with her. I can't see how she would have given up on that."

I could feel my temper rise. "You do know that if you had told the guards that, they may not have closed the investigation? They got some other idiot of a psychiatrist who didn't know her from Adam to say that she was a suicide risk because of her cult history."

Quinn had the grace to look uncomfortable.

"You could still talk to them. Tell them what you know," I said.

"You know I can't do that. They'll investigate my connection with her. And remember, I hadn't seen her for six weeks before she died. I can't be sure she wasn't a suicide risk after that."

"Okay," I said, unable to conceal my disgust. "If you won't go to the guards, I want you to help me."

"How?" He looked at me warily.

"The guards have closed their investigation."

"So you've said."

"I think they're wrong. I think it's possible Marguerite was murdered. If she was, I'm going to find out who did it. And if she wasn't murdered and she took her own life after all, I'm going to find that out for sure. I feel that I owe it to her," I added pointedly.

Quinn sat back. "How on earth do you think you're going to do that?"

"By finding out everything I can. How she lived. Who she was close to. Who would have wanted to hurt her. You can help by telling me everything you know about her. You must have found out a lot during your counseling sessions."

"I can't do that, Ben. You know I'm bound by patient confidentiality."

"You didn't seem to be so concerned about the rules when you wanted her in your bed."

He winced. I knew it was a low blow but I didn't care. I took another pot shot. "And how will you feel if it turns out that she did commit suicide? Won't you feel some degree of responsibility for that?"

Quinn put his head in his hands. Neither of us spoke.

Eventually, he said, his voice weary, "Very well. What do you want to know?"

"Thanks, Brendan. I know this isn't easy for you."

"Don't." He glared at me.

"Okay. Tell me when she came to see you first of all, and why."

Quinn took a deep breath. "She came to me exactly a year ago. She was referred to me by her GP in Glendara. It was shortly after Alain Veillard died. His death was in the media quite a bit at the time, I don't know if you remember. Having to deal with that threw up quite a few issues for Marguerite, issues she had buried for a long time."

"Like what?"

"Each person's experience after a cult involvement is different. Some people seem to walk away relatively unscathed while others are tremendously damaged. In Marguerite's case a number of factors counted against her recovery in the immediate aftermath of her involvement with the Damascans."

"Family being one of them?" I prompted. "Or lack of family. She told me her parents were dead."

"Yes. She joined the cult after her parents had been killed in a car crash and she was living with her grandmother. By the time she left, her grandmother had also died. In fact, Marguerite inherited quite a bit of money from her grandmother. She gave it all to Veillard. So she had neither family nor security when she came out."

"And that has an effect?" I waited for Quinn to confirm what Michaela had said.

He nodded. "The availability of a network of friends and family as support has a huge bearing on a person's reintegration after a cult involvement. Marguerite had no one. Also, her immersion in the cult was absolute. She was in a relationship with Veillard himself so she was part of the inner circle, and she had a child with him when she was still very young. She was completely controlled by him."

"But she managed to leave. That must have taken some strength."

"Yes, but without her baby. She told me that she tried to leave with her baby, was found, and brought back. Not surprisingly, this angered Veillard, and she was ultimately rejected by the group and removed from it and her daughter. That would have been profoundly traumatic."

"I can imagine."

"She felt considerable guilt and shame at having to leave her daughter behind. She grieved for the loss of her daughter but also for the loss of the group even though she tried to leave them. And she never dealt with this grief. She was afraid to. She was afraid of Veillard and she remained that way until he died."

"That's a long time to suppress your feelings."

Quinn nodded. "Emotional suppression would have been a way of living she was used to in the Damascans. It was her position of default. After she left the cult, she moved frequently, never became close to anybody, and eventually ended up in Inishowen – possibly because of its proximity to where her daughter is now. Norway, I think, isn't it?"

I nodded. "So she pretty much lived a life of emotional isolation until last year when she heard that Veillard had died, when she came to you?"

"Yes. Cult members are also generally encouraged to shun medical and mental health professionals, but when Veillard died, she felt that she could finally open up, talk about what had happened to her."

"Which was a good thing?"

"In the long run yes, it would have been. But in the short term, it meant that all of her suppressed memories were returning and she was having to deal with them. She started to have nightmares and flashbacks. She also started to engage with people."

"A good thing too?"

"Yes and no. One of the most common difficulties people experience on leaving a cult is issues with intimacy – difficulty trusting people but also inappropriately trusting or trusting too much, resulting in unstable personal relations or promiscuity."

I raised my eyebrows.

"Yes, yes, I know. Do you not think I've been over and over this in my head since she died?"

"Sorry. Go on."

"Marguerite was taking down the walls she had built around herself and maintained for over twenty years. But it wasn't easy. It was like learning to walk again."

"Are you saying she had relationships with other men apart from you?"

"I can't be sure about her sexual relationships. She didn't talk to me about that area of her life after . . ."

"After your affair."

"Yes. But she was learning to trust people again for the first time since leaving the cult. Her instincts would not have been great to begin with. I have a sense from what she told me that she'd rebuff people who were trying to be kind to her and then trust the wrong people. It was a learning process for her."

"Tell me about your affair."

Quinn lowered his voice. "There's not much to tell. It didn't last very long. It started a few months after we met, only happened a few times, ended more than six months ago. We both got over it. I carried on counseling her because she wanted me to," he said defensively.

"Until six weeks ago?"

"Yes. I don't know anything about her sexual life after me. But I do think her only relationships of any kind were with men. She had difficulty relating to women. The Damascans were a patriarchal cult; Veillard kept the women servile and unseen. Marguerite seems to have been an exception. As his chosen consort, she mixed with the men in his inner circle."

"And yet she had a baby girl."

"Yes. Her daughter. She wanted so badly to have some kind of relationship with her. She was attempting to contact her all the time I knew her – writing letters every week. I don't suppose she ever succeeded?"

"It doesn't look like it. Although the guards managed to track the daughter down and she came to the funeral. Which you'd have known if you'd bothered to come yourself."

"Yes," he said shamefacedly. "That would have meant a lot to her, her daughter being there."

"When was the last time you saw her?" I asked.

"As I said, about six weeks before she died. Around the beginning of August. I can check my diary to confirm that. She rang me out of the blue and said she wanted to stop our sessions. No warning."

"How was she when you last saw her?"

"Good. She was making progress. The initial trauma she suffered when we started the counseling only lasted a couple of months, the nightmares and flashbacks. She was over that a long time by that stage. She seemed stable, as content as I'd ever seen her, actually. But . . ."

"What?"

"A lot can change in six weeks. Remember, she was away from counseling for all that time."

"And you're sure you didn't know she was pregnant?"

"No. You said she was two months' pregnant when she died so she probably didn't know herself the last time I saw her."

"Do you think that might have changed things?"

"Possibly. Depending on the circumstances."

"And you have no idea who the father might have been?"

"No, I'm afraid I haven't." He looked at his watch. "Look, I have to go. I have an appointment at half past three."

"Are you sure you didn't prescribe anything for her? No drugs of any kind?"

"No, nothing. I told you that. Why?"

"She had clonazepam in her system when she died. The epilepsy drug."

Quinn frowned. "Marguerite didn't have epilepsy."

"Panic attacks? It's used for that too apparently."

"No, she didn't have those either. I'm sure of it. She would have filled in a questionnaire when she came to see me first. I don't know why she was taking clonazepam, but it didn't come from me." He got up to leave.

"One more thing," I said. "I spoke to someone who used to be in the Damascans, and she told me that Veillard had his followers believe that they need to die by drowning to get to the afterlife. Do you think that was something that Marguerite might have done?"

Quinn's face registered confusion. "Marguerite was afraid of the sea."

"And yet she chose to live near it?"

"It was a sort of challenge for her. To face it. To some day be able to walk on the beach, or even go for a swim."

"Some day?" Now I was confused. Molloy had said that Marguerite liked to walk on the beach.

"Yes, she was a long way away from that. She was still petrified of water the last time I saw her."

"Okay," I said, standing up. "I'll be in touch if I need anything else."

Quinn gave me one last look before he left. "I promise you, that wasn't me at the beach the night she died, Ben."

Chapter 24

As I DROVE back to Glendara, I wondered why Quinn was suddenly allowing for the possibility that Marguerite might have committed suicide. Was he covering himself? Was it possible he could have been involved in her death? I only had his word for the fact that he had returned from his holiday the Friday after she died. And without Molloy's involvement, I had no way of checking. Quinn had good reason not to want his affair with Marguerite getting out – two good reasons, in fact: his career and his marriage. And despite his insistence that he hadn't seen Marguerite for six weeks before she died and had never been to her cottage, his car *had* been seen at the beach on the night she died. I trusted Maeve's powers of observation.

But could I seriously imagine Brendan Quinn – a professional I had known and respected since I had moved to Glendara – murdering someone to protect his career and marriage? It seemed impossible. But desperate people did desperate things, and a week ago, I wouldn't have imagined him to be capable of sleeping with one of his patients. How little we truly know about each other's lives.

My mobile rang. It was Leah. "Are you finished in Letterkenny?"

"On the way back now. What's up?"

"Two things. One, I wanted to remind you about that farmers meeting tomorrow night. The chairman just rang to say that the time has changed from seven o'clock to eight."

I groaned. Every year I am asked to put together a short talk on legal issues of concern to local farmers and fishermen – issues such as land, inheritance rights, rights of way. The most difficult part of the evening is always the question and answer session afterwards; it is impossible to predict what I will be asked and I dread it.

"Okay. What's the second thing?"

"Can you see Clodagh O'Connor at ten tomorrow?"

"Really?"

"Yep. She just called in."

Jesus, I thought. *I'll have the whole pack.*

Later that evening I was sitting on the floor in front of the fire, surrounded by contracts and title documents for a sale I had taken on weeks before; one I had been putting off. The title was old, unregistered, and complicated, and required a lot more attention than I was giving it. My mind kept wandering back to Marguerite . . . which was the very reason I was falling behind in my work in the first place. I had been so distracted during the past couple of weeks that I had begun to find it almost impossible to make even the simplest of professional decisions, the kind of judgement calls a small-town solicitor has to make every day, and work was piling up as a result. I suspected that there were any number of time bombs ticking away in files in the office just waiting to go off if I didn't defuse them soon.

As far as Marguerite was concerned, I was going around in circles; the more I discovered, the less things seemed to add up. Maybe it was time I admitted to myself that I was failing in what I had set out to do and limit my task to delivering her letters to their rightful owner before I succeeded in losing them, too.

I had just managed to convince Guinness that the cushion I had left for him by the fire was far more comfortable than the map he insisted on sitting on, when a knock at the back door gave me a jolt.

Molloy stood on the doorstep, his brow furrowed with concern. "Have you a minute?"

"Sure. Come in."

Maeve always says that my house is designed for little people, of whom Molloy is not one. He stooped to get through the low back door and followed me through the hallway into the sitting room where I cleared a space for him on the couch. This included removing Guinness, who had returned to his chosen spot on the map as soon as my back was turned but who leaped on to Molloy's knee as soon as he sat down.

"Coffee?" I offered.

"Please."

I went back into the kitchen. To my annoyance, my hand shook a little as I filled the kettle. Molloy's presence unnerved me. I had an almost irresistible temptation to tell him everything that had been happening; all that I had discovered about Marguerite, Simon, the phone calls, Luke. But I knew I couldn't. Molloy had made his feelings clear on a number of issues, and I had to respect them. I had to learn not to rely on him any more.

He looked up when I returned. "So how have you been?"

There was something about the way he said it that made it sound as if it wasn't a general inquiry.

"Fine," I said, avoiding his eye by throwing some extra fuel on the fire – unnecessarily, I realized, since Molloy had already done it while I was in the kitchen. "Why?"

"We're trying to trace the silver car that ran you off the road, but it doesn't help that we don't have a numberplate, or a make."

"I'm sorry. I know I wasn't much help. If anything comes back to me, I'll let you know."

"It was a pretty strange thing to happen, don't you think?" He paused. "Seemed almost deliberate."

I looked up. "You think? I thought maybe the driver was just drunk."

"You really can't remember anything else about it?"

"Nothing other than what I've already told you. Why?"

"It's an odd coincidence, what with the face at your window the few days before. Has there been anything else?"

"Like what?"

"I don't know. You tell me."

I smiled. "You think someone's after me? An unsatisfied client? I'm not exactly a high-profile criminal lawyer. I have no dangerous clients that I know of."

"You're quite sure there's been nothing else?"

He didn't believe me, I could see it.

"Just try and be careful, would you? Don't take any risks. And talk to me if you need to."

"Of course." I stood up. "I'd better get that coffee."

His tone had changed when I walked back into the room. An attempt at levity – not Molloy's strong point. "So I hear you were away for the weekend?"

I stopped in my tracks, nearly dropping the tray with coffee pot and mugs. "How did you know that?" My voice sounded odd.

"McFadden saw you boarding the ferry at Greencastle."

"It was just for the night." *Why the hell did I feel the need to clarify that?* I thought. *What difference did it make?*

"Right." Molloy tickled the cat's chin and was rewarded with a loud purr.

For a minute neither of us said anything. I placed the tray on the coffee table, avoiding his gaze again, busying myself pouring coffee and milk.

"Nice time?"

I nodded. "Yes." Where was this coming from, I wondered. This wasn't like Molloy. He didn't do small talk. Was he trying, albeit somewhat clumsily, to see if we could be friends?

"New man, I hear?"

I shook my head. I couldn't do this. There was no way I could have this kind of relationship with Molloy, where we would discuss each other's love lives like old mates.

"The small-town information-superhighway never fails, does it?"

He smiled, a stiff kind of a smile. "You okay?"

"Why wouldn't I be?" I said, sharper than I had intended.

He didn't respond.

"Sorry," I said.

He gazed into the fire, his brow furrowed. "It's fine. You're right, it's none of my business."

Five minutes later, he had drained his mug and was on his way to the door. Before he reached it, he seemed to remember something and turned back.

"By the way, those dangerous driving charges will be struck out."

"Which ones?"

"Hugh O'Connor."

"Oh, right." I was surprised. "How come?"

He smiled. "Are you complaining?"

"'Course not. Just wondering. You seemed to be pretty gung-ho about it."

"I can't say I'm happy about it, but the farmer refused to make a statement, and we can't proceed without it. There were no other witnesses."

"Okay. I'll let him know." I paused. "Tom . . ." I said, unsure whether I should continue.

"Yes?"

"Do you mind if I ask you something? Just out of curiosity, nothing else."

Molloy looked at me cautiously. "Go on."

"Who was it who told you that Marguerite Etienne used to walk on the beach?"

"Why?"

"Because she was afraid of the sea."

"Ben, you have to drop this," Molloy said strongly. "It's not your concern."

I looked down. "I know. Forget I asked."

He sighed. "I'd have to check the file to be sure, but from what I can remember, it was your new man."

I wasn't sure whether it was hearing Molloy refer to Simon as my "new man" but suddenly I was lost. "Sorry?"

"It was Simon Howard who told us that Miss Etienne used to walk on the beach."

Chapter 25

THERE WAS A figure perched on the wall outside my cottage when I emerged the next morning, with Guinness sitting contentedly beside him. Bloody treacherous cat.

"You're running late, aren't you?" Simon jumped down on to the footpath and matched my stride as I walked towards my car.

"Yes, I am." I opened the driver's door. "I haven't time to talk. You know how it is sometimes."

He grinned. "Oh, look. I know you're bloody furious with me. And I'm sorry. I just get that way when I'm working. I can't take interruptions."

"I've managed to figure that one out for myself."

"Forgive me? I thought you might want to do something on Friday night?"

"I won't be here."

"Going somewhere exotic?"

"No. I just won't be here."

"Do you mean *you won't be here* for me or *you won't be here* in general?"

"Both."

"Oh, come on. I sent you a text. You didn't reply." Simon crossed his arms and leaned against the car.

"Correct." I sat in, closed the door and put the key in the ignition.

He whistled. "Lord. I must remember not to cross you again." Then he knocked on the window. Reluctantly, I opened it.

"Is there nothing I can do to make it up to you?" he said, a mock-mournful expression on his face.

"Actually . . ." I turned to face him.

"Go on." He smiled. "Anything. Ask me anything at all."

"Did you tell the guards that Marguerite used to walk on the beach?"

The smile disappeared. "I have no idea."

"Did you ever see her there?" I persisted.

"David used to run into her on the beach when he was walking the dog. I may have told them that."

"Thank you." I wound the window back up and started the engine.

"Hey?" He knocked on the window again. "Am I forgiven then?"

I ignored him and pulled away from the curb. I could see his reflection in the mirror, looking exasperated.

"Isn't that a rather extreme reaction to a bit of artistic temperament?" I bumped into Maeve on the street outside the office. "I thought you had a good time with him last weekend?"

"I did, but it was all moving a bit fast. I've too much going on at the moment."

Maeve sighed. "Jesus, Ben. When are you going to take a few risks?"

I changed the subject, suspecting I had taken one too many risks already. "So what's happening about this yoga class?"

"Oh, I think that might have died a death. The others reck-
oned they couldn't face listening to a Derry accent. Made out
they wouldn't find it very relaxing." Maeve chuckled.

"I suppose they might have a point."

She crossed her arms, back into interrogation mode. "You
didn't let David put you off, by any chance, did you? With
Simon?"

"Nope."

"Because I reckon you might have been a bit hard on him.
I think David might be kinder than you give him credit for."

I took my keys from my bag and turned towards the
door. "You'd find it impossible to dislike anyone who was a
dog-lover."

"It's not that. I saw him helping Marguerite's daughter clear
out her cottage after the funeral."

I spun around. "Really? I had no idea they even knew each
other."

"It doesn't mean they did. He could have just offered to help.
It reminded me of something. I saw him helping Marguerite
once too. At the book shop."

"Really?"

"Yes. She was taking a delivery of some books, and he carried them in for her. Actually I wondered if she might be ill —
she seemed a little dizzy. Anyway, David came to her rescue;
they appeared to get on well." Maeve then added, "We could
do with a bit more of that kind of neighborliness at the moment. I'm off to visit a farmer who had his barn burned down
at the weekend."

"God."

"Complete accident apparently, according to him, but he's
in a bad way. No feed for the animals, so all his neighbors are

pitching in to help. A bit of kindness can make a hell of a difference sometimes."

There was no chance for me to absorb this latest development
because as soon as I got back to the office Clodagh O'Connor
was waiting for me. She followed me upstairs without a smile
and arranged herself carefully on the seat I offered her.

It was only when I sat down opposite that I realized how
awful she looked; she had huge bags under her eyes and her
skin was red and blotchy as if she had been crying. She wasn't
wearing any make-up and she looked very different without
it – older.

It seemed trite to pretend I hadn't noticed. "Are you okay?"
I asked.

She was brusque. "I'm fine. I want to know what's happening with my son's case."

"I'm sorry, but I'm afraid I can't discuss his business with
anyone else."

"I'm his mother."

"I know, but he is over eighteen." I tried to keep my tone
conciliatory. I had left a message for Hugh on his voicemail
after talking to Molloy the night before. "I'm sure he'll be able
to tell you himself if you ask him."

"I'm asking you to tell me now," she said rudely.

"And I can't. Not without your son's consent. That's just the
way it is."

She glared at me. "I know my husband has already been to
see you. I wonder if you were more helpful to *him*!"

I gazed back at her as if I had no idea what she meant. I got
the impression that Clodagh O'Connor was not accustomed to
hearing the word *no*.

"What was he talking to you about?" she demanded.

I shook my head. "Again, Clodagh, I can't talk to you about anyone else's business."

Her tone softened a little — a change of tack. "Was it Hugh? I presume it was. That's why I thought I'd better come and see you myself. Aidan is not the most effective of people."

"Your husband seems to be very well liked," I said.

Her eyes flashed. "What is *that* supposed to mean?" She placed her bag on the floor with a gesture which said *I'm not going anywhere.* As she did so, her sleeve rode up and I was distracted for a second.

She leaned forward. "Don't believe everything Aidan says. He's weak. He's never been any good at standing on his own feet."

"You're obviously concerned about him."

She snorted. "Aidan's fine. Hugh is the one I'm worried about. Hugh's the one who has a big future ahead of him." There was that word again. *Fine.*

"So I hear."

"He's special — born to it, like his grandfather. That's why this stupid charge mustn't be allowed to stick. I can't let his future be destroyed by some Mickey Mouse driving offence."

Suddenly something snapped and I just couldn't listen to her any more, confidentiality or not. "They've been dropped."

"What?"

"The charges have been dropped. I've left a message for your son."

For a brief second I thought she was going to hit me. I'm sure she wanted to. Instead she picked up her bag, barked, "Why the hell didn't you say so to begin with?" and stormed out, slamming the door behind her.

Chapter 26

I KNEW I could have managed my meeting with Clodagh O'Connor better. I knew too that I had been deliberately provocative in my comment about Aidan being well liked. But as I walked to the Oak to grab a takeaway sandwich and coffee, I wondered what a woman like her would be capable of and how she would respond to someone she really had a problem with – someone who was having an affair with her husband, for instance? A husband who had given both her and his mistress the same bracelet. For that was what I had seen when her sleeve had ridden up.

I was greeted, as I was about to leave the pub, by a large orange figure. I felt a pang of guilt; I had been avoiding Phyllis ever since Marguerite's things had gone missing. She had entrusted them to my care and all I had managed to do was to have them stolen from me within days of getting them.

She smiled broadly, oblivious of my guilty secret. "Lunch on the run isn't good for you. Stay and have it with me."

I agreed, conscious that I didn't have much time. I stood shifting from one foot to the other while she put her glasses on to examine the sandwich fillings on offer and after some complicated discussion about the merits of olives over cucumber I followed her to a table by the window.

"So, how have you been?" Phyllis took the couch, managing to spread herself over a fair bit of it. "The last time I saw you, you were quizzing me about Marguerite. Have there been any developments?" She said quietly, "I'm dying to help."

"Actually, I would like to ask you something, if you don't mind."

She leaned in towards me. "Go on."

"It's about David Howard."

She scowled at the mention of his name. "What about him?"

"How well did he know Marguerite?"

She snorted. "I always thought he had a bit of a crush on her. He was always in the shop when she was there. Always up at the counter talking to her in that odd way of his, calling her over to the bookshelves to give him advice. I thought she gave him way too much time, frankly. Couldn't really understand why she was so nice to him. I even heard her arranging to meet him a couple of times."

"That seems odd. I had no idea they were close."

"It *was* odd. But she seemed almost anxious to please him."

"He was unhappy about his father's contact with her. I wondered if maybe he was jealous."

Phyllis frowned. "His father being Simon, that sculptor fellow?"

"Yes. Marguerite's cottage was close to where Simon lives, and David is there at weekends. I presume that's how he got to know her."

"Of course, that's right." Phyllis took her glasses off again and scratched her chin thoughtfully. "That cottage again."

I felt my phone vibrate in my pocket – it would be Leah, letting me know that my next appointment had arrived. But I decided they could wait.

Phyllis was deep in thought. "I still think it's an odd coincidence that Aidan and Clodagh both had relationships with people living in that house. I mean, I know the two were nearly twenty years apart, but still . . ." She sighed. "Poor Seamus. Clodagh was absolutely crazy about him."

"Why didn't they stay together?"

"God, it seems such a long time ago now. We were all still in school. Seamus was a bit older, nineteen; he was a handsome boy back then. He lived in that wee cottage with his mother. Lived there all his life, as it turned out. Short life that it was," she added grimly. "Anyway, Clodagh kept the relationship from her father, as she didn't think he'd approve. She kept it from everyone, as a matter of fact, as she didn't want him to find out from someone else. Seamus wasn't up to the father's standards. I think I was the only one she told, even though it went on for a good year."

"Did her father ever find out?"

Phyllis nodded. "Oh yes. One day, she decided to take her courage in her hands and tell him herself."

"And?"

"All I know is that it didn't go very well. I'm not sure exactly what happened, but she ended things with Seamus straight away and within weeks she was going out with Aidan. And she married him very soon after that."

"Really?"

"Yes. It was weird, I thought. Aidan was no less from the wrong side of the tracks than Seamus, and yet she married him. With the father's permission, it seemed. But I don't think she ever really got over Seamus. She was heartbroken when he died, years and years later. You could see it."

"And she never told you what happened with her father?"

"Never. I just assumed he was against it. We were great friends all through school, but she kind of distanced herself from me after that. I never knew why."

Leah buzzed me to put through the last call of the afternoon. "It's that woman Michaela."

Michaela got straight to the point. "I just wanted to let you know I've had contact with some people who have recently left the Damascans and I thought you might be interested in some up-to-date information?"

"Absolutely."

"It seems your client's daughter, Abra, is having some problems."

"Oh?"

"You might remember that I told you that the Damascans were an utterly patriarchal organization – that women had no power whatsoever?"

"Yes."

"Well, obviously an exception had to be made for Abra, as Veillard's only offspring. But it doesn't mean that his lieutenants were exactly pleased about it. They have been making things very difficult for her since her father died. Talking to the members, trying to turn them against her. They will get rid of her if they can. I suspect she will hold on though."

"You think?"

"She has the ultimate requirement to hold the reins of power. Veillard's blood."

"I'm going to try and see her this weekend."

There was a sharp intake of breath. "You're going to Norway?"

"Yes. I have some letters I want to deliver to her. Letters her mother wrote to her over the years."

"You'll have your work cut out for you. Be careful."

"I will. By the way, I meant to ask you when we met – Marguerite had a strange tattoo on her thigh: would that have been connected with the Damascans?"

"Did it look like a fish?"

"Yes, a crude one."

"I have one on my forearm. We all got them at our birthing ceremony. It's an old Christian symbol – Greek, I think. If you were one of Veillard's inner circle you got one on your thigh. *And on his robe and on his thigh he has a name written, King of Kings and Lord of Lords,* Revelations 19 chapter 11 verse 16," she quoted. "Revelations was a favorite of Veillard's."

"Hmm. He strikes me as a Revelations kind of a bloke all right."

She laughed. "I think he chose the fish insignia on purpose too. It fitted in with his theory about the sea."

"Good job, Miss O'Keeffe." The pink-faced chairman pumped my hand that evening. "That was all very informative."

"I'm glad," I said, hoping my relief that the damn thing was over for another year didn't show on my face.

"There's some tea and sandwiches if you're hungry?" He shepherded me towards the back of the hall where the members' wives had laid an enormous spread of cakes, sandwiches and cold meats on two long trestle tables. I was just trying to work out how I could negotiate my heaped plate of food and full cup of tea without dropping one when Liam McLaughlin appeared and grabbed the cup.

". . . and he rescues me again," I said. "You have no idea how happy I was to spot your face grinning up at me earlier."

"Ah, you should be used to this caper by now. It's a good old turn-out all the same, for a wet Wednesday." He nodded towards the edge of the stage. "You even managed to get some politicians."

Following his gaze I saw Aidan Doherty accept a cup of tea from one of the women while deep in conversation with a large man. From where I was standing, he looked even worse than the last time I'd seen him, if that were possible. He was clearly perspiring and he had lost so much weight that I wondered for the first time if he might be ill. He caught my eye and smiled weakly. As he did so, the man he was talking with turned too and dipped his head in recognition. My heart sank. It was Sean Dolan. Suddenly I realized I needed this day to end.

"I'm going to leave before I have to have another conversation about those bloody contracts," I said.

Liam gave Dolan a wave. "I know what you mean. They're not exactly pleasant to deal with, are they?"

"That's an understatement." I lowered my voice. "What's their story? Are they going around buying up cheap land? Is that what they do?"

"I have no idea." Liam shrugged. "I never had any dealings with them before this. They've been away for a long time."

"I thought you said Gallagher bought Seamus Tighe's old cottage – the one Marguerite Etienne used to live in?"

Liam shook his head. "I said he owned it. He didn't buy it, he inherited it. They were cousins, him and Seamus."

"Really?"

"Tighe's mother and Gallagher's were sisters. Seamus's mother never married. Seamus was born out of wedlock, you know." He tapped his nose. "Wasn't so acceptable back then."

I tried to absorb this. My struggle must have been obvious.

"You look wrecked," Liam said with a grin. "Go home to bed, why don't you?"

Raised voices could be heard from behind the hall as I turned the key in the car door outside. I locked the car again and went to peer around the corner of the building. Two men, one considerably taller than the other, were arguing in the moonlight. I didn't need to see the taller man to know who he was; I recognized Gallagher's voice immediately, the accent was unmistakable. But I couldn't make out what he was saying – the wind was carrying the voices in the other direction. I briefly caught sight of the other man's face, but didn't recognize him, and I moved away before one of them saw me. Luckily they were both far too engrossed in their disagreement for that to happen.

Back inside the hall, I found Liam talking to the other man. He looked up in surprise to see my return.

"Liam, can I have a quick word with you? It's work," I added apologetically to the chairman, who wandered off affably. "Can you come outside with me for a minute?" I whispered.

Liam followed me with a bemused look. On the doorstep, I stopped for a second to listen – I could still hear the voices. I motioned to Liam to stay quiet as we crept towards the corner.

"That man?" I breathed. "The one talking to Gallagher. Who is it?"

Liam had a look. He frowned. "Uh-oh. That doesn't look too good."

We returned to the doorway of the hall.

"Well?" I asked. "Who is it?"

"It's Jack McLaughlin Dancer. He's the nephew of the man selling them that land in Malin Head."

Chapter 27

THE FOLLOWING EVENING I stood in the arrivals hall at Torp airport, about ninety-five kilometers south of Oslo, waiting to complete some paperwork at a car-hire desk. We'd been delayed taking off and the flight, which had taken us over dark coniferous forests, red wooden farmhouses, and lakes like pools of mercury, had lasted about two and a half hours, all of which had given me plenty of time to think. And to make some decisions.

I was hoping that this trip would resolve matters one way or another. I hadn't wanted to acknowledge it, or face it, but I knew that my quest to find out what had happened to Marguerite was a way of seeking some kind of redemption. Redemption for how I had treated Marguerite certainly, but also for the way that I had failed my own sister.

The reason I hadn't answered Faye's calls on the night she died was jealousy, plain and simple. She had taken a man I cared for. And though I had learned to live with it, the truth was I had never forgiven myself and never would. But somehow I had convinced myself — without even acknowledging what I was doing — that if I managed to make up for failing Marguerite, it might lessen the guilt I felt about Faye. That sickening feeling of regret in the pit of my stomach that I lived with every day.

But I was failing Marguerite again. All I had done was un-
cover parts of her life that might have been better left hidden.
I knew she had had two affairs, with Quinn and Aidan Doherty. I knew that people had known about the second. I knew
that she had been pregnant when she died, probably by Aidan
Doherty, although I had no idea whether he knew about the
pregnancy. I knew Marguerite had been distressed and behaving strangely before she died, that she had been taking clonazepam, and that she was still affected by her traumatic past with
the Damascans. And I knew she had been trying to contact her
daughter, apparently without much success.

But how had she died? If not by her own hand, then who had
killed her? A married lover who wanted to protect his career
or his marriage? A jealous wife? I was no closer to finding out
the truth than I had been three weeks ago. I had uncovered co-
incidences and connections: the bracelet, the cottage, Quinn's
car. But I had no idea what any of it meant. What the hell had
made me think that I could do any better than the guards?

Leah was trying to hold things together at work, but there
was a limit to what she could do if I didn't manage to get back
to working properly soon. As the plane taxied along the run-
way, I resolved that on my return I would talk it through with
Molloy. I would push my personal feelings aside, tell him everything that I had discovered, leave the whole thing entirely in
his hands, and let it go.

As I handed my driver's licence to the very blond woman
behind the desk, I sensed someone behind me, standing a little
too close for usual queueing etiquette. I turned to look. Standing there with a wide grin on his face and a bouquet of flowers
in his hands was Simon. I nearly jumped out of my skin.

"Surprise!" he said.

"What on earth are you doing here?"

The grin stayed in place. "Not exactly the response I was looking for."

"How did you know I was here?"

"Leah told me. I managed to get on the flight after you. Nearly overtook you in the air as it turned out, since yours was delayed."

I kicked myself for not telling Leah to keep where I was to herself.

"Are you on your own?" he asked, looking around.

There didn't seem to be much point in denying it. Before I could reply, the car-hire woman coughed to get my attention. I signed the contract and took the keys she handed me.

"It's a Ford Focus, silver, parked at space number 15. Just go out of the airport and follow the signs to the right," she said, pointing to the exit.

I turned back to Simon, walked a couple of meters with him towards the door and then stopped, placing my bag on the floor and crossing my arms.

"What *are* you doing here? Are you following me?" I asked.

He laughed. "You make me sound like a bloody stalker. I thought you might like some company, that's all. I have some making up to do." He handed me the flowers. "These were supposed to be a start."

"And what am I expected to do with them?"

"It's called a romantic gesture. As was my coming here. I thought we could spend some time together."

"I'm here for work. It's not a holiday."

"What kind of work are you doing in Norway? I thought solicitors were limited to practising in their own country."

"I don't have time to discuss it." I struggled to pick up my bag without dropping the flowers.

Simon leaned in to help. "I'm coming with you."

"No, you're not."

"Why not?"

"Why would you want to?"

He grinned. "For the craic. I've never been to Norway. It's supposed to be amazing — somewhere every artist should see some time during their lives. And maybe you'll allow me to treat you a bit, to make up for Monday night." He tilted his head with a winsome expression on his face.

"There's no need. I'd rather be on my own."

"Come on. Surely you could do with the company? You can do whatever business you have to do, and we can still have some time together. You can't tell me you're going to make me get back on a plane to Belfast after I've come all this way?"

I felt cornered. I was alone in Norway and I didn't trust him not to follow me anyway if I refused to bring him along. At the moment I didn't trust him, full stop. What was his real reason for being here?

He took advantage of my confusion and picked up my bag. "So it's decided, then." He hoisted it on to his shoulder and led the way towards the exit. I followed him out into the sunshine.

My research had told me that the Children of Damascus had located their headquarters in what appeared to be an old sanatorium just north of Bergen, so I had decided to stay overnight a little way out of Oslo and do the long drive in the morning. I estimated it would take about six hours.

With his usual cat-like ability to land on his feet, Simon managed to bag himself the last room available in the hotel I had booked in Holmenkollen. Not without the usual suggestion to share, of course.

The dining room was closed by the time we arrived so dinner consisted of a cheese sandwich and a glass of very average wine in the bar. A spotlight brightened and darkened on a huge snowflake sculpture by the door as Simon went to order more drinks. I watched while he chatted to the tall blond behind the bar, laughing and joking with her as he seemed to be able to do with everyone he met. It was hard not to be seduced by Simon's easy manner. Just as I would have found his persistence flattering – if I chose to believe his reasons for being here, which I didn't. Instead I found his presence claustrophobic, as if he were trailing me without bothering to hide his presence.

He turned towards me and smiled disarmingly before strolling over to the table with two cognacs. "I've been promised that these are a cut above the wine."

"They'd need to be." I took a sip. They were.

"So," he said, "are you going to tell me why we're here?"

"You're here because you followed me."

He didn't deign to acknowledge that. "And where we are going tomorrow? Because I think I might have an idea."

"Really?"

"Marguerite's daughter lives in Norway, doesn't she?"

"How do you know that?" I took another sip.

"I heard someone saying it at the funeral."

There was a pause.

"Oh, come on. It's a bit of a bloody coincidence surely, you asking me all of these questions about Marguerite and then suddenly you feel the need to take a trip to Norway for the weekend. You're going to visit the daughter, aren't you?"

"Yes," I conceded eventually.

"Any particular reason?" He raised his eyebrows. "Are you going to start asking her questions, too?"

"I have some belongings of Marguerite that I want to give her, that's all. It's all very straightforward." I tried not to look at the small bag at my feet in which I had put Marguerite's letters. I wasn't going to let them out of my possession until I had handed them over to Adeline.

"Belongings?"

"Jewellery, that sort of thing."

"Couldn't you have posted them, whatever they are?"

"I could, but I wanted to deliver them personally. Wanted to make sure she got them."

He sat back with his arms crossed. "Isn't that over and above a solicitor's call of duty?"

The following morning we set off while it was still dark. Light came as I drove along a wide smooth road cut through the rock. On the left were dark coniferous forests as high as the eye could see and on the right, deep gorges filled with water. I discovered that in Norway, water was everywhere. It made me think of what Michaela had said about its significance to the Damascans.

Simon switched the radio on to search for an English-speaking station and found one which happened to be playing U2. It seemed this morning as if he was willing to treat the trip as "the craic" he had claimed it to be; Marguerite had not been mentioned since last night. I, on the other hand, was nervous, unsure of my ground. I had no idea what kind of reception I would get from Adeline when I found the cult headquarters, or even if I would get to speak to her at all.

Perhaps it was the U2 track, but as we drove along the edge of the Hardangerfjord, the landscape began to take on a rather Irish look, Donegal in particular. One stretch of wild rocky moor, with tiny lakes dotted along on either side, could have been cut from the mountain road between Buncrana and Glendara, the only difference being the wooden posts lining the road on either side, with reflective strips on top. It seemed that the Scandinavians were a more careful people than the Celts. Slatted wooden houses came into view high above the road, rust-colored with small white windows, some with grass roofs that were neatly clipped. Everywhere was immaculately clean.

We arrived in Bergen at lunchtime after six hours of driving – Simon doing the bulk of it. With some effort, I managed to be grateful for the help.

Bergen turned out to be a striking coastal town with wooden buildings brightly painted in shades of orange and gray. We parked the car in the square beside the town hall and made our way through the sheets of rain to the old quarter and the first restaurant we could find. I turned down the whale toast on the menu and settled for some very unNorwegian pasta while Simon had whitefish.

"So, are you all set for your good deed?" He poured me some water.

From our table by the window we watched the market outside. It was busy and seemed completely unaffected by the downpour; the locals were clearly used to it.

"Feeling a little apprehensive, to tell you the truth."

"I'm not surprised. The daughter was a bit sniffy the day of the funeral, wasn't she? Are you sure you want to do it?"

"Yes."

"You could always post the stuff from here, and we could have a wee holiday." He mimicked the Inishowen lilt.

"No. I'm here now. I'm going to try and see her."

He sighed. "I don't get it, to be honest. Why you're so bothered by it."

Suddenly I felt angry. Surely the question was: why wasn't Simon *more* bothered by it?

"Why did you really follow me?" I asked.

"I told you."

"I don't buy it."

He looked up, a forkful of fish halfway to his mouth.

I knew I was being reckless but I couldn't seem to stop myself. "The incident with Marguerite, when she appeared in your bed . . ."

"Yes?"

"Was that your only encounter of that kind?"

"What do you mean, *of that kind*?" He emphasised each syllable, all of his previous bonhomie washed away by the rain. "What are you implying?"

I had no idea what I was implying. Too late, I tried to reverse. "Well, she was very attractive. I thought maybe you might have . . ."

He put down his fork. "Fucked her? Or killed her?"

I felt as if I had been slapped. "That's not what I meant."

"Did I or did I not tell you that I didn't know her very well?" He addressed me as if he was speaking to an idiot.

"Yes."

"Well, it's the truth. And, for the avoidance of doubt, in case I haven't made myself clear on this point – I did not fuck her and I did not kill her." He looked furious. "What the hell is wrong with you? Is this some kind of screwed-up jealousy or something?"

I could feel my own temper rising to meet his. "God, the arrogance of you. Do you really not care what happened to her?"

He stood up. "Marguerite was a lonely, middle-aged woman who committed suicide. She had some bad things happen to her when she was young which affected her later in life. It's all very sad, but that's the end of it. It's over. Her suffering is over. Mine, on the other hand, seems to have just begun." He rooted in his pocket for some notes, flung them on the table, and stormed out of the door.

I mouthed an apology at the woman behind the counter, who nodded back. I got the feeling that such outbursts weren't exactly commonplace in Norway. The other diners kept their heads down, concentrating hard on their food while I stared at the remains of my pasta, red-faced.

It had been a mistake, asking Simon again about Marguerite, but his reaction confirmed my decision to cut contact with him when we got back to Inishowen. What I needed to do now was to calm things down, do what I came to do, and then go home. I gave him a few minutes then followed him outside. I found him walking down by the water looking at the boats with a surly expression on his face. I approached him with a conciliatory smile.

"Look, I'm sorry. Let's just get this over with."

He didn't reply. We walked back to the car in silence.

While Simon followed my directions without a word, I tried to lighten the mood by reading snippets from the guide book.

"They found a gold torc buried on a farm about eight kilometers from here and were able to trace it back to a monastery in Dublin. Imagine! They reckon it must have been brought back by a young Viking from an Irish raid as a present for his mother or sweetheart." I spotted a right turn. "Oh, this is it. Take this one."

Humoring people isn't my strong point, but as Simon took the turn without responding, I knew I had to fix things.

"Look, I really am sorry for asking you all those questions about Marguerite."

He kept his eyes fixed on the road. "As you said – let's just get this over with."

After the turn, the road began to incline steeply through ubiquitous spruce forest. Here and there through a gap I caught glimpses of a stark rocky peak rising above the mist. The road snaked towards it in a series of heart-stopping hairpin bends.

"Are you sure this is right?" Simon asked, initiating an exchange for the first time since we had left Bergen.

"Positive," I said. "The old sanatorium is marked on the map. It's at the top of this hill."

After about twenty minutes of dizzying bends, we were rewarded with the first sight of a fine red-brick building with large windows and two gothic-looking towers at either gable. It was surrounded by boulders which reminded me of what I had read in the guide book about farmers' children on the shores of the Geirangerfjord, being tied to boulders to prevent them from falling down the precipice while their parents worked.

After a few miles the road came to an abrupt end, and we were greeted by an iron gate blocking off a rough laneway. A hefty padlock indicated it was locked. There were no signs. Simon switched off the engine, leaned across me, and opened the passenger door.

"The car won't go any further. Out you get. Go and do your good deed."

Chapter 28

I GRABBED MY bag, climbed out of the car, and closed the door, clambering over the gate and setting off up the laneway. For one brief panicky moment it occurred to me that Simon might not be waiting for me when I returned; we had encountered very few cars on the route up so I would be marooned here in this lonely place.

The laneway snaked through dark coniferous woods. I checked for CCTV cameras but could see none. If there were any, they were well hidden. It was eerily quiet. Surely it couldn't be this easy to gain entrance to the cult's headquarters, I thought; any minute now I would be halted in my tracks by some heavy in a white robe. But eventually the ground beneath me became rougher, the laneway less obvious. It was like walking on a lumpy mattress. One minute it was soft and springy, the next hard and jolting where the roots and branches of the spruce and fallen cones had decayed underneath; in places, the ground was almost completely black. Distracted by a clump of Fly Agaric toadstools with their red and white spotted caps, I tripped over the root of a tree, fell in the mulch and dropped my bag, spilling the contents on the ground. I cursed loudly, picked myself up, and started to gather up my belongings.

Luckily, the bundle of Marguerite's letters had landed on a pile of cones and were completely untouched. This was my last opportunity to see what they contained, I realized. There could be something in one of these letters that held the key to her death. Should I really hand them over to a person who could easily just destroy them, without even taking a look?

I sat down by the tree that had tripped me up and took the most recent letter from the bundle. I slit open the envelope and extracted the notepaper; it was that tissue-like airmail paper – paper I hadn't seen in a long time.

My hands were shaking slightly as I started reading. It felt so intrusive. Marguerite had written her address and the date in her neat hand. The letter began *Chère Adeline, j'espère que tu répondras . . .*

My heart sank. The letter was in French, of course it was. I couldn't believe that hadn't occurred to me before. I skimmed through it. I could grasp the odd word, but it was no good, my French was lousy. So I folded the letter back and stuffed it into the envelope. It would be obvious that it had been opened, but I suspected Adeline would not even notice.

Frustrated, I continued my way up towards the house. After about ten minutes, I emerged on to a surprisingly manicured lawn, and the old sanatorium appeared in front of me, perched on a hill, an enormous red-brick building with Victorian eaves and balconies, straight out of an Alfred Hitchcock movie. It seemed deserted, so I crossed the lawn and approached what appeared to be the entrance. Suddenly, I felt a little spooked, as if I was being watched. I imagined I could hear chanting somewhere at the back of the building as I neared the huge front door.

I was still looking for a bell when the door opened: I had been right about my arrival being observed. Standing smiling at me was a tall, dark-skinned man dressed in loose trousers and a tunic.

He spoke softly. "Can I help you?"

"Oh, hi. I was wondering if I could see Adeline. I mean Abra . . . for a few minutes. If it's convenient," I added.

"Of course." He gestured for me to enter.

I followed the man into an entrance hall with high ceilings and corridors leading off in all directions, a smell of incense lingering in the air. The walls were completely bare apart from one large portrait photograph in a gilt frame in prime position above a grand old fireplace. It was Alain Veillard.

The chanting was louder now that we were inside. I hadn't imagined it. It was coming from above the hallway. I looked up to see a wide staircase leading to a landing on the first floor, continuing on three sides and fronted by a wooden railing. At the top of the staircase was a large double door.

The man followed my gaze. "Abra is at service at the moment. Service will be finished in fifteen minutes, if you would care to wait."

"That's fine."

"What is your name?"

"Ben O'Keeffe. Thank you."

The man showed me into a sort of parlor off the hallway. Dominating the room was another photograph of Veillard above the fireplace, this time with a lit candle in front of it. It reminded me of the Sacred Heart pictures from my convent school days. The man bowed and left me alone. I sat on a rather uncomfortable, high-backed chair, with a coffee table in front of me strewn with leaflets on the Children of Damascus; the same happy smiling faces I had seen on the website peered out at me, imploring me to consider giving up my worldly existence for a purer, more harmonious and brotherly life.

The room was cold, and five minutes passed like an age. I walked to the door and peered into the corridor, but there was no one there. The chanting had stopped. I crept out of the room and along the corridor towards the staircase. Slowly, I began to tiptoe up the stairs. I knew it was risky; as with the laneway, I expected at any moment to feel a firm hand on my shoulder. If that happened, I decided to plead my usual excuse: needing the bathroom. I thought I could pull that one off easily. It was partly true.

I reached the top of the stairs and walked quietly over to the double doors from where the chanting had come. One was slightly ajar, only seven centimeters or so. I could hear voices, though it felt as if my heart was beating loudly enough to drown out any sound.

I peered through the gap into a large hall with a high ceiling and a huge white cross at one end. A row of solemn-looking men in the same tunic and trousers as the man who had greeted me downstairs stood in front of the cross, facing towards me. All had shaved heads. Addressing the men with her back to me and similarly garbed was Adeline; I recognized her voice.

She sounded angry, displeased. She was speaking slowly in French. I managed to catch the odd word, words that are similar in English like *incompetence* and *collection*, and one or two I remembered from a prayer we used to say before French class in school. After a couple of minutes she switched to English, and her tone changed. She seemed to have composed herself; her voice was calm, measured.

"Brothers, you hold honored and trusted positions. Do not forget that. With this comes responsibility. Do not take it lightly. Your duty is to serve the Lord. Exodus 35 verse 4 says, '*This is the thing which the Lord has commanded. Take from among you an offering to the Lord; whoever is of a generous heart let him bring the Lord's offering.*' You have been chosen because of your generous hearts and your ability to bring out the generosity in others. But you must do better if you are to continue to hold on to your privileged positions. Is that understood?"

The row of bowed heads nodded; a picture of humility. She dismissed the men and they filed out of the room. I couldn't see her face from where I was standing, but I could see her hands clasped behind her back. Since I had started watching her, they had not stopped trembling. She walked over to the cross, knelt down and started to pray quietly, looking very much alone.

A noise behind me made me whip round, but there was no one there. I hurried back down the stairs as silently as I could, along the corridor and back into the room from which I had come. I returned to the chair and picked up one of the brochures.

Some minutes later, the door opened and Marguerite's daughter walked in. She looked no more pleased to see me than the last time we had met. Still, she was polite; she offered her hand and I took it. Her handshake was cold and limp.

"Miss O'Keeffe. I didn't expect to see you again. All of my business in Ireland is complete."

"I'm sorry to bother you, but I felt I owed it to your mother to come."

"I see. I have some recollection of you saying you were my mother's solicitor. Do I have that correct?"

"Yes, I was. I have some letters to give to you."

There was a barely perceptible raising of one eyebrow.

"They are letters that your mother wrote to you. Over the past year."

"Before you go any further, Miss O'Keeffe, I should make it clear that I have no interest in my mother. I'm sorry if that sounds harsh to you. I think I told you at the funeral that I did not know her."

"Yes, you did, and I know you had no contact with her for many years. But you see, she wrote you all of these letters." I retrieved the bundle from my bag and held them out to her. "Almost one a week."

Adeline made no move to take them from me so I placed them on the coffee table beside her.

"My mother left me when I was a baby. I was nine months old."

"She may not have had much choice."

She bowed her head. "We all have free will, Miss O'Keeffe."

"Sometimes it's not as simple as that. I don't think it was easy for her."

"I never heard from her again after she left. Not once."

"But she tried to get in contact with you in the last year. A lot." I pushed the letters towards her, but she didn't even glance at them.

"How well did you know my mother?"

"Not very well, but . . ." I faltered.

"My mother was not a good person, Miss O'Keeffe. It is an unfortunate thing to accept but it is something I have had to learn to live with. Luckily, I had my father."

"Did you know your father made her leave you?"

She gave me a cold smile. "Do not labor under the illusion that you can tell me anything my father has not, Miss O'Keeffe. He has told me everything. He did not consider my mother fit to take care of me. I am grateful he was here to protect me."

I saw the first real glimmer of emotion in her eyes as she said, "It is his loss I feel, not my mother's."

"Your mother loved you, too. I know she did," I said firmly. "She wanted to make a will leaving everything to you. She gave me instructions for it but she never had the chance to . . ."

Adeline smiled. "And what did she have to leave?"

"Well. Not very much . . ."

"Not very much. Can I just clarify? I am her only child, am I not?"

"Yes."

"And she did not have a spouse."

I shook my head.

"Then surely a will would be irrelevant in those circumstances. Or are the laws of Ireland different?"

"Well, no, but . . ."

"So, it was a meaningless gesture on all fronts."

"No," I insisted. "It wasn't. It shows that she was thinking about you before she died."

"Guilt at the end, after a life of sin and self-indulgence and vice."

"I think she had been thinking about you all her life. I think she even came here to see you . . ."

"She did not come here. I would have known if she had. Look, Miss O'Keeffe, I'm sorry you have wasted your time, but my mother betrayed my father and she betrayed me. She betrayed the whole family. If I hadn't had my father, I would have had nothing. Death brings regret, Miss O'Keeffe. I accept that even my mother may have had some regret at the end. She seems to have made some attempt to make amends by attempting to return to the family through her mode of death. But again it was meaningless and too late."

"You don't understand. She didn't commit suicide."

"I did not use that term and I would not use it. But the fact remains that she took her own life. It was probably the most honorable thing she ever did."

I was shocked. It must have registered on my face. What kind of poison must Marguerite's daughter have heard over the years to say something like that about her own mother? I realized that there was no point in arguing any longer. I had done what I came to do.

"I hope you read the letters. I'll show myself out."

Walking back down the hill, I was shaking with anger. Not with Adeline – I felt phenomenally sad for her. But the power that Veillard had had over Marguerite's daughter had been absolute and he had abused it. What must he have told her, for her to hate her mother so much, I wondered. The cruelty of it appalled me. I was sure that she would never read the letters. Simon had been right about one thing – I should have just posted the damn things.

By the time I made it back to the gate, I was relieved to see that the car was still there.

Simon opened the passenger door. "How'd it go? Not so good, by the look of you."

"No. Not great. I'd rather not discuss it, if you don't mind."

He reached over to put his hand on mine.

I managed a smile. "Thanks, but it's done now. Let's just forget about it."

"Happy to. No mention of Marguerite for the rest of the journey, then."

"Agreed."

As I drove us back towards Oslo, I saw that Simon's mood had changed. I was grateful for that at least, after the encounter I had just had.

We stayed the night at a pretty little hotel where we succeeded in spending a whole evening without discussing Marguerite. We talked of nothing of any consequence and our laughter was forced.

Beneath the laughter I felt bleak, as if I had finally failed Marguerite. It was time to let the guards do their work and go back to the job I was supposed to be doing. If I'd done that in the first place, I would have saved myself a lot of grief.

Chapter 29

BY THE TIME we reached Derry on our way back to Glendara, it was late on Saturday night. Simon had taken a train and taxi to the airport in Belfast on the way out and was car-less when we landed so I felt obliged to give him a lift. A distance had grown between us since I climbed back into the car after my encounter with Adeline – an unspoken acceptance that we would see little of each other once this episode was over. And I was relieved. I couldn't wait to be back in my own bed.

My phone rang on the dashboard. It was Molloy. "Can you talk?"

I told him I could; although Simon was beside me and would be able to hear every word, I wasn't sure what the alternative was.

"Where are you?" Molloy said. "I've been trying to get hold of you."

"Driving through Derry. I'll be home in half an hour. Why?"

"Good," he sounded relieved. "Look, I don't want to worry you but I called to your house earlier and the lock on your front door has been broken."

"What?"

Simon looked over at me with concern.

"Now, don't panic. Nothing seems to have been touched."

"Are you sure?"

"Pretty sure. We've had a good look around. But I wanted to catch you before you got back. We've secured the house, but I don't want you staying there alone with no proper lock on the door. Is there somewhere you can stay tonight?"

Simon overheard the last question. He mouthed the words *stay with me*. I shook my head. That was the last thing I wanted.

"What about Maeve?" Molloy asked, as if he had witnessed the exchange.

"I'll be grand," I said. "I'll make some kind of arrangement. What about . . . ?"

I could hear Molloy's half-smile as he cut across me. "Guinness is fine. I fed him. Thought about bringing him back to mine but couldn't catch him. He was a bit spooked."

"Thanks."

"You sure you'll be okay?" There was a pause. "You could come here if you like."

"To the garda station? Are you going to put me in a cell?" I joked.

"I'm at home."

My stomach did a strange little flip. I had never been to Molloy's house; it was a line of intimacy we hadn't crossed. He came to mine, but usually on some work-related errand. I realized that I wanted with every fibre of my being to go to him. But I also realized that it would be unwise.

"That's okay," I told him. "I'll be fine."

"Give me a shout in the morning then, will you? I want to talk to you about something."

"Sure."

"Look, stay with me," Simon repeated when I ended the call.

"Thanks, but I couldn't. I'll give Maeve a shout – she won't mind." I reached over to dial her number, but Simon put his hand out to stop me.

"It's late," he said, "and she has small kids, doesn't she? You can't wake them up."

"She's a vet. She's used to being woken up in the middle of the night."

"Seriously, it's no problem. You can sleep on the couch."

Simon's house was the last place I wanted to be, but he did have a point. Reluctantly I agreed. "Okay, then. Thanks."

I flung my bag on to Simon's kitchen floor and flopped on to the couch as he headed straight for the kettle.

"Coffee?"

"Tea, please. I need to sleep soon, don't you? That was a lot of traveling for one weekend." I glanced at the beanbag. "Where's Sable?"

"Locked up for the night, by the looks of things. I noticed the shed door was closed when we drove in. I presume David's in bed." He tossed tea bags into two mugs. "That sergeant seems very fond of you."

"Molloy?" I shrugged. "I've known him a long time. We work together a bit."

"He's very protective of you."

"He's protective of everyone. It's his job." I yawned. "Thanks for putting me up, by the way. I appreciate it."

"Anytime."

Simon made the teas and handed me one. Then he went to an old hot press to the left of the fireplace, rooted out some blankets and bedlinen and left them on the couch beside me.

"Right, I'm off. I'm up early, I have some work to finish off for an exhibition in Derry. Bathroom is on the left at the top of the stairs."

For the first time there was no mention of my sleeping anywhere else. I wasn't entirely sure I wasn't a little disappointed; apparently I'm as contrary as the next person.

"Thanks. I'll be gone early too. I need to get home."

"Okay. 'Night." He disappeared up the stairs.

I drank my tea in a few mouthfuls, set about putting together a makeshift bed on the couch as best I could, pulled off my jeans and curled up under the blanket in my shirt. The room was warm – there was some heat left in the fire – and I was completely exhausted. I was asleep within minutes.

By five a.m., I was wide awake. The room was cold. It was still dark, but a chink of moonlight from the window gave the room an eerie light. I pulled the blanket around me and stared at the ceiling, unable to sleep. My mind was racing. Why had someone been trying to get into my house again? Who was it and what were they after this time?

I closed my eyes and tried to go back to sleep again, but it was impossible; my neck and shoulders were sore – couch or tension, I wasn't sure. After half an hour of turning over and back and flipping my pillow, I finally gave up.

I wrapped the blanket around me and headed for the sink, filled the kettle, and put it on to boil, pacing the kitchen while I waited. My head was beginning to hurt now too. When the kettle boiled I made some tea and curled up in the armchair to drink it, but it didn't help. I needed some painkillers, to help me get back to sleep.

The bathroom door was slightly ajar. I switched on the light, walked in, and closed the door behind me as quietly as I could. There was a small cabinet above the hand basin which I opened. It was full of bottles and plastic containers with various types of medication. I picked out one or two likely suspects, read the labels and put them back again. There were no painkillers.

I splashed some cold water on my face. As I gazed at my reflection in the glass, something occurred to me. I opened the cabinet again, took out all of the medicine containers and placed them along the edge of the bath. One by one, I picked them up and examined them: cholesterol medication, antihistamines, vitamins. The last one was a small brown bottle with a white lid containing some kind of drops. I couldn't read the label; it was stained. But, when I turned the bottle over in my hand, there they were: the very words I had been looking for *contains clonazepam*. I looked to see if there was a patient's name on the bottle but there wasn't any. Whose was it? David's or Simon's?

I recognized the pins-and-needles sensation traveling up my shoulders as the beginning of panic. I needed to leave straight away. I put the rest of the medicines back into the cabinet and snuck back down the stairs, put the glass bottle into my wash-bag and pulled on my jeans and boots as fast as I could.

I had seen Simon lock the back door before he went to bed – but where the hell had he put the keys? Frantically, I searched and finally, I caught sight of his jacket hanging from a hook by the back door. I found the keys in one of the pockets. The second one I tried fitted, but still it seemed an eternity before the key finally turned in the lock, every click sounding like a gunshot.

The sun was rising and the lemon and ink-stained sky mirrored in the water as I drove back along the coast road, relieved to be out of that house. The garda station opened at eight. I would try Molloy's mobile when I got to Glendara. If he didn't answer, I would simply wait.

Malin was like a grave as I circled the green, Guinness perched on the wall outside my cottage, his eyes radioactive in the strange morning light. I parked on the footpath and checked my watch; another hour and a half before the garda station opened. I could spare a couple of minutes to feed a disgruntled cat.

The lock on the front door was smashed as if it had been hit with a sledgehammer and the guards had placed a makeshift bar across the frame to secure the house – effective, but it also meant that I couldn't get in either. I would have to go around the back. I called to the cat, but he'd turned away from me.

I put my bag on the back doorstep while I searched for my key, down on my hunkers. Suddenly, I sensed a presence behind me . . . felt someone's breath on my neck. I stiffened, stood up slowly, afraid to turn around. Before I reached my full height there was a loud crack, a flash – and a sharp pain to the back of my head. I felt my knees give way.

Chapter 30

MY OWN COUGHING woke me up. I could barely breathe; it was all I could do not to gag. Wherever I was, it was pitch black. I was groggy and the back of my head was throbbing. I tried to reach behind to see if I was bleeding, but I couldn't get my right arm back and my left was trapped beneath me. I was curled up in a foetal position with my knees almost touching my chin.

The smell of petrol was overpowering. I felt a rush of panic; I was in the boot of a car, a moving car. I could hear the engine. How long had I been unconscious? By shifting forward slightly, I managed to pull my left arm out from under me to look at my wrist. I pressed the button to light up the screen – 6.45 a.m. I had been unconscious only a matter of minutes. But who the hell was driving the car? And why had they knocked me out?

Tossed from side to side as the road beneath me twisted and turned, I was suddenly thrown back as the car took a sharp left and traveled uphill, the gradient getting steeper all the time. I checked my watch to time the journey. The uphill section continued for about five more minutes before the road levelled off and the car slowed down and came to a stop.

The engine ceased. I held my breath, heart pounding, waiting for footsteps. But after a few seconds the engine started up again and the car turned left, climbing again for some minutes before suddenly veering right and continuing to climb, more steeply this time. The road surface became rough, twisting and climbing continuously for about ten minutes.

Suddenly with sickening certainty, I knew where the car was headed. We were on the road leading to the viewing point at Knockamany Bends, the cliffs high above Lagg Beach. Cliffs with no safety rail, nothing but an old barbed-wire fence between you and infinity. A beautiful, windswept place with a violent sea hundreds of meters below.

The realization terrified me. Oh, why the hell had I decided to wait till eight o'clock to see Molloy? And why had I let my foolish pride prevent me from going to him last night?

The car slowed down, and I was pitched to the right as we turned a sharp left. I heard gravel beneath the wheels. Finally, the car came to a stop and the engine was switched off. The vehicle swayed slightly as the wind battered the lid of the boot.

I heard the driver's door open and slam shut, followed by footsteps crunching in the gravel coming towards me. I held my breath. A key turned in the lock above me and I shrank back, as slowly the boot was opened. Light blinded me for a second, but my eyes adjusted, and I saw gulls screeching and circling high above. A pale face peered down.

"Still breathing, are we?" The face came into focus.

"David? What the hell . . . ?" I struggled to prop myself up on one elbow.

"Stay where you are. I don't want you to move."

"What's going on? What are you doing?"

David Howard turned away, head in his hands. His voice was muffled. "You've ruined it all."

"What do you mean?" I tried to climb out of the car, but he spun round and pushed me roughly back into the boot. I hit my head painfully against the side.

He glared at me. "Those letters. Why did you have to give the letters to her?"

"You mean Marguerite's letters?"

"We were all right. We would have been all right. Now everything is falling apart. Everything we've worked for." His face was wet, his eyes reproachful.

"You know Adeline?"

"Abra!" he shouted. "Her name is Abra."

"Abra."

"She was groomed all her life to take over; it was her destiny, her birthright, no matter what others said. And I was beside her. We would have done it together."

"I don't understand."

"Of course, you don't understand," he said scornfully. "You have no idea what you've done. She read those letters after you left. Everything I did was to prevent her doing that, and then someone like you just gives them to her, hands them over with no care for the consequences."

"How do you know Abra?"

"Abra is everything to me. The Teacher took me in to the family when I had no one and gave me to her when we came of age." His voice broke. "She saved me."

Realization finally dawned. "You're in the Children of Damascus."

"He knew I would protect her. And until her whore of a mother decided to return, I succeeded." David's voice hardened in disgust. "The second the Teacher died, she crawled out from under her stone. She was a coward – she wouldn't face her daughter while he was alive – and then suddenly letters, letters every week."

"She wanted to see her daughter," I said. "That's all."

"She wanted to destroy her, take everything away from her. I wasn't going to let that happen."

"You were the one who kept the letters from her daughter?"

"After the Teacher died, I was the administrator – I opened all the post. So when I opened the first one and discovered the poison her mother was trying to spread, I had to protect her. But that woman wouldn't give up. She even tried to see her, but I managed to get Abra away, so they didn't meet. I knew then she wouldn't give up." He shook his head. "Why couldn't she just stay away? Abra didn't need her. She was fine without her, happy."

"Did you kill her?" I said quietly. "Did you kill Marguerite?"

David looked away into the distance. "She finally realized that she needed to return to her home. There was nothing for her here." His voice trailed off.

"Tell me what happened, David." I hauled myself up on my elbow again. My voice was shaking. I was terrified of what lay ahead, but I needed to know what had happened. "Did Marguerite know who you were? Did she know you were with Abra?"

He turned to face me. "I told her I'd arrange for her to communicate with Abra if she would just be patient and stop trying to contact her. I said that Abra had refused to accept her letters, but that I might be able to persuade her. The woman was a fool – pathetic, grateful for any attention, believed anything I told her."

"But you were drugging her though, weren't you? With clonazepam."

"Not at first, no. But she became impatient, and I was afraid she would try to harass Abra again. I had epilepsy when I was a child; it wasn't difficult to pretend the seizures had returned. Clonazepam made it easier to get her to do what I wanted her to."

"And you were the one who told her to stop seeing Quinn, weren't you? Because you knew he would be able to tell."

"I couldn't have her exposed to any other influence. That fool of a politician saw sense and got rid of her, so when I got her away from that quack, she had no one. Other than me."

I suppressed the pang of guilt I felt. "What about your father?"

David laughed contemptuously. "My father didn't care about *her*. He cares about no one but himself. When my mother was dying of cancer, he was screwing all around him. Thinks he's Scotland's answer to Picasso."

I had a sudden flashback to Simon's kitchen and a tea bag stuck to a bag of coffee beans. "It was the tea, wasn't it? Clonazepam tastes like mint. You put the drops into the peppermint tea." I was beginning to piece it together. I remembered what Phyllis had said about Marguerite's strange behavior. "And because you couldn't do it consistently, because you were only here on the weekend, you gave her stronger doses when you could and she suffered withdrawal symptoms."

"She began to get suspicious, frightened. She knew the effects of Valium."

"It was you who broke into my house, wasn't it? You took the box with her belongings. You were looking for the letters."

"I knew she had kept them, the ones that were returned. It was a mistake marking them Return To Sender, but I thought it might discourage her from writing if she knew they weren't being accepted. But she kept them, hoping I would give them to Abra someday. They weren't in her house when we cleared it out, so when I saw that bookseller woman going to your office with a box, I guessed that you must have them."

"But I thought you were away the night she died?" I said. "Didn't your father say he had just picked you up from the airport that morning at the office?"

David was dismissive. "I have no idea why he said that. My father is a despicable human being. He lives an utterly selfish life – all he has ever cared about is his art. He broke my mother's heart and never even noticed. Give him a lump of rock to play with, and I could drown ten women a week and he wouldn't notice. Even if it is one he's been screwing."

He spat the words out and a wave of fear washed over me. I felt sure this time he wasn't referring to Marguerite.

I shrank back as he reached in, grabbed hold of my arms and lifted me roughly out of the boot – he was a lot stronger than he looked. I tried to struggle, but my legs had been in the same cramped position for too long, and they gave way as David wrenched my hands behind my back and tied them with rope. He began to drag me towards the barbed-wire fence and the edge of the cliff. The wind battered the wire like the string of a kite. I did the only thing I could think of; I tried to keep him talking.

"How did she die?" I shouted into the wind. "How did you kill her?"

"I told you, I didn't kill her. She was getting suspicious, impatient. She didn't trust me any more. When I called to her that night, she was writing another letter to Abra – after I had warned her not to. She needed to be taught a lesson."

He stopped at a break in the wire. We were less than two meters from the edge. I tried desperately not to look down;

it was enough that I could hear the waves crashing on to the rocks below.

"I slipped some extra drops into her drink and made her change what she was writing into a goodbye letter. She did what I told her. Then I took her down to the shore. My intention was just to frighten her, but I had given her more than I thought; she was staggering about like a drunk. We got as far as the stones before she passed out." He peered over the edge of the cliff. The dark patch of stones was visible in the distance.

My throat was dry, my heart pounding in my mouth. "You just left her there?" I twisted my head to look at him, but his face showed only contempt.

"I didn't expect her to die. I expected her to come round on the beach and know how close she had come to the afterlife. She was terrified of the sea. But somehow she must have found the courage to take the final path." He tightened his grip on my wrists. I could feel his breath in my ear. "All of the chosen must take it."

"But why did you want to keep her away from her daughter? I don't understand."

His eyes flashed. "You know why. You had the letters."

"I never read them. They were for Abra."

"That whore wanted to tell her the Teacher wasn't her father."

"*What?*" I tried to twist around to face him again.

"Abra has a birthright. It doesn't matter what some bitch who gave birth to her says. She was born to lead the Damascans and I was born to be beside her. But there are those who would have seized on that information and used it against her. Taken away her right to lead. I couldn't let that happen."

"Is that what Abra wanted?"

"She knew nothing of it. It was my role to protect her." He shook his head. "But now it's too late. She has read the letters and she has told the Children that she does not wish to lead, that she cannot bear false witness. She knows now that I kept the letters from her. She thinks I betrayed her." His voice was flat. "There is nothing left for me now in this life."

He took a step towards the cliff. I opened my mouth to scream, but no sound came out, my voice lost in the wind and the screech of car brakes. And a siren. David spun round, clutching me in front of him like a shield, as Molloy's car thudded to a halt in front of us, followed by the squad car.

Molloy and Simon leaped out of Molloy's car simultaneously, McFadden from the squad car behind. Molloy approached first, his hands outstretched, palms down, his face tense, Simon directly behind him.

David pulled the rope tighter. I could feel the skin on my wrists burning, the blood roaring in my ears.

"It's okay, David," Molloy said. "Stay calm. There's nothing to get excited about."

"Why is *he* here?" David glared at his father.

"Because he's worried about you. We all are," Molloy said.

Simon stepped forward. "Don't, David. We know what you think you did."

David's voice was harsh. "I didn't kill her, you fool. She took her own life. She chose to move on to the next life, just as I am about to." He took a step further towards the cliff, taking me with him.

"But why would you want to hurt Miss O'Keeffe here, David?" Molloy spoke to him as if he were speaking to a child. "Do you want to tell me what this is all about? Why are you so upset?"

If I hadn't been shaking so violently, I would have been impressed.

"Why should I?" said David. "I told you there is nothing left for me now."

"Of course there is. Just talk to me, calmly, and I'll listen."

"I'm not going to be trapped in a prison."

"Why would you go to prison, David? Your father is right. We know you didn't do anything. Someone else has confessed to Miss Etienne's death."

I felt David stiffen.

"It's a lie. You are trying to trick me. You're going to blame me for it."

"I'm not. We have them at the station right now."

I felt David's grip on my wrists loosen. He let out a long slow moan and suddenly he shoved me back towards Molloy. Molloy caught me in his arms and held me.

Simon and McFadden appeared beside us as we turned to face the cliff. David raised his right hand in the air and marked out the sign of the cross. Slowly he took three steps towards the cliff face. Simon ran towards him, calling his son's name. But he was too late.

Chapter 31

WE STOOD THERE, the four of us, at the top of the cliff looking down at a sea that was green and frothing and hundreds of meters below. Helpless. There was no sign of David; it was impossible to tell if he had landed in the sea or fallen on to the rocks.

Molloy moved first. He instructed McFadden to take Simon to the squad car and told him to call all emergency services, including the coastguard station and lifeboat service. I watched as they walked away, Simon silent and hunched as if he had shrunk in height in the past few minutes. He didn't look at me. Molloy took off his jacket and put it around my shoulders.

"Do you think he's . . . ?" I said, knowing the question to be a stupid one.

"There's no way he could have survived that fall. Are you okay?"

"No, but at least I'm not down there." I shivered. "How did you know I was here?"

"Your sculptor . . ."

"He's not my sculptor," I replied automatically.

"Come on. Let's get you into the warmth," Molloy said gently as he walked me over to his car, arms around my shoulders.

"What did he know?" I asked as Molloy turned the car's heating up full blast. "Simon, I mean."

"He's known for a while that his son was having problems. At first he thought there was something going on between David and Marguerite – a relationship of some sort – or at least that his son had a crush on her."

"So that's why he backed off . . . why he didn't finish the sculpture of her," I murmured.

"Okay," Molloy said slowly. "I'm afraid I know nothing about that."

"Sorry, go on."

"The night that Marguerite died, Simon saw David calling at her cottage, so when her body was found the following day, he suspected that his son had something to do with her death. Then when he saw David with Marguerite's daughter on the day of the funeral, it became clear that his son must have some involvement in the cult. He challenged him about it, and I don't think David even bothered to deny it."

"So Simon has known all along."

"Suspected, at least. This morning, he had an altercation with David that concerned you – so when David took off in his car, Simon felt sure he had gone to find you. Simon called 999 and they got us. He was worried about you, sufficiently concerned to tell us everything he knew. He actually told us he thought David had killed Marguerite, before we informed him that someone else had confessed."

"How did you know that David had taken me here?"

"Simon saw him drive back up past his house after he had been to yours, heading in this direction. There's only one reason to come up this road."

I glanced at the squad car where McFadden was still on the phone. Molloy was right. No one could survive a fall from

Knockamany Bends. The emergency services would be searching for a body. Simon knew that too; he sat beside McFadden
with his head in his hands.

Molloy saw me look. "Do you want to talk to him? I know
you are close."

I shook my head. It wasn't the time to say it, but Molloy
was wrong, Simon and I were not and had never been close.
He had stayed close to me physically, true, to ensure that I did
not discover his son's secret, and I had spent our time together
trying to extract information from him. For both of us our
priorities and our loyalties had been elsewhere.

Molloy left the car. I was dimly aware of him speaking briefly
to McFadden and then getting back into the driver's seat.

"I'm going to take you back into town."

"What about McFadden?" My voice sounded very far away.

"He's staying here with Simon. We've called for back-up and
the lifeboats are on their way."

We didn't speak at all on the drive back into Glendara. I was
grateful to be left alone with my thoughts and Molloy seemed
to sense that.

I still had no idea whether Simon had ever had a relationship
with Marguerite, but it seemed likely now that he had made up
the story about finding Marguerite naked in his bed to deflect
attention away from David. He had known of his son's connection with the cult and suspected his involvement in Marguerite's death, which was why he tried to get me to back off,
even following me to Norway in case I discovered something.
The saddest thing of all was that David had been wrong about
his father. Simon clearly cared about him very much. He had
been trying to protect his son all along.

It was only when we turned into the garda station that I remembered. I couldn't believe I hadn't asked the question earlier; I must have been in shock.

"Who confessed?"

Molloy pulled the keys from the ignition and turned to me. "A kid named James Quinn. As a matter of fact, his father's asking for a solicitor. He says he knows you so he's asked for you specifically. The father is Brendan. Are you up to talking to him?"

"Brendan Quinn, the psychiatrist?" I struggled to grasp what Molloy had said. My brain seemed to be frozen. "His son's confessed to Marguerite's murder?"

"Yes. He's a minor – seventeen, I think. So his father will be with him. But he wants you as his solicitor."

I walked into the garda station to be greeted by a face I could have done without – DS Frank Hanrahan, although I thought I saw a hint of sympathy in his expression: I assumed he had been told what had happened on the cliff.

He pointed towards the little interview room at the back of the station where we had had our first encounter. "The kid's in there."

"We're holding him under Section Four," Molloy said. "He came to us. Just walked into the station about an hour ago."

"His father wants to speak to you first," Hanrahan added.

I followed his gaze. Brendan Quinn was sitting in the narrow waiting area, hunched over with his head in his hands – a carbon copy of Simon Howard. For a split second I was glad not to be a parent.

I walked over to him and put my hand gently on his shoulder. "Brendan."

He looked up, his expression wretched. "They tell me he's confessed to murder," he said. "He's seventeen, for God's sake. What's going on?" His face searched mine for answers I didn't have.

"I don't know, I'm afraid. That's all I've been told. They're holding him under Section Four of the Criminal Justice Act 1984, which means they can hold him for an initial six hours to question him, then a further six if ordered by a Superintendent, and a further twelve after that if ordered by a Chief Superintendent."

Quinn hadn't taken in a word. I could tell by his face.

I distilled it down. "Unless they charge him, they can only hold him for twenty-four hours."

"He's only been here an hour," he said vaguely. "I had no idea he even knew her."

"Look," I said, "he's a minor so he needs to have you present with him. So let's go in and see him, shall we?"

With a mammoth effort, Quinn hauled himself out of the chair and followed me towards the interview room. Molloy opened the door for us but didn't come in. Hanrahan was there already, sitting at the table with his back to us with a thin-looking boy in a gray hoodie sitting opposite. The boy had his elbows on the table and his head bent, a curtain of greasy brown hair covering his face. He didn't look up when we came into the room, nor when his father sat down beside him. I took the seat beside Hanrahan.

Hanrahan spoke. "You are entitled to have a solicitor present, James, along with your father. Your father has asked Miss O'Keeffe to be here."

The boy glanced up for the first time. He was deathly pale and he looked as if he hadn't eaten in days – not what you would expect of the son of a prominent wealthy psychiatrist. With a jolt, I realized I had seen him before. He was the gangly-looking youth who had been sitting beside Hugh O'Connor that day outside Phyllis's book shop, and hanging about in the Oak on the day of the Wax Auction.

I smiled at him and offered my hand. He shook it and gave me a weak smile. There was fear in his eyes.

"I'm just going to turn on the tape recorder," Hanrahan said as he reached over to flick the switch on the old machine. He leaned forward. "Now, James, I want you to tell us again what you told me earlier. Take your time, and in your own words."

James spoke in a whisper. "I did it. I killed her."

"You'll have to speak up for the tape, James," Hanrahan said.

"I killed her," he said again, marginally louder. "It wasn't suicide like they said."

"We need you to be clear, James. Who are you talking about? Who did you kill?" Hanrahan spoke gently to him.

"That French woman."

"Marguerite Etienne?"

"That's the one."

"And why are you telling us this now?"

"Because I can't live with it."

"Thank you. Now, James, just tell us what happened."

"I took Dad's car," I heard Quinn's sharp intake of breath to my left, "while he was away. And I followed her."

"You followed her from where?"

"From Glendara. She came out of," he nodded in my direction, "your office."

Hanrahan interrupted, "For the purposes of the tape, can you clarify what you mean when you say 'your office'?"

"Miss O'Keefe's," James said.

"Thank you, James. Please continue. What happened next?"

"The French woman went to another house and then she went home."

"Was this something you had done before, James? Follow her?"

"No."

"So why did you do it that night?"

"Don't know," he shrugged. "Just for something to do."

"Was there anyone with you?"

"No one. I was on my own."

"Are you quite sure about that?"

"Aye."

The door opened and Molloy came in. He shut the door behind him.

"And what did you do then?" Hanrahan asked.

"Sat in the car down the road from her house for a wee minute. I saw a man go in."

"Can you describe the man?"

"Skinny."

Molloy and I looked at each other. David Howard.

"And what did you do then?"

"Drove down to the beach. Walked along the shore." He paused. "Smoked a joint." He glanced uneasily at his father. *Something didn't add up*, I thought on seeing this. The boy had just confessed to murder and yet he was afraid to admit to smoking a joint in front of his father.

"How long were you down there for?"

"Half an hour. Then I walked back up the beach towards the stony part."

"And then what happened?"

"She was just lying there, passed out on the beach. Drunk or something. Down at the road end, where the rocks are."

"And?"

"I picked up a rock and I hit her. On the head."

"Why would you do something like that, James?"

"I don't know," he muttered. "I had been smoking. I wasn't thinking straight."

"You had no other reason? Did you know Ms. Etienne?"

He shook his head. "No."

"What did you do after you hit her, James?"

"I panicked. I took off her clothes and I dragged her into the sea. I thought it would look like suicide."

Distressingly, he started to cry, burying his head in his arms on the table. When he spoke again, his voice was muffled. "I had to tell you. I can't live with it."

"Was there anyone with you, James – at any point during the evening?" Hanrahan asked again.

James raised his head, tears smeared across his cheeks. "No," he said firmly. "I was on my own."

"And you've kept it to yourself all this time? You've told no one?"

"No one knows but me."

"And you had never met Miss Etienne before this happened?"

"No." He hung his head again. "I don't know why I did it. It must have been the dope."

"Okay, James, we'll leave that for the moment." Hanrahan switched off the tape recorder.

We left the interview room and Molloy headed off to get James a glass of water while his father and I went outside to get some air. The interview room had felt like a cell.

"Did James know about you and Marguerite?" I asked.

"No," Quinn replied. "There's no way he could have known."

"Are you sure?"

He gave me a look of horror. "Why – do you think he found out? Do you think that's why he did it?"

"I'm not saying that. I just want you to be sure."

"Oh, Jesus Christ, what have I done? Should I tell the guards about it?"

"Maybe. Let's wait and see what happens."

Molloy emerged from the station. I left Quinn pacing up and down in the car park and went over to talk to him.

"What do you think?" I asked.

"Well, his story has lots of holes in it. There seems to have been no motive and Hanrahan thinks that he would have found it pretty difficult to lift a dead body on his own, let alone undress Marguerite down to her underwear. He's not the biggest kid in the world."

"What's he thinking?"

"Well, he agrees with me. If the kid's telling the truth, it seems very unlikely he was on his own."

The arrival of the squad car interrupted our conversation. McFadden climbed out of the driver's seat looking wet and dishevelled. "Need a change of clothes, then I'm heading back up there."

"Any news?" Molloy asked.

"Nothing yet. We're searching the cliffs and the lifeboat service are searching the sea. We'll keep at it till we find him."

Five minutes later, Hanrahan confirmed that they were suspending questioning James for an hour so he could have something to eat. Molloy tried to make me go to the hospital to have myself checked out, but I resisted. I was fine physically, bar a little bump on the head. So I left the station and walked back out onto the street.

I looked at my watch. It was half past ten. I wondered if I should try to talk to Simon, to offer him some comfort, but I doubted what good it would do, since it was clear now that there had been nothing real between us in the first place. Also, I couldn't go too far – I might be needed again at the garda station if they resumed questioning.

So I went to the office.

I made myself a coffee and sat at Leah's desk. I couldn't be-lieve that James Quinn had killed Marguerite; it just didn't add up. But James was Hugh O'Connor's friend and both boys' fathers had had relationships with Marguerite. Affairs, in fact. Surely that couldn't be a coincidence.

The guards thought that James couldn't have done what he said he did on his own. Could Hugh have been with him? I went to the filing cabinet and fished out the file on closed dis-trict court cases, pulled out Hugh's sheaf of charge sheets and ran my finger down through the descriptions of the offences. I checked the date they had occurred and immediately felt that pins-and-needles sensation traveling up my neck again. The date on the charge sheets was 13 September – the date Mar-guerite had died. I couldn't believe I hadn't checked before.

Finally, I knew what had happened. But there was one last piece I needed to be sure.

I rang Quinn.

There was fear in his voice when he answered. "Hello?"

"Brendan, it's Ben. What is your car registration number?"

He replied without hesitation. "DL 09 98788. Why?"

I checked the charge sheet. The number matched. Hugh O'Connor had been driving Quinn's car the night Marguerite died, not James.

"Did you notice any damage to your car when you came back from holidays?"

"No, none. If anything, it was in top shape. Looked like it had had a paint job. I thought James had given it a good going over with the wax. What's this about?"

"I'll let you know."

I dialed the number of the garda station at high speed. Hanrahan answered. I asked for Molloy.

"He's gone back up to Knockamany Bends with Garda Mc-Fadden. Do you want me to give him a message?"

"No. It's okay, thanks. I'll track him down myself. I need to get hold of him fairly quickly."

I hung up, tried his mobile, but the call went straight through to voicemail.

I raced down the stairs and out the door, charge sheets in hand, crossed over to the County Council car park and searched frantically for my car until I remembered that the Golf I had borrowed from Hal was still outside my house. I ran back into the office, grabbed a note from the petty-cash box and made my way to the taxi rank in the square. I opened the passenger door of one of the cabs.

"Paddy, can you take me back to my house, please? I need to collect my car."

The driver grinned. "Big night last night?"

"Something like that."

We were back in Malin in five minutes. I rummaged around in my bag which Molloy had given me from Simon's car and found my car keys, but I couldn't find my phone. Where the hell was it? Could I have left it in the car? I searched the Golf, but it wasn't there, and I didn't want to leave without it. I would need it to get hold of Molloy if I couldn't find him on the cliff.

I tried to think back. I was sure I'd had it in my hand before I was knocked out, so maybe I had dropped it somewhere outside the house. I walked up the path, searching as I went, but there was no sign of it on the path or on the doorstep.

Might it have been kicked under the back door? I went round to the back of the house, unlocked the back door and walked through the porch and into the kitchen, but there was no sign of it there either. I dropped the bag and charge sheets on the table while I searched the pantry, then returned to the kitchen and started up the hallway towards the sitting room. But my way was barred.

Chapter 32

HUGH O'CONNOR WAS standing in the doorway, leaning casually against the door jamb, one hand in the front pocket of his jeans. I swallowed. My heart felt as if it was about to stop.

I feigned a lack of concern. "Hugh. What are you doing here?"

He gave me one of his movie-star smiles. "I heard you were down seeing Queenie."

"Queenie? Oh, James Quinn, your friend."

He nodded in approval. "My friend. You've made the connection, well done. I hope that doesn't mean you're going to start interfering."

"Interfering?"

"Sticking your oar in. Telling him what to say."

"I can't tell him what to say, Hugh. But it is my job to represent him."

"You're not needed. Queenie knows what he's doing. Just let him be." His tone was indolent, disinterested.

I shook my head. "I can't do that."

He looked away. "We have our own way of doing things around here – I told you. We take care of ourselves, in our own way. We don't need outsiders. Queenie knows that."

He withdrew his hand from his pocket and placed it against the wall. If the action was designed to emphasise his considerable height advantage, it worked. He glanced over my shoulder into the kitchen and his smile faded. He had seen the charge sheets on the table where I'd left them.

"What are you doing with them?"

I didn't respond.

He took a step towards me. "You heard me."

I stood my ground. "I know you were driving James's father's car that night. The night Marguerite died."

The smile returned. Contemptuous now, cocky. "Was I fuck."

"The registration number is on the charge sheets. The car was seen, down by the beach."

"Queenie was the one at the beach, sweetheart."

"The guards are sure he couldn't have killed Marguerite on his own."

"The guards know fuck-all. That boy has psycho tendencies. Goes a bit mental sometimes. Doesn't like women, you see." Hugh waved a limp wrist at me.

Suddenly, it all made sense: why James would confess, the adoring look I had seen that day outside the book shop, the evasiveness, the lack of motive.

"James would do anything for you, wouldn't he? Even take the blame for something you did."

"You're full of shit."

"Or did you do it together? Did you make him help you?"

Hugh's face took on an arrogant sneer. "He wouldn't have the balls."

"So it was you." Fear wrapped itself around me like a damp coat. "Why would you want to hurt Marguerite? What had she ever done to you?"

His eyes hardened. "I told you, we don't need outsiders telling us what to do. Knowing things they shouldn't."

He took a step towards me and I backed slowly into the kitchen. He came after me. I reached the sink and gripped the counter-top behind me with both hands. Only the table was between us. He placed his hands on the table and leaned towards me, lip curled. Suddenly he wasn't so handsome any more.

"All I did was put her out of her fucking misery. Found her lying in a drunken heap on the shore and hit her over the head with a rock."

I tried to keep the quiver out of my voice. "Why would you do that?"

He tilted his head to one side. "Did the same thing when I ran over a cat once. Kindest thing. Did you never have a sick cat that keeps you up all night yowling? That bitch couldn't keep her mouth shut."

"What do you mean?"

"Mouthing off about family, how important it was to know where you come from, who your parents are. In that horrible fucking accent of hers. Donegal people know how to keep their mouths shut." He banged his fist on the table.

I shrank back against the sink. *If I ever get out of this I'm going to have a panic button installed right here,* I thought.

"She was talking about her daughter. Marguerite had a daughter she hadn't seen for a long time," I said quietly.

Hugh's eyes darted about the room. "She knew things she shouldn't."

"What things?"

He shook his head and suddenly, as if someone had flipped a switch, his temper was gone; the smile returned and his voice became silky again. "But you'll know how to keep your mouth shut, won't you, being a solicitor an' all. You'll let Queenie do what he wants to do for his *best friend.*"

"What things did she know, Hugh? Things about you?"

His smile faded again. "I wasn't going to let her ruin things. Some outsider. That's not going to happen. I have a future." He had an odd, distant look.

With a horrible jolt, I realized the kid was insane, I could see it in his eyes. There was an absence, a lack of focus, that frightened me. Hugh stared at the ceiling, distracted for a second, while I edged slowly towards the door – an act of pure desperation. I hadn't a snowball's chance in hell of getting past him.

It was a stupid mistake. The movement seemed to bring him back. He leaped forward, grabbed both my arms, twisted them behind my back and pushed me head-first into the sink. I could smell his breath on my neck – toothpaste again.

"I wouldn't bother trying to fight it, sweetheart."

I struggled, but it was utterly futile. He was at least one and a half times my weight.

"It's no trouble, you know, I can kill you easily. Make it four. Even number."

I heard a noise at the back door – someone knocking, my name being called. I felt Hugh's muscles tighten behind me, and in my peripheral vision, I saw Simon's sculpture sitting on the counter-top. I heard footsteps.

Distracted, Hugh loosened his grip on me. As he turned his head to see who was behind him, I managed to pull my right arm free and grabbed Simon's sculpture. Somehow I lifted it and swung it towards the side of Hugh's head. With a loud, sickening crack it connected and he fell to the floor.

I looked up to see Molloy standing in the doorway of the kitchen, an expression of disbelief on his face. He looked down. To my horror, blood had started to seep from Hugh's head.

Malin's little green was a mass of flashing lights, sirens and on-lookers. I sat on the wall in front of my house wrapped in one of those tinfoil blankets they give to marathon runners, drinking a cup of strong sweet tea they'd brought out from Caffrey's. It was disgusting.

Molloy emerged from the crowd. "He's alive. Lost a bit of blood, but he's going to be okay."

"Thank God."

"Jesus Christ, Ben. Twice in one morning."

"I know."

"I'll have to take a formal statement from you when you're feeling up to it."

"Sure."

He darted off to talk to one of the uniformed guards at the gate. Suddenly I became aware of someone else pushing their way through the crowd. It was Aidan Doherty, fear etched across his face.

"What the hell happened? I've just seen Hugh in an ambulance."

"I'm sorry, Aidan. He's confessed to Marguerite's murder."

Aidan said nothing, just stared at the ground, ashen-faced.

"You knew, didn't you?" I said, horrified.

He shook his head. "Not for sure."

"But you're not surprised, are you?"

"I suspected."

"How, for God's sake?"

He sighed. "I lied to you. I did go out to the beach that night when she called. I could never have turned my back on her if she was in trouble. I just couldn't."

"Did you see her?"

"She wasn't at her house – I couldn't find her. When I was on my way back to Glendara I spotted Hugh and his friend driving up from the beach. I didn't want Hugh to see me so I left. Hugh knew about the affair, he knew I had told his mother it was over, and I didn't want him to think I was breaking my promise. But the next day, when I heard what had happened, I was afraid."

"Why the hell didn't you say anything?"

"He's my son." He held his hands out in a gesture of help-lessness. "But it's been torturing me. Just yesterday I decided it was time to talk to Sergeant Molloy. And I told Hugh I was going to do so."

"That's why he persuaded his friend to confess – before you had a chance. But why? Why would Hugh kill Marguerite?"

Aidan didn't meet my eye. "I don't know. Because of my relationship with her? For his mother?"

"No, I don't think that was it. He said she knew something. She talked to him about family, the importance of knowing where you come from. That seemed to upset him."

Aidan's mouth opened in horror. "Oh, Jesus, he thought she knew . . ."

"Knew what?"

He covered his face with his hands and then slumped down on the wall beside me. "Marguerite didn't know anything. I would never have told her. I made him a promise I wouldn't tell anyone. I'd never have broken that."

One of the paramedics appeared suddenly beside us. "Excuse me, sir. Are you Hugh O'Connor's father?"

Aidan looked up anxiously. "Yes."

"Good. We'd like you to come with us in the ambulance. He's going to be okay but he may need a blood transfusion. I presume you would be willing . . ."

Aidan paled. For a second I was confused by his hesitation, until something clicked.

"You're not his biological father, are you?"

"No."

The pieces finally fitted. "Seamus Tighe was his father, wasn't he?"

The paramedic was still waiting, looking confused. "Mr. Doherty?"

"His father is dead, I'm afraid." Aidan's voice was dry with exhaustion. "I'll call his mother. They have the same blood type."

The man nodded and left. Aidan withdrew his phone from his pocket and walked away.

While Aidan made his call, Molloy reappeared. I told him what he had missed.

When Aidan returned, he slumped on to the wall between us. He ran his fingers through his hair and said, "I've only known for a couple of years."

"But why keep it a secret?" I asked. "What was Hugh so paranoid about?"

Aidan took a deep breath. "When Clodagh told her father about her relationship with Seamus, she also told him that she was pregnant. He responded by telling her that Seamus was *his* son, the product of an affair. Which meant that Clodagh was eighteen and pregnant – by her half-brother."

I stared at him. "Jesus."

"No one knew but Clodagh and her father. It all but destroyed her. She only told me when she had no choice. I thought

Hugh was mine for fifteen years." There was real sadness in his
eyes. "I think it was the beginning of the end for us when she
told me. But she was right not to tell anyone. No one needed
to know – especially not Hugh."

"But he does?" I asked.

Aidan bowed his head. "Yes. I told him. It was the worst
thing I've ever done. That was when everything started to go
wrong."

"Go on," Molloy said.

"Seamus Tighe was a great footballer and he still came to
see all the schools games. When he saw Hugh's ability on the
pitch, he started to ask questions. Hugh looked like him too,
you see. He asked Hugh to come and see him. Clodagh didn't
want him to go, she was terrified it would all come out, but
Hugh was insistent, would never be told what to do." Aidan
smiled bitterly. "Anyway Clodagh finally told me the truth
and made me follow him. She wanted the meeting stopped at
any cost."

"What happened?" Molloy asked.

"I was too late. I met Hugh leaving Seamus's farm. Of course,
Seamus hadn't been able to resist telling him his suspicions, that
he thought he might be Hugh's father. Hugh seemed almost
elated by it. He'd never had any respect for me, always thought
I was weak. He was happy to have anyone replace me, I suspect. But Seamus had no idea that Clodagh was his half-sister;
she had never given him a reason why she had ended things
with him. And his mother had never told him who his father
was – she had died a few years before.

"Hugh was ready to tell the world. But I knew it would destroy his mother if it came out. So I told him why they could
never have a relationship." Aidan looked down. He muttered,

"I was wrong to do that. I should have realized what it would do to him."

"Seamus Tighe falling into a slurry tank wasn't an accident, was it?" I said.

"No," Aidan said quietly. "I tried to save him, but it was too late. Hugh pushed him. He was fifteen."

My voice was shaking. "So that's why you were afraid he had killed Marguerite. Because he had done it before."

"And you kept that information to yourself, Mr. Doherty," Molloy said.

"I was trying to protect him. I didn't even tell Clodagh until recently. I hoped he would just be able to get on with his life."

"I see."

"I was wrong. I can see that now." Tears welled up in Aidan's eyes. "I've made such a mess of things. It's just as well I never had any children of my own. I'm sure I'd have made a mess of that too."

At that moment, I hoped to God he didn't know that Marguerite was pregnant when she died. I couldn't see how knowing that would do him any good whatsoever.

Chapter 33

I HADN'T INTENDED to fall asleep. But by Wednesday evening, after three days of back-to-back appointments with each and every client finding some way to segue from the matter at hand to the events of the day before, I was exhausted. And so, when I lay on the couch after eating, intending to close my eyes for five minutes, that was it.

I sat up, rubbed my eyes and tried to work out what had woken me. Then it happened again: a buzzing noise coming from the coffee table in front of me. It was my phone, on silent. I answered it.

"So are you going to let me in?" It was Molloy.

I yawned, struggling to grasp what he meant. "Sorry?"

"I've been at your door for ten minutes."

"Oh shit. Sorry, I fell asleep on the couch. I'll be there in a sec."

He stood at my newly-repaired front door with its brand new lock, fitted by Hal that morning, looking pretty much as I felt. Tired eyes with heavy dark shadows underneath. Unshaven too, which was most unlike him.

"You look as if you've had the same kind of day as I have," I said.

"Something like that. How are you doing?"

"Fine. A bit wrecked."

"Sorry." He made a face. "Have you time for a chat? I can come back later if you're not up to it."

"No. Come on in."

He stepped over the threshold and followed me into the kitchen.

"Tea, wine?" I offered. When he hesitated, I started to smile. "Whiskey?"

He sighed. "I'm tempted to say yes to all three to be honest, but I'd better stick to the tea."

I filled the kettle. "I hear Aidan Doherty got bail?"

Molloy stood beside me with his arms crossed. "Yes, he did. He's been charged with perverting the course of justice. But he's co-operated completely."

"I can't help feeling sorry for him."

"I wouldn't waste your sympathy. If he'd spoken up, he could have prevented two murders."

"Two?"

Molloy nodded.

"Iggy McDaid?" I asked, afraid to hear the answer.

"Yes. Iggy took a bracelet from Marguerite's body, a bracelet Aidan had given her. He thought he was doing Aidan a favor. But he got himself killed for his trouble."

I tossed some tea bags into the pot. "Why?"

"He tried to get Hugh to pass the bracelet on to his father, but made the mistake of trying to give it to him in the court-house, in front of people."

I had a flashback of Iggy with his dirty handkerchief. "God. I saw him with it. The same morning you warned me he was drunk."

"That's why he did it, I presume. Probably wouldn't have if he'd been sober. Hugh recognized it as coming from

Marguerite's body and was so paranoid at that stage that he became convinced Iggy knew what he had done."

"So he pushed him off the ferry?"

Molloy nodded. "Poor old Iggy made it easy for him. He never learned to swim."

"God love him."

"By the way," Molloy added as I poured boiling water into the tea pot and went searching in the fridge for some milk, "we've arrested your clients, Gallagher and Dolan."

I turned. "Really? What for?"

"Blackmail of Aidan Doherty. They needed him to sort out that re-zoning issue, apparently. You're acting for them in buying some property in Malin Head, I believe?"

I didn't react.

Molloy smiled. "It's all right. We know you are. Anyway, while Hugh was running around town thinking everybody knew the truth about him, he didn't figure where the real danger lay. The only people who knew anything about his parentage were Gallagher and Dolan, Gallagher being Seamus Tighe's cousin. Gallagher knew Seamus suspected he was Hugh's real father, although I don't think he knew anything else."

"Right."

"Still, it was enough for them to be able to get Aidan Doherty to use his influence to obtain the planning permission they needed. Aidan was terrified of it all coming out. He had to call in favors owed to his father-in-law from decades before."

I poured Molloy a mug of tea and handed it to him. "What about James Quinn?"

"Though he was almost certainly with Hugh on the night Marguerite died, I think we're happy enough that he had no involvement in the actual killing. He'll be charged, all right, but he may get away with a suspended sentence."

"Good. And Hugh himself? Out of hospital, I hear." I frowned. "I'll never forget seeing that blood seeping from his head after I hit him."

"Out of one hospital and into another. He's been detained in the Central Mental Hospital in Dundrum and is going to be there for a long time. He may not even go to prison. All the reports seem to point to psychopathy."

"Has he been charged?"

"Three counts of murder, one of unlawful imprisonment and arson."

"Arson?"

"He burned down the barn at the farm he crashed into, the night of the murder. That's why the dangerous driving charge was withdrawn. He scared the old pair half to death. Killed one of their cattle."

I remembered Maeve mentioning something similar. I wondered if it was the same barn.

"He was threatening Marguerite, too, from what we can gather," Molloy continued. "Trying to get her to leave the area. All in that semi-charming way of his."

"But, of course, she was never going to leave when she thought David Howard was her only way to her daughter," I said. "God, that's why she was so nervous at the office. Between Hugh O'Connor and David Howard it looks as if she was being scared half out of her wits."

Molloy looked grave. "Yes, it seems I owe you an apology for that one. You were right. They still haven't found David Howard's body, by the way."

I shook my head. "Poor Simon."

Molloy gave me an odd look. "I'm sure you'll be a comfort to him."

Embarrassed, I said. "I think you have the wrong idea. There's nothing between Simon and me."

He looked confused. "But I thought . . ."

"It never really started, to be honest."

He looked away. "I'm sorry."

"It's fine." I shrugged. "Shall we take our tea in by the fire?"

Molloy took the armchair while I sat on the couch, the coffee table between us. I watched him as he stared into the fire, his profile in silhouette. All that had happened in the past few days had helped me come to a decision about Molloy. I realized that more than anything, I wanted him in my life, and so if friendship was all that was on offer then I would be fine with that. It was time to put that decision into practice.

"So how is it going with Laura?" I said brightly. If I'd managed to get through the events of the day before, then I should be able to tackle this, I thought.

Molloy placed his mug on the coffee table. He avoided my eye. "Actually, that's something I wanted to talk to you about."

At that point I realized that I couldn't do it, after all. "It's fine," I said hastily. "You don't need to tell me anything."

He sat forward. "No. Listen to me, Ben. Please, I need you to hear this. Laura hasn't had an easy time of it lately, and I wanted to be there to support her. But she . . ." He paused. "Well, she wanted something I wasn't sure I could give her. Wrongly perhaps, I felt I owed it to her to try."

"I see." I held my breath.

His eyes met mine. "But I'm afraid it didn't take her very long to realize that I was more concerned for someone else. That I had feelings for someone else."

He reached across and touched my face, the tips of his fingers cool against my hot cheek. It was all I could do not to close my eyes and lean into his touch, but I held his gaze. His face was tense, his eyes anxious.

"Ben, I know I've hurt you, I have no reason to . . ."

I placed my hand on his. His eyes softened and remained fixed on mine as he leaned across the table to kiss me. I felt the pressure of his lips on mine, gently at first, teasing. I found it hard to breathe, the dizziness of a first kiss. I closed my eyes as he pulled me towards him.

Molloy grinned as he surveyed the couch some time later. There was a lightness about him I hadn't seen before. I liked it.

I feigned indignation, but threw the cushion on which I had been sleeping to the floor for Guinness. As I curled up in Molloy's arms, with my head on his chest, I wondered if he would stay the night, if I should ask him to. But before I did, there was one loose end I needed to be tied up.

"So do you think it was David Howard then who was peering in my window?"

Molloy tensed. He didn't reply.

"Tom?" I pulled away from him so I could look at his face.

His expression had changed; the lightness had gone. I tried to ignore the sense of dread in the pit of my stomach.

"I'm afraid it may not have been." He paused. "Ben, there's something I need to tell you."

"Something else?" I smiled, trying to retrieve the earlier mood.

He touched my hand. "It's Luke Kirby. He's been released from prison."

I froze. "When?"

"He was released that morning, the day you saw the face at your window."

My mind began to race. I couldn't think straight. How long ago was that? Was it before or after his phone call to me?

"How long have you known?" I demanded.

"Only a few days. After your accident it occurred to me that I should check. It seemed such an odd thing to happen. And from what you had told me, I thought there was a possibility he might be due for release."

I stood up, as if that would clear my head. "Why the hell didn't they tell us?"

Molloy stood too. He took my hand in his. "You know they never do, Ben. It's just odd that the media didn't get hold of it."

"And you've known for days and haven't told me?" I could feel my temper rising. I needed someone to blame.

Molloy stayed calm. "He left the country, Ben. He was gone by the time I knew he was out, so I didn't see any reason to worry you." He waited. "But there is a possibility he was in the area before he left."

An hour later, I was alone again. I told Molloy I had some work to finish for the next day and assured him I was fine. I could tell he didn't believe me, but I didn't give him much choice.

But as I gazed blankly at the television news, I knew I had made a mistake. Memories returned like spools of film, blocking out the scenes on screen. I turned the volume as high as I could bear as if that would drown out my thoughts, but it didn't help. And as the images blurred in front of my eyes, my head began to spin. I gripped the arms of the chair to stop myself from passing out. Suddenly my stomach contracted and

I ran to the bathroom, where I threw up violently and repeatedly for ten minutes.

When I emerged, the doorbell was ringing. I stood in the
hallway paralysed, unable to answer it. It rang again, more urgently this time, and I watched as Guinness padded silently past
me to the door where he sat on the doormat expectantly, tail
wrapped neatly around him.

I took a deep breath and walked to the door. I opened it.

Molloy smiled. "You're going to have to try much harder
than that to get rid of me this time."

Acknowledgements

Thank you to my agent, Kerry Glencorse, and to Ella Munn-Giddings, Mark Kessler, and all at Susanna Lea Associates. Thank you also to Krystyna Green, Grace Vincent, Amanda Keats, Joan Deitch and all at Constable/Little, Brown; to Siobhan Tierney and all at Hachette Ireland; and to Bob and Pat Gussin, Lee Randall, and Autumn Beckett at Oceanview Publishing.

Thank you to Paul Gaster for the head-shots. Thank you to Henrietta McKervey, who again read an early draft of *Treacherous Strand*, as did Lily McGonagle. Thank you also to Fidelma Tonry, Brid Gallagher, Roisin Doherty, Myra Cahill, Donal McGuinness, Emile Daly, Caroline Tynan, Tom and Brenda O'Grady, Paul Gunning, Marc Thompson and Geraldine Biggs for their advice, friendship and support in matters Donegal, legal, veterinary, pharmaceutical, and otherwise. All errors are entirely my own!

I will always be grateful to Frank McGuinness for his kindness and encouragement and to Éilís Ní Dhuibhne and James Ryan of UCD.

And to the Irish Writers Centre whose support has been invaluable to me on more than one occasion.

You will (still) not find Glendara on the map of Inishowen, but many of the other places frequented by Ben O'Keeffe do exist. In particular, the beach at Lagg, or Five Fingers Strand, remains one of my favorite places on earth, as it is hers. Do visit. But don't swim!

Finally, thank you to my family: Jack and Gloria, Nikki, Tom and Christopher, and Owen and Jean.

And to Geoff who I hope will forgive the dedication.